# A
# WORK
## OF
# ART

# A WORK OF ART

## MICAYLA LALLY

a novel

She Writes Press, a BookSparks imprint
A Division of SparkPointStudio, LLC.

Published 2017

Printed in the United States of America

Print ISBN: 978-1-63152-168-3
E-ISBN: 978-1-63152-169-0
Library of Congress Control Number: 2016959053

For information, address:
She Writes Press
1563 Solano Ave #546
Berkeley, CA 94707

Cover design © Julie Metz, Ltd./metzdesign.com
Formatting by Katherine Lloyd/thedeskonline.com

She Writes Press is a division of SparkPoint Studio, LLC.

# ONE

The lock disengaged and the door clicked open, squeaking gently. Samson pushed it shut behind him. The air wasn't stale but the place itself might have been. He set down his badge and gun on the small table beside the door and made his way through to the kitchen, ignoring all save for the drinks in the door of the fridge. He pulled the ring tab on a can of beer, foam covering the top of the can and one of his fingers before he slurped it.

Dinner was a drab state of events and he tried not to think of how it used to be. He fell asleep on the couch with the television on.

# TWO

Julene drove aimlessly through the city streets and beyond, down past all the bay shops, the slow and rumbling trams, to the Port of Adelaide. She parked the car in a forgotten 'No Parking' zone and threaded her way toward the boats and noise, her thick, dark hair whipping around her face before she could lash it behind her with a clip. The sight of the water helped clear her mind, even with all the noise, or perhaps because of it. Certainly it had done this past week as she'd sat in the same spot and lost herself almost every day.

The noise blocked out everything—thoughts, feelings, memories—so she was free to sort out what was going on inside her. Right now it was a lot of confused thinking and probably a second heartbeat. She'd suspected she was pregnant for a while now but hadn't done anything about it. Hadn't told David she suspected anything, hadn't told him anything at all since they'd parted a month ago.

Julene broke one of her own rules and allowed herself to think of him as she walked the length of the pier, avoiding detritus and coils of rope, not minding the smell, though she would complain of it on her clothes when she got home. She wondered what he was doing now; possibly typing up one of the reports he hated or interviewing a witness to a crime. Or maybe, just maybe, he was thinking of her, wondering what she was doing or thinking, missing her, too.

# THREE

I t burned.

"Another."

The bartender was a pretty blonde woman by the name of Sally.

"My name is Anita and I think you've had enough." She slapped his tab on the bar in front of him.

"Sally."

"Anita, now why don't I pour you a coffee, instead?"

Samson's reply was quiet and probably unintelligible. He bowed his head over the bar, thinking of the burning feeling in his throat and how it overshadowed everything else. He could feel it burning in his stomach as well, and should he admit—even to himself— there was a burning somewhere a little higher? Could it be it was his (heart)?

"Samson!"

A headache. It was going to be a nightmare.

"Man, you look terrible. Have another drink, it's the only cure." The barstool creaked as his friend Matt, AKA Moose, dropped onto it.

"Make it two and you've got a deal." Samson lifted his head and gave his friend a weak smile.

"Make it three and I'll join you."

Elbowing and shouldering their way over to a miraculously free table away from the threat of coffee, a waitress followed with a loaded tray.

"Hey, watch it!" She slapped a hand and Moose looked chastened.

"Moose, you really should keep your mitts off."

"Talking from experience?"

A ferocious laugh burst forth from his chest, not surprising from his generous frame. He was sobered by Samson's look.

"Which one?"

"All." Samson's tone was philosophical.

"Uh, enough said. Look, get those into you and then let's get out of here. What's say we head down Hindley Street? I know some of the door men."

Hindley Street was well-known as *the* red light district.

"I'd shake my head in the negative but it would probably explode. Just take me home."

Water on the skin in the wee hours can actually sting if your skin is still oozing scotch fumes. It might have been dew or he might have been rained on at some point. He was wet and it only added to Samson's pain and discomfort. He cracked his eyes and found himself laying on the grass in his backyard. He groaned and closed his eyes again. He swore disjointedly and tried to drag himself up. A comment from an open window of the neighboring house recalled to mind that this had been his routine for far too long, and it was purely luck that kept his superiors in the police department in the dark about it. It might also have been pity on the part of his neighbors because they'd also loved her. But no, he would not pursue that thought.

Samson collapsed onto the battered sofa next to the back door, his body having moved itself as far as it was interested in going before giving him up as a bad joke. His eyes drifted closed even before his head was settled uncomfortably against a convenient cushion.

# FOUR

Julene walked out of the doctor's office and nearly into the path of oncoming traffic. Horns blared at her and cars swerved away from the curb where she stood perilously at the edge of the pavement. She stepped back quickly, her mind frantic with the next six months—things to be bought, books to be read, money—of course—and where it was going to come from because she'd decided that her nursing career wasn't what she wanted anymore.

But above all else, she wondered whether or not she would tell David Samson, the man who had been the love of her life until recently, now that she knew for sure. She remembered the day she thought it might have happened. They were—*had been*—so careful with birth control except for that one time, that one romantic and day-dreamy time. But then she shook herself out of the reverie, her thoughts turning instead to their last night together. Her brow furrowed. She wouldn't tell him, but she couldn't hide the news from her mother. Well, she could until she found somewhere a little inane in which to lose herself—and somewhere with snacks. She drove to the local shopping mall and bought herself a smoothie and a cookie before making the call.

"Julene, it's good to hear your voice again; it's been so long! Your father and I have just come back from the theatre, it's lucky you caught us. We're getting ready to go to Paris for the weekend. What have you been up to?"

"Julene!"

She looked past the potted plants where her friend Moose greeted her as he walked toward her from a few stores down. She was surprised to see him and wondered if it was his new hairstyle that made him look even taller. She said her good-byes to her mother and ended the call.

"Moose! How are you? Oh my gosh, I haven't seen you in ages!"

She was pleased to see him, regardless of the fact he was Samson's closest friend; they'd been quite close themselves. She asked him about his hair as he enveloped her in a hug.

"It's all anybody can talk about, as if it's the only thing that I've done recently." He laughed to show he wasn't bothered by it.

"Well, what else have you been doing?"

"Actually, not much different. But they say change is as good as a holiday, and since I can't get away from work this summer, the haircut will have to be it until further notice."

"I like it."

He gestured toward a café and they seated themselves at an outside table, their hot drinks thumbing their noses to the early warmth of the spring. A squall of errant blossoms battered themselves on the glass window of the café, waving their good-byes before skipping off down the street.

"So what have you been doing with yourself?" Moose asked after Julene gave her order to the bored-looking waiter. "I mean, the last time I saw you was at, well, it was at the Italian Festival with Samson."

"Right, the pasta-eating competition and the zeppole."

They both cast down their eyes but Moose lifted his in time to see a glimmering sheath over Julene's. It quickly disappeared, but not quickly enough for him not to see it had been there initially.

"Julene, I'm sorry."

Julene glanced at him and then away; she nodded. There was a hard look in her eyes that Moose had not expected as she attacked a pastry. Julene wondered what he knew. His steady gaze was disconcerting.

"I'm pregnant."

Moose wasn't sure what, if anything, he had expected her to say but it wasn't that. Among other things Samson had been babbling about last night when they had made it back to his house—and the only thing coherent—was how much he missed Julene, how he'd ruined it all.

Moose ate his pie floater—an Adelaide specialty comprised of a meat pie in pea soup—in silence while Julene pushed her small salad around with her fork.

"Are you going to tell him?"

Julene shook her head shortly.

"You have to, he has a—"

"I don't have to do anything, and you don't, either."

"How can I not tell him?" Moose could only shake his head at her.

"Because you're my friend, too."

Moose pushed his plate away, recalling his friend's adamant rejections that Julene still loved him, that he should call or contact her somehow. He'd also told Moose what to do with his "well-intentioned sticky-beaking" in no uncertain terms and he had resolved not to bring up the subject again. He remained true to his resolution now, with Julene, adding to her misery with every anecdote of their mutual friends, perhaps more so because he didn't actually relay a skeric of real news. They parted with intentions to keep in touch more regularly but they both had other things on their mind, the same in fact.

# FIVE

It was late in the day before Samson was roused from his position on the sofa outside. Was it the pounding in his head, the beads of sweat and tension in his neck, or the lawn mower next door that caused an unwelcome consciousness? He fumbled the door open and poured himself a glass of water, wishing for headache relief.

In the bathroom cabinet he searched in vain for something that might be a suitable match for the feeling in his skull before settling on a handful of vitamins and a scrounged ibuprofen in a bottle hiding behind a box of tampons. He frowned and slammed the door, genuinely surprised when the mirror didn't break.

Although he felt like shit, Utter Shit, with capital letters, Samson was intent on being useful, on making up for lost time. He had resigned his job with the police force the previous week and needed to find something new, if only to keep his mind occupied and to avoid being arrested by his previous partners. Staring at the ceiling from the leather couch, now that the headache had dissipated, was hardly going to help, especially since the drapes were open and the sun was blaring at him, mocking his discomfort.

His knees creaked when he peeled himself off the leather and walked around. He tested the state of his head by taking deep breaths and stretching his arms. Stretching his hamstrings would have been too much. From his vantage point in the hall, he could see the state he'd been existing in—it could hardly be called living. The house was a confirmed bachelor pad, if bachelors lived in squalor. After a tall glass of dissolvable vitamins Samson found in the pantry, he turned to face things, literally and figuratively.

The dishwasher, the vacuum cleaner, the mop and everything in between, were used to capacity and then discarded. Eventually Samson was ready to face his messages before deleting them, and then the scary fridge with its congealing contents. Dirty clothes from the pile on the bed, and in the wardrobe, the office, hanging in the bathroom, went into the washing basket.

"I have a wash basket?"

No, it was Julene's, but she had neglected—or not bothered—to take it with her when she walked out. His body sagged and he crawled onto the bed, craving oblivion. He imagined he could smell her on the sheets, the pillow. Even after nearly a month. When was the last time they had been washed? The comforter, the throw cushions—*throw cushions?*—even in the air, for Christ's sweet sake.

There could be no relief while his face was buried in something he could no longer have. There was some air freshener in the bathroom and he brought it back to the bedroom. After spraying it generously around the room he glanced at the label. Lemon something or other, her preferred brand.

"Is there nothing in this fucking place that's mine?"

Books and cushions and bits and pieces were thrown to the floor from shelves and cupboards, including a bra that conjured more than mere memories. Samson caught a glimpse of himself in the coffee table glass and was hardly inspired. He ought to have a shower and then go to bed since the room now seemed devoid of all personality, let alone that of his ex-girlfriend.

He sagged onto the couch again, lost. He could forgo the shower and just sleep right here but he was uncomfortable and seemed, after his cyclonic cleaning of the house, to lack the energy needed to roll sideways and lie down. Food, then? Out of the question. His stomach was an acid pit, likely to erupt at the slightest provocation. As it was, he was lucky it hadn't objected to the proximity of the detergents for the previous few hours.

What did he normally do for a hangover? Because cleaning the house in almost a state of mania was just not cutting it. But of course, Julene used to make an organic concoction that worked every time. He did lay down, uncomfortable again, the brown leather of the couch creaking beneath him, and reached for the stereo remote. The low music drifted until twilight when his eyes opened again. They betrayed him and tears fled down his cheeks.

"Fuck," he whispered.

The next morning Samson awoke unlike most others, ready for the day after his three cups of coffee and not thinking about heading out to drown his sorrows. A list of jobs on the fridge announced that first he must take care of the dirty washing and think about apologizing to his neighbors for his almost continued intoxication. Eventually he decided against apologizing and assumed renewed good behavior would trump all.

"First, a job. My primary setback to life as a confirmed bachelor."

Grocery shopping, steering his cart clear of all that reminded him of better days, kept him busy. Later, perusing the employment ads with espresso coursing through his veins at a café marginally helped his state of mind, since it was still frustratingly free of bulletproof grain alcohol. The newspaper didn't hold his attention for long, and he watched a bus on the main road drive past with a large poster for the next clash of sporting teams. He wondered if joining a football team would keep him occupied as well. His mind wandered toward getting laid properly with one or another of the players' wives.

"Now there's a challenge," he muttered, wondering when he had become such an asshole.

After another day of self-imprisonment, Samson set to work washing and refinishing the outside of the house and fixing some loose tiles on his roof when he could no longer ignore the blatant sunshine, mocking him through the window. As he worked, he reflected that he hadn't felt this clear-headed for a while. Of course, he hadn't had this much free, and sober, time on his hands. And before that he had been much occupied with work and—

But enough of that. Back to mindless physical labor, that would keep him honest.

And honest it kept him. For a week, Samson did little else than hard physical labor: cleaning and repainting the in- and outside of his house, mowing lawns, gardening as though possessed, and jogging daily—wearing himself out to the utmost. By the time he had eaten a hearty, huge by most standards, evening meal and cleaned the kitchen to hospital grade, Samson would shower and be asleep before his head hit the pillow. His sleep, dreamless.

"So tell me, David." He glanced up from his steaming plate, fork half raised. "What makes a man like you tick?"

Chewing his food, Samson tried to affect a look of deep thought. In reality, he was thinking how disappointed he was with the whole evening, and what a stupid remark that was.

"Same as any man, Doctor." She raised her eyebrows. "Food, shelter, and sex."

"No love?" An arch smile.

"Not if I can help it."

"Perhaps I can rectify that." Her foot brushed his leg under the table, touched his foot more forcefully.

"You can certainly try." *Fat chance.*

Dr. Ashton's home was a penthouse apartment in the heart of Adelaide, too close to everything in Samson's mind. His own house was only on the other side of the park but it was far enough to be *away*, even from such a small city. The apartment décor was bare, sparse; calico rugs and pale wooden furniture; incense burned somewhere. Soft lighting and softer music made him think of leaving. She handed him a glass of wine and smiled at him as she sipped hers.

"Nice place, Doctor."

"Victoria, please."

"Victoria."

Samson had been invited to give an opinion on updating the interior of the apartment over dinner, but he had seen from the beginning of the night that she had other ideas. He set the glass on a blond wooden table and traced her jaw with his finger, her face drawing up to his in a hungry kiss. His hands were in her hair and her fingers unbuttoned his shirt.

Victoria's bathroom was just as bare as the rest of the rooms, though it was more appropriate in the bathroom, he thought. Wood-grain standing boards, white tiles reflecting nothing because of the steam. Samson's shower was hot, very hot, and Victoria yelped as she stepped in with him. Cooler water sluiced down their skin and flattened her hair, turning it the color of dishwater. She took him in her hands and gasped in pleasant surprise as he pushed her against the wall, mouth on her breasts, hands on her skin, molding her to him yet again. This time he was gentler and she didn't correct him when he absently whispered a name that wasn't hers.

He awoke in her sparse bedroom, underneath a white quilt with her ash blonde hair covering her face. She smelled sweet but he was not interested in pursuing anything further, including that thought.

The truth was, all he wanted was to disconnect, to not think, and what better way was there other than physical work? Including sex, but he doubted he would see Victoria again.

Gathering his rumpled clothes to his chest he padded quietly to the kitchen. He left an apologetic note to zero effect on the dining table because there were no magnets on the fridge. She was the only person he'd ever met with no fridge magnets.

At home after a long hot bath in which he fell asleep and awoke prune-like, Samson had little else to do and he was in danger of thought.

"Not for long!"

In loose shorts and a long-sleeved shirt against the sun, he set off down the street, first walking, jogging, and then running as his thoughts threatened to overtake him. Eventually Samson began to feel his muscles—a dull ache—and a whiff of breeze had the heavy scent of man from beneath the shirt wafting to his nose. He was sweating profusely. He turned for home, arriving shortly before Moose pulled into the driveway in a tiny Mazda.

"Samson, I don't know how you do it. I can barely get out of bed in the morning."

"Take a look at yourself, that should give you some motivation, you fat bastard."

"I'm big boned and you're jealous."

"I've got a big bone of my own. I don't need to be jealous."

"Anyway, there's usually a gorgeous woman sleeping at my side and that's encouragement enough to stay in bed."

They both chuckled and walked around the side of the house; Moose readying the barbecue while Samson headed inside to shower.

Moose was ready with the oil and condiments and a couple of plates on the wooden table outside when Samson came out, smelling considerably fresher than before.

"Do you know what I heard some woman on the bus talking about today?"

"What were you doing on a bus? And what happened to your car? That Mazda is tiny." Samson glanced away from their dinner to look at his friend, sitting well away from the hot mess of the barbecue burners.

"My car broke down."

"That's a laugh! With all the money you pour into it, the damn thing should be running like a wet dream."

"Ok, well, I crashed it."

Hilarity from Samson.

"Are you happy now? I only bought the damn thing a year ago and it's irreparable. At least, it looks that way to me."

"You with all your mechanical know how. When was that, and how'd it happen?"

"Apparently I took a corner too fast and skidded on some gravel, took out a pole on the other side of the road and rolled. It was a week ago."

"Holy shit! But you're okay?" He did spare a glance for his friend's well-being. "I told you not to buy an imported model." They hemmed and hawed.

"I know, but tell me, honestly, what car isn't imported these days anyway?"

"Yeah, ok everything's imported." It was tantamount to admitting defeat.

"Are you going to the motor show?"

Moose ducked into the kitchen for silverware and then sat down on the bench-seat, waiting for Samson to bring over the meat. Samson absently turned the sausages, rustled the onions, and looked over at the table as he pulled the meat off the flames.

"What, no salad?"

Moose wrinkled his nose and waved his hand for Samson to continue.

"I'll be there tomorrow morning, ticket in hand. How 'bout you?"

"Hell yes, wouldn't miss the new Mercedes for all the famed women of Hindley Street."

"That's a big call."

"Yeah, maybe that's taking it too far, but I'll be there. Anything in particular I should keep an eye out for?"

"Other than the Lexus girls?" Samson was thoughtful for a moment before replying. "The Sandman. Just like the old ones, except it's the latest Pontiac. I always wanted one when I was a studly young man. I probably wouldn't have had a chance in hell of getting anyone in there of course, except for the boys with a six-pack of beer."

They were quiet as they ate and moved only to get more beer from inside.

"Speaking of houses, what do you think? I've been hard at work. Look any different?"

"Cleaner, newer even. You did a great job, man. Love the new stain on the floorboards."

Samson nodded his thanks and then forked more steak.

"Anyhow, I saw Julene the other day, looking radiant as always."

"Oh." Samson tried to ignore the feeling of meat sitting unpleasantly in his gut, all of a sudden. "With someone, no doubt." Samson refused to meet his friend's eyes and steadfastly watched what he was doing. Knife, fork, mouth, plate, repeat.

"Quite the opposite. She was alone, wandering about the place. We had brunch at that pie place on the corner."

"Jeez, you'll even invent a meal so you can eat."

Moose ignored the comment and continued.

"She seemed kind of sad, to be honest."

Samson didn't reply straight away. "And what about you. Are you seeing anyone special?"

"No, but if I played my cards right, and with some sweet talking, I could otherwise be married by now."

"That's bullshit. So why aren't you, then?" Samson wiped his face with a napkin and leaned back, his hands behind his head.

"Man, the real question is, why aren't you?"

Samson dropped his hands but Moose persisted.

"Now if I were you, I would've chased after Julene like a man possessed. And I can tell you that if a woman half her caliber had the great misfortune to come my way, I certainly wouldn't be here tonight, shooting the shit with you, my friend."

They stared at each other, eyes level. It was high time Samson leveled about what had happened or moved past it already. They both knew it; Moose relented first.

"I just never understood why you didn't try harder to win her back."

"Well she's not a trophy for one thing, she was always adamant about that, but she was right to leave me, had every right." Samson pushed back his chair and lifted a foot onto the chair beside him. "Don't think I wanted to let her go, but I would've done the same."

"What are you saying?" Moose read his expression. "So you didn't just have a fight. You did something; you stupid prick." Moose rolled his eyes.

Samson nodded, defeated, and relayed the story.

*It was a Saturday evening and there was a whole heap of people at Sean's house, only a handful of which he actually knew. After a few drinks they started talking about drugs. They knew, of course, that he was a cop. He wouldn't arrest them—drugs weren't his area—but they shouldn't get out of hand. They'd cajoled him about trying something himself, which he'd declined. Obviously they thought it would be a lark.*

"I still don't know how they did it, I thought I was careful with my drinks for exactly that reason."

*But he had ended up flying, the whole world his playground. He could*

*only remember vague illusions of color and patterns in front of his eyes.
Sean had later told him the rest.*

*It may have been Linda who slipped something to him, because she
was playing up to him all night. Of course he hadn't minded the attention
but remained unimpressed with her, otherwise. Up to a point. Almost
everyone else had left or was leaving, so it was only Sean and Julene who
walked back out to the patio, and saw Linda on top of Samson in a corner
of the backyard, their simultaneous cries echoing off the fence. The one
fact in Samson's favor—almost but not quite a saving grace—was when it
was over he had said, "I love you, Julene." But that was beside the point.
Sean had sent Linda home, she, too, not properly herself, and Samson
had walked the half a block to his own house.*

*In the morning he had found a note stuck on the fridge. "Good-bye"*

*Just the finality of the word and the fact that there was no explanation
or anything else had set alarm bells ringing in his head. In the bathroom
he had smelled another woman and after showering profusely, had called
Sean. Sean had been reluctant to speak to him at all and only eventually
relayed the evening to him, his voice laced with disdain.*

"Since she left me, I've fucked nearly everything I can, a way of
filling the gap, I suppose, but it's not done anything useful. For all I
know, I've sewn plenty of wild oats." He smiled bitterly.

"Dude, that's so fucked up, I'm sorry. But you need to tell her
you're sorry, beg for her forgiveness, throw yourself on her mercy
and all that."

"Don't you think I've done all that?"

"No. Otherwise, I've no doubt she'd be here instead of me, and
instead of pining for love lost, you'd be on the couch with Netflix
in the background."

Samson sighed and stared into his beer, looking drunk and
skeptical.

"I've no reason to doubt that she still loves you, misses you, and
wants you back. She didn't say as much but," Moose swallowed the
lie, "the tone of her voice, and, stuff."

"For bloody hell, man, don't talk about the tone of her voice." Samson poured them both new drinks. He avoided his friend's eyes. "Tell me about her eyelashes or how her clothes smelt." He set his elbow on the table to lean his chin on his hand.

"I'm sure her friends tell her to at least call you, if only to give you a bloody ear full. I would have done the same if she hadn't told me, something."

Samson's eyes were closed and his breathing was a little heavy. He nodded slowly against his palm and then lifted the other hand and waved it for him to keep going.

"Are you even awake, man?" Moose didn't get a real response and he couldn't bring himself to say what came next in more than a whisper. "She's pregnant."

Samson stirred, his head rising slightly off his hand, drool in the corner of his mouth, he grunted.

"What?"

Moose shook his head; it was nothing, of course.

They woke late Saturday morning, Samson dragging himself out of the bedroom and Moose sitting up on the couch, uncaring about the general discomfort he must have experienced the entire night. Neither remembered much of the end of the previous evening and it was just as well. Moose was no longer sure Samson was good enough for Julene, and Samson wasn't sure he wasn't better off without her, now that he was back to his "I'm king of the world even though I've no one to share it with" frame of mind.

# SIX

Since the time she'd resigned her nursing job and before she'd flown to London to pay her parents a convenient visit (she refused to admit that she'd been running away), Julene had decided to indulge her old love of the arts to keep herself busy. In no time, her pencils had rediscovered the talent of the hands, flowing over the pages. Sketches, landscapes, and soon abstracts, oils and water colors. Initially it had been purely for recreation and perhaps to flatter her vanity in her own abilities, but it had soon flourished into more. Had she had the concessions of wealth when she was younger, she would have pursued her love to a career but circumstances had not been in her favor. It wasn't until after she finished high school that her parents had begun taking well-paying international consultancy jobs, Julene thought wryly.

Her conveniently-timed visit had ended up becoming a full-fledged holiday and she'd stayed with her parents in their London townhouse for the last four months. During that time, she steadfastly ignored their attempts to discuss what had happened, instead visiting galleries and museums as often as they were open. Her parents relented on the conversation and cleared a space in the small sunroom for her to paint since she was most relaxed when she was doing it.

Though painting was not overtly physical, her parents—read, her father—had initially been alarmed at the rate at which it wore her out. Concerned but supportive, he had introduced her at the galleries of their neighborhood and eventually further afield and into London. Julene was encouraged to join a class where she could be taught correct techniques (and constantly observed, though he would never admit this to his daughter or his wife), so as to place as little stress as possible on her body.

It was at one of these classes that Julene had met Claude—a typically arty name, she'd thought at the time. He'd introduced himself as an art dealer who was looking for fresh *artistes*, new talent. Apparently she was a perfect example. After a period of getting to know and understand him, there came a period of acceptance—though he was flamboyant to the point of annoyance, Julene soon learned he was critical where criticism was called for yet vastly encouraging at the same time. As she'd spent more and more time indulging her hands with paints and pencils, Claude had quietly been establishing her a reputation with the small and shrewd group of art dealers he preferred to work with. It came as quite a surprise when he suggested she sell some of her work, or he sell it for her, and more of a shock when it sold so quickly. More than a dream come true, it was the life she had always wanted, the only lacking feature was a significant other to come home to, someone to share it all with; the father of her baby.

As she disembarked from the international flight, all the painful memories she had softened into cotton wool dreams returned to her tenfold and she scolded herself inwardly for letting her tumultuous hormones direct her mind. Now that she was home, Julene would be working full time on her art and preparing for the much-awaited arrival. She didn't know the sex of her baby—tradition had held firm there—but gifts were pouring in from all quarters for both boys and girls. She could only wonder what she would do with all the frilly dresses if she delivered a boy.

It was strange travelling from winter to winter, as if she was following Jack Frost from one side of the globe to the other. Though it was cold and windy in South Australia, it was a far cry from the English winter she had experienced with her parents. She was glad to be back in Adelaide, even if it was just below freezing and there was mist in the streets as they drove.

A thin layer of early morning ice crackled under her shoe as she alighted from the taxi, a task proven difficult by her sensitive belly and aching back. It was silly and petty that Julene no longer felt graceful. Yes, she glowed and was radiant with health and love, but she didn't feel there was grace in her step. She'd always been rather slim, skinny, some might have said, and she was used to feeling lithe and light. She felt clumsy and cumbersome now. Skipping around London at five months pregnant, she'd only just begun to show and perhaps that had given her a false sense of how the rest of her pregnancy would go. But now, at seven months, she felt enormous and was a little bulbous, and required the driver's help to the curb.

Similarly shocking were all of the suitcases and bags—some stand-out vintage pieces among them—the driver pulled from the trunk of the car; she should have noticed them before she left Heathrow but she'd been in a daze, people like fog all around her, and having had only fitful sleep on both legs of the journey had not helped.

Once inside her house, with the door closed against the chill and the heater emitting persistent warmth, Julene left a short message on her parents' voice mail a million miles away, a million miles she still couldn't believe she'd just finished traveling, and headed straight up to her bed, hopeful it was as comfortable as she remembered it.

Sleep now, was almost as fitful. The major difference was the soft mattress and warm blankets enveloping her like a hug. Though she was asleep, Julene wasn't sure if she was dreaming or remembering, but David Samson featured heavily in her mind's motion pictures, always smiling, touching her, laughing with his goofy grin, and, later, carrying a child with him. She thought it was a girl, judging by the color of the blanket.

The telephone cut through her sleep. It was a distant sound, distant but no less constant. It was still dark, could that be right? No, it was dusk. No, it was just her eyes adjusting as she came slowly awake. Just as dimly, she wondered why she hadn't turned the stupid thing off rather than leave it in the kitchen. If it was important, they'd ring back. It could really only be her parents calling back or Claude, and besides, it was too damn cold to get out of bed.

The next morning Julene found it had been Claude who had called. After leaving another message for her parents, she set to work checking the kitchen and wiping a thin layer of dust from the red composite counter and steel appliances. Julene listened to Claude's soft but commanding voice relay details of an art "viewing" and she made a mental note to phone while looking earnestly through the pantry for a scrap of edible food.

"Nothing. I should have had some delivered."

Other than some tea and a lot of empty containers, there was nothing with which to wake up.

A dejected reflection stared back at her from the steamed glass door. As hot, condensed water dribbled down the shower screen, flashes of David Samson recurred to her over and over. Perhaps she had a headache. He kept asking her why she hadn't told him about her pregnancy. Why hadn't she contacted him; why hadn't she let him know; why had she just run away.

"Because you probably wouldn't have called, anyway."

Her broken voice echoed off the white tiles, bouncing back to her sullen ears once or twice before evaporating like the water now puddling around her wrinkling toes. Though it was pure pain, Julene sunk down to the bottom of the shower and balled her pathetic little eyes out, quiet sobs wracking her, hot water needling.

It was a time before her eyes ran dry but she felt better for it and reached for the fancy shower gels and lotions her mother had packed. Opening each bottle was an exercise in the olfactory; rubbing only a small amount of each onto her skin was restraint itself. Each new scent, each new pooling of the fragrant liquid in the palm of her hands invigorated, restored her mind to its usual positive state. She relished the feel of the heat around her and on her skin. She found herself humming a recent song, hands ever-increasing in massaging motions until her breasts became tender, nipples swollen. Were pregnant women supposed to become aroused over nothing? She thought about it as she leaned against the wet tiles, goosebumps all over.

"I'm going to have to start reading up on these things."

Julene giggled to herself as her hands moved lower. She massaged the small of her back, felt the rounded curve of her belly, fingers moving ever lower to where her baby had been created, and she was consumed by a feeling of self, of power that she could be carrying another life within her delicate body, that she had the power to deliver this new life into the world and shape it, help it grow, nourish it, and love it. She loved herself.

It must have been hormones because Julene felt hyper-sensitive to even the smallest touch. As she dressed in thick cotton pants and a thicker woolen sweater, her skin was aflame. The fabric brushed against it, caused static with her hair and tingled her fingertips as she pulled the material over her body.

Outside, the streets were preternaturally silent; the sky low and colored a crystalline pastel, the smell of coming rain thick in her nose. Walking seemed the order of the day and it was a short distance to the shops. Slowly, sounds became louder and sharper—the crisp crackle of leaves underfoot—and she seemed to become real, she knew not how to describe it but now she was *there*, whereas before she'd not been.

"Just hormones, or jet lag."

Already she was at the plaza and people were everywhere, some with children, some with dogs, the cutest little dogs with matching coats and leads, their owners dawdling in the fruit shops or window shopping at the bookstore. Would her child be like theirs, the people not the dogs? She absently rubbed her belly through her navy coat and reached for a cart, pushing it toward the entrance to the store. Fluorescent bulbs poured pallid light over everything, every person, and Julene felt it like a cold sweat. Faces became anonymous as she reached out for some potatoes, her fingers grappling and then grabbing desperately as her treacherous feet gave out beneath her. She went down.

Julene awoke in an uncomfortably soft bed, the smell of antiseptic in her nose. She tried to sit up but her head protested. A nurse in the corner came to her bedside, a soft and warm cloth in her hand, insisting she lay back as she applied it to her forehead. A doctor entered the room and came straight to her side, rather than to the foot of the bed where the chart hung from a rail.

"Good morning." His voice was deep and rumbling, like distant thunder or rolling surf. "Do you remember what happened?"

"Not really." Julene's voice sounded weak and small to her ears, like a child.

"Apparently, you collapsed in the fruit and veg department of the market just around the corner. I've run a few tests and they confirm what I first thought." The doctor moved to the foot of the bed and retrieved her paperwork, stepping close to her again. "Believe it or not, you're a little on the malnourished side. I can see you've been putting on weight but nutrition is a concern." He checked the chart again.

Julene's eyes widened in alarm. The doctor placated her with his large, gentle, ideally masculine hands.

"We'll be putting you on a course of dietary additives to turn things around, and I want you to start seeing a specialist."

She nodded her compliance.

"Julene."

She turned to look at the doctor and really saw him for the first time. His dark hair was run through with a bit of grey at the sides and she guessed his age to be maybe mid-thirties. His eyes were amazing and his open collar betrayed his suntan, even though it was the middle of winter. For the first time she wondered how she looked and what she was wearing underneath these hospital linens. He was holding something out to her, a card.

"This is for a specialist whom I've been working closely with for a while. I'd like you to see her as soon as you can."

He patted her arm and left the room, the nurse at his side. Julene looked down at the card in her hand, brought it to her nose and sniffed. It was probably only hand soap on the card, but the very idea of him had her thinking of shower gels.

The next day Julene was allowed to leave the hospital and once again, she arrived home in a taxi. This time, though, she called an old family friend to shop for her and when she entered the house, she could smell a hot kitchen. She called out as she closed the heavy door behind her and leaned against it, standing still for just a moment.

"In the kitchen, honey. I thought you could use a home-cooked, hot breakfast."

"Thanks, Janet, but I did eat at the hospital."

"I know, but I also spoke to your doctor yesterday after visiting hours were over, what a honey of a man, by the way! So here I am."

Janet greeted her with open arms wrapped inside a heavy woolen cardigan and guided Julene to the couch where she arranged her between the soft cushions.

"Now, where is that little table of yours?"

Julene fiddled with the cushions and then turned her head to see what exactly Janet was fidgeting with. Janet's ass could be seen poking around a corner of the cupboard as she looked for the lap table with the bean bag base. Julene couldn't figure out what she was looking at or a polite way of asking.

"Janet, what have you been doing with yourself?"

"Nothing. Why do you ask?"

"Your ass . . ."

"Oh! It's these pants!" She stood up with the little stable table and laughed, walking back into the kitchen. She returned with a plate in her hands. "Everyone says something like that when I wear them, stupid things. I don't know why I haven't thrown them away. Now, get this into you."

She thrust the plate, heaped high with grilled vegetables plus eggs, under Julene's nose and sat down beside her to watch her eat.

It wasn't necessary to tell Janet about her holiday because she still kept in contact with her parents. Julene was also sure her father would have been on the phone to Janet as soon he left the airport. She told her about some ideas she'd had for some new art projects instead, and they discussed how many canvases she might be able to fit in the back room. Gradually the discussion led to Claude, her parents, the flight, the doctor, and then to David Samson. Throughout the whole, Janet was up and down preparing tea and toast as fast as Julene could consume it. Julene protested but Janet rebuked her with words from the good doctor. This inevitably led to a discussion about him and his availability or lack of.

They were interrupted by a knock on the door and who should it be but the good doctor himself, looking good in jeans and a heavy grey coat unbuttoned over a well-loved sweater. Both women were taken back and blushed with embarrassment. He stepped awkwardly into the room past Janet and produced a goody basket full to the brim. Julene pushed herself up from the navy corduroy couch and walked over to meet him. She appreciated the touch of his fingertips as he gave her the basket and then Janet took it gently out of her hands and whisked it away to the kitchen.

"Hi," he said with a forced smile. "I hope this is a good time. I'm not interrupting any-"

"Dr Litton. It's nice to see you. I didn't realize the hospital did house visits."

"Well, no, they don't. I just." He fidgeted with his coat. "Do you mind if I take this off?"

He sloughed the thing off when Julene shook her head and handed it awkwardly to her. Julene gestured to the room at large so that he might move away from the door or from her or whatever else might be making him stammer. She draped his coat over the side of a chair and watched him walk stiffly away from her.

"Sorry to barge in like this. I don't. I didn't. I mean, I don't usually make house calls either. I didn't see anyone visit you, and I didn't want you to be going through anything. Alone. I mean, I live nearby and I was on my way home and thought, I don't know what I thought, I just. Grabbed that. Life can be hard, sometimes, you know? Harder than it needs to be and, it's nice to have someone to talk to. I'm not saying you don't, but you didn't. You know. The other day." He scratched his head. "Sorry, what was the question?"

After such an explanation and the ensuing silence, it was obvious he had more personal concerns in mind than that of a doctor for his patient. She wouldn't delay their pleasure any longer, Julene thought, so she slid her arms around his neck and thoroughly kissed him.

He looked aghast as he gently pushed her away from him.

"Oh no!" Julene was horrified, and then burst out laughing, apologizing profusely.

He, however, wouldn't hear of it and apologized for giving her the wrong idea. He introduced himself properly to Janet as she stood staring at them both after having come back into the room. He stuttered a little.

"I'm Doctor Darcy Litton."

Janet looked to Julene. Both had dancing eyebrows and Oh Mr Darcy! expressions.

"I think we met briefly this afternoon, or yesterday, rather. I'm sorry, I was a little busy."

"Oh my, don't you worry about that. I'm glad Julene has someone to talk to besides me. I've got to get going so don't you get into trouble between now and tomorrow afternoon." She kissed Julene on her cheek and gave Dr Litton a big cheesy smile as she left.

"I really am, very sorry, and very embarrassed. I don't usually do that."

Julene edged back to the couch and busied her hands with a cushion.

"Don't even worry about it. I don't want to say it happens all the time but I'd be lying if I didn't say that I don't mind when a female patient plants a smacker on me unawares." They both laughed. "But don't tell my boss I said that."

He wandered into the kitchen and Julene could hear him opening cupboards and drawers while the kettle boiled. He brought two steaming mugs into the lounge room.

"So how are you? And what have you been up to, or, are going to be up to? That's a gorgeous kitchen, by the way. The red countertop is amazing."

Julene smiled at the kitchen comment and then told him about her plans for the second bedroom. Now she was home again, she'd be working full-time on her art projects and was going to convert the back bedroom into a proper studio. Some new equipment was being delivered tomorrow and she was sure Claude was going to start calling her every forty-five minutes.

"Wow! That sounds amazing. And you've really had so little formal training. It must be in your soul, then."

"I like to think so. Now, I appreciate you dropping by but since I can't get busy with you, I think I ought to get to work so my hands, at least, can get busy."

He left his cup on the table and wished her well as he grabbed his coat. She could only sigh disappointedly after he left.

# SEVEN

Three miles due south, Samson slept soundly in his bed. The previous day had been a long one, rubbing down and staining the floorboards of a stunning terrace apartment in a suburb renowned for them, and then a surprise visit from Victoria.

A short time after Julene had gone overseas, though he knew nothing about it, Samson had decided against a proper job and set to work on his house so as to sell it and move on. Of course, he saw it as an opportunity to make some money (for he'd added considerable value to his property) but also to get a change of scenery, though he didn't examine his reasons for wanting one. He'd been toiling for a few weeks when he realized he was procrastinating and decided to shelve the idea of the sale. He got himself registered and licensed as a Building Contractor, and started working on other people's houses instead.

Victoria, meanwhile, had become something of a fixture in his life. She was an assertive woman and he seemed to have been an impartial decision-maker in what had become their routine. She would sometimes come with fixings for dinner or take out from somewhere downtown, or sometimes she'd drop by late at night. He was trying to be indifferent to her presence but he certainly didn't mind the company at night.

Samson was anticipating a tough day today, not because of any work that was underway but because of a delay. Days that weren't completely full with physical work were harder for him, and he sometimes ran for an hour mid-way through the day if there was a lag in his schedule, lest his idle mind dwell on the past.

One of Samson's clients had met with their architect and made changes to the original plan, so everything was on hold until the new permits were granted. After a meeting with the permit office and a rep from the architect's office, Samson met up with Moose for a quick lunch, then it was home to change out of the office threads and back into his heavy duty King Gee work clothes.

His mind was gloriously still while his hands were full of activity. The late afternoon was eaten up by phone calls with new clients anxious about their projects, whereas Samson was anxious about when he would have time to eat. He had a night out with friends planned, and he didn't do the whole "shit-faced on a school night" thing anymore, so he really needed to eat something. He could ill-afford late starts since his business had really taken off. Originally, he'd started out doing a bit of work for a friend and then a friend of a friend, and now he was busier than he could have imagined. He made it into town as night fell.

Moose stood and waved Samson over to the table. He made his way through the throng of people and threw a glance at the bar before sitting down. There were a few drinks on coasters already and a few more were ordered. There were one or two people from Moose's office, whom Samson had met briefly before, and a few guys from high school as well. He also waved over a few guys he'd been working with recently that he spied on the other side of the room, and the wooden tables were merged noisily.

Conversation mainly consisted of jokes about how clean and well-turned out everyone was, until a group of women sat down at a table not far away and the conversation turned to possible happy consequences of said cleaning up. Samson remembered Joey from high school, looking basically the same but with a few added pounds and longer hair. He asked if anyone was still with their high school or university sweethearts and who had moved on to meeting women in bars. One of the other guys from school piped up.

"Hey, Samson, tell me did you ever get together with Julene Somersby?" All eyes at the table turned his way. "You and her had the hots for each other for ages. There were bets going round on graduation whether or not you'd propose before she ran off overseas."

Everyone laughed, though Samson's was ginger and Moose's was quiet.

"Yeah, you know, we actually did, get together. No ring, though." People booed. "But that was a little while ago now, and she's off doing I don't know what these days."

"Oh mate, how'd you let that happen? Bar flies are a dime a dozen but I'm pretty sure she could've been the one." Joey missed the look in Samson's eyes.

"Yeah, I don't know what happened. It just didn't work out, in the end."

He avoided looking in Moose's direction. The conversation moved on to the other might-have-been relationships from the past ten years, and then a few of the guys went over and bought drinks for the women at the other table. Moose gestured for the barman to bring another round.

In spite of his good intentions, Samson was feeling worse for wear the next morning on his run around the neighborhood. He had a bit of a headache as he jogged and he dropped a few business cards accidentally. He always brought a few cards in his pocket so he could pop them into the mailboxes of any houses he saw that could use some TLC. He had left a few that morning and turned around to find himself at the end of the street from Julene's house. Joey's comment must have appealed to his subconscious mind. He'd run clear across town without even realizing. Samson checked his watch and ran to the end of the street to flag down a cab.

He was only a little late to start work and he made it up by working through lunch. His mind was as busy as his hands, which was a
relief – he needed to delete last night's conversations from his mind.
He was getting calls from people who had received business cards in
their mailbox that very morning. His schedule for the next month
filled quickly with appointments for inspections and estimates, and
he'd have to refrain from heading out with the guys until after these
new jobs were well established. He replied in kind to a message from
Joey who invited him to hit the town on the weekend, and who was
still teasing him about letting Julene get away. He allowed himself a
short sigh and then headed home for a shower and dinner.

Victoria walked in that night not long after he arrived and she
brought wine. She hung her coat noisily in the hall closet and
walked up behind him in the kitchen, wrapping her arms around
his waist and laying her head on his back. He 'hmmm'ed a hello and
kept on stirring, slowly easing out of her embrace.

"How was work, today?" He spared her a glance as he pulled
another plate from the cupboard and divided the food between the
two.

She talked about patients and nurses and an argument she'd
had with a technician while she poured the wine. He 'hmmm'ed
as he ate and wondered if she would be staying over tonight. He
was kind of tired. She ended up finishing the wine and fell asleep
pretty heavily on one of the leather couches after dinner. There was
nothing to watch on television so Samson tried to read a book but
couldn't really get into it. He sighed and hefted Victoria into the
bedroom. He stayed awake late, staring at the ceiling as she lightly
snored; it wasn't loud but it hurt his brain. He got up and headed
for the study with the idea of a scotch but hit his jaw on the lamp.
Samson thought he'd moved it into the corner of the lounge room.

He'd have to tell Victoria to stop moving his bloody furniture. He might lose an eye next time.

The scotch had soured in his stomach and after twenty minutes of trying to sleep, on his back, his side, his feet under and then out of the blankets, he was still awake. Samson opened his eyes and turned toward Victoria next to him. He ran his hand from her chin to her thigh. Her hair fell across her face as she started to wake and it looked grey. He followed the shape of her fingers with his fingers, until they curled around his hand and he saw her eyes open. He looked at her before moving in to kiss her. She blinked and raised her eyebrows.

"Don't fall asleep, now," she whispered.

# EIGHT

Julene had just woken up and the sun was peeking through the trees when she heard a truck pull up outside. She peeked through the curtains and spied a couple of workmen opening the back of a white box truck. Her heavy navy coat thrown hastily on, she walked outside to ask them if they wanted a hot drink when they were done. She held the door for them as they brought in a couple of large easels, print racks, a couple of stools, a drawing table, an art horse, and a metal flat file drawer. As the coffee steamed in the mugs, they went out and brought back a large box each of brushes, pastels, and paints. They assured her, as their hands warmed up around the hot drinks, that the paper would be delivered soon after they left.

Later, when she was moving the easels around for the tenth time, the paper arrived and she was almost light-headed with glee when it was safely installed in the flat files. Julene pulled on a large apron and set to work immediately with the pastels. Eventually, she stopped because she was so hungry. Remembering the advice and direction from Dr. Litton, *sigh*, and the specialist, she sat down and had a proper meal and made a large thermos of tea to keep on hand in the studio for later. In the meantime, she stirred the miso soup on the stove. Janet was coming over later with her multi-bowl slow cooker so she could make her meals ahead. When the pot was off the hotplate, she checked her messages. Claude was on a flight *right now*, and would land in a few hours. That was much sooner than she'd expected but at least she could stay home right until the last minute. And she did. She didn't even hear Janet come in and set up the slow cooker but she smelled the evidence of her visit after a while. It reminded her to drink some of the tea but she didn't pause long.

The phone rang and it was Claude. *Claude!*

"Oh my goodness, Claude! I'm so sorry! I'll leave straight away."

"Nonsense, I am already in a cab and coming into the city. The driver assures me we'll be there in no time. Just make sure you aren't working in your pajamas again, please."

After a hasty shower, Julene threw on some clean clothes just in time for the doorbell to ring. Claude swept in and hugged her, and then unceremoniously—or ceremoniously—dumped his coat and scarf and bags in a heap and told her to take him to the studio.

They walked through to the back room and he was pleased to see her pastel drawings from the morning and the fact that she had a dedicated studio.

"It's beautiful. Just beautiful. Now, get ready, we have appointments downtown to decide when and where to host your coming out party."

"I am ready. I just got dressed."

He gave her a dubious look and shook his head.

"No, no. Let's see what else we can find."

After a visit to her wardrobe and the required change, he was satisfied. It was a bit flashier than what she would normally pair, but Claude assured her she looked like an *artiste* announcing herself to the world and they had no more time left to spare. He hurried her out the front door.

It was brisk outside but it was bright rather than overcast and they had the requisite coats. A taxi drove past and Julene lifted her arm to wave it down.

"Oh, no need for that," Claude motioned for her to follow him.

"We're just going around the corner here first. We'll go into the city later. I spoke to the owner a few times over the phone after you left London and I feel very confident this will be a perfect fit."

It really was only a short walk and Julene realized they were going to The ArtCaf, where she had occasionally hung out with Samson for a year or so before she went overseas. She pushed the memories out of her mind.

Inside it was bright and airy, windows making up one wall. The rest of the décor was comprised entirely of paintings or drawings by local artists. They were told by the maître d' that the current exhibit would be taken away by the end of the week and three-quarters of the work had already been sold. A woman with a bold shock of auburn hair and wearing a haute navy dress came to meet them.

"Hi. I'm the owner, Catherine Thomas. Please, call me Cath." She shook both of their hands.

"I'm Julene Somersby and you've been speaking to my manager Claude Martin over the phone."

"I think I used to see you around here a while ago?"

"I did used to hang out a bit before I went to London. I don't remember this much art, though, the last time I was here."

Cath gestured for them to sit at a table by one of the large windows and opened a thin folder to show them photos from previous events.

"That's right. I only used to have a handful of pieces here at any given time, but we had such great interest from the community as well as the local art fraternity. I've amped it up and everyone is better for it. Friday and Saturday nights here are really packed. It's a great atmosphere, especially when an artist comes in with their own group of friends and can see how well people in general respond to the work, rather than an exclusive art crowd."

They talked about menu options and Claude asked questions about the guest list and asked for recommendations of the local up and ups so he didn't miss anyone or tweak any noses. He also pulled out a few photos of Julene's work to give Cath an idea of their size and the palettes she was using so the light would be to the best advantage of each of the pieces. The wait staff brought out some small plates of each of the items they'd chosen and Julene wolfed them down.

"Woah, make way for the hungry person. Let's get some proper food. You've obviously been working through snack time." Cath grinned at her and gestured for a selection of teas and snacks for three.

"So, does the collection have a name, or is it part of a series? And how do you want it promoted, in terms of scheme or design? I can work with a local designer if you like, but some artists prefer to design the promo material themselves."

Julene deferred to Claude since she had a mouthful of tea and cookie, and was eyeing off the aromatic plates a waitress was bringing out of the kitchen.

"Julene has such an amazing natural talent, there can be no doubt of that. However, this will be her first exhibit and I would rather her keep working, rather than getting involved in the minutia of promotions."

Julene nodded around forkfuls.

"I had a chance to look at a few new pieces this morning, and I think the promo materials should be fairly minimalist but with bold lines. Because, as you can see from these pictures, her work is very bold right now." He made a few sketches on a napkin and Cath put it in her folder.

"I can send a mock up later today and we should be able to get them out tonight if there aren't too many changes. I think that's it from my end, unless you have any questions."

Julene had finished her meal and Claude had finished his tea, so they were ready to go since Cath was clearly busy, with wait staff and managers queuing patiently in the background, many with notes or clipboards. They gave their thanks and good-byes as they wrapped their scarves and arranged their coats against the wind, which had picked up while they sipped and savored inside. Claude made some calls as they walked back to Julene's house, clouds threatening them with every step.

It had just begun to rain when they got through the front door and Julene's phone rang. She expected it to be her parents but it looked like the hospital number on the display. She wondered if she would get another chance with Dr. Litton after all. She answered the call with a bit of a strut. Claude quietly went into the studio room.

"Hellooo, Doctor."

"Hello? Julene?"

"Yes." She paused. "Is this call on speaker?"

"Yes. Julene, this is Dr. Litton from The Royal Adelaide Hospital, and I'm with a few of the members of the senior management." Awkward pause. "Is this a good time for you?"

Julene covered the handset as she laughed and then coughed, and started picturing her eighty-year-old neighbor gardening in the nude to regain her composure.

"Yes, this is a good time. What can I do for you?"

"Julene, I hope you don't mind, but after speaking to you the other day I heard the board here was looking to install some artwork around the hospital, and so I mentioned your name to them. We're wondering if you're available to come in for a meeting today? Perhaps you could bring some of your work, or copies of it, and we could discuss it."

She was completely taken aback.

"I would love that. I'd be honored. My manager just flew into town today, actually, and he'd welcome this opportunity."

They agreed on a time that very afternoon and Claude was jubilant at the news.

"This is the most amazing timing imaginable. Just think, if it all works out, this will launch you into the artistic stratosphere, not to mention local history!"

Julene laughed at his outburst.

"Seriously! You might be contributing to the artistic upgrading of the *hospital*, Julene. Your work would stay there for years, decades! This is enormous!"

His delight finally transferred to her and she was equal parts electrified and disbelieving.

"This will require another wardrobe change."

He shuffled her off to the bedroom and began huffing and puffing over her lack of appropriate garb. While Julene was changing, Claude made a few calls and informed her when she came back to the kitchen that she had an appointment with *the* local authority on all things *a la mode* later that evening.

"Her name is Ursula Litton."

"Oh. I dare say she might be related to my doctor."

The rain had ceased and was not meant to return until the wee hours so they risked the walk into town. Claude was happy to see the contrasting colors of the sky and garden foliage along the way. They stopped for more tea before continuing on to the hospital.

They were met in the pale reception by a service manager who ushered them upstairs. There were certainly plenty of open spaces since the restoration and renovation had been completed, and it was all quite drab. Julene could see why they were looking to liven up the place a bit. The service manager indicated which bland room they should go into and a large group was just sitting down at a boardroom table.

Introductions were offered and it seemed to take a long time as there were far more people present than Julene had expected. Of course, there were multiple sources of funding for the hospital and so there were interest groups, and user groups, and plenty of other interested persons, not to mention a large group of artists. Julene had to excuse herself halfway through a presentation because she'd drank so much of the lemon water. Claude filled her in on her return but she really hadn't missed much. There were a handful of artistic opportunities and a large number of artists being considered for the tenders, and so they would wait and see.

After what seemed like forever, everyone thanked everyone else and then most people left. There was Dr. Litton remaining, talking to a handful of suits near the door and then he walked over with two of them for personal introductions. Julene thanked them for their interest in her work and assured them of a speedy reply with regards to the paperwork handed out during the meeting. Claude tagged along with a few of the suits and waved her off. She smiled at Dr. Litton and clasped her hands in front of her chest.

"I cannot thank you enough, Doctor. This is, a dream come true and I feel like it wouldn't have happened without you. Thank you so much."

"Seriously, it was nothing. It was a lucky coincidence you told me about your work and I was in the right place at the right time to promote it. How are you settling in, by the way? You haven't been exhausting yourself with your projects, I hope. Your nutrition works best in conjunction with rest," he gently chided her.

"I know, I know. I appreciate your concern, however I might be of the opinion that I should be getting myself ready for no rest so I'm ready for that when the baby comes." She smiled up at him and he laughed. "Also, I was wondering, since you really aren't my primary doctor anymore, if you would join me for dinner one night this week?" They were both surprised by her question.

"Um, not like a date?"

"Well, how about like a date?" Julene felt her cheeks flush, but she pushed on. "I haven't had a date in a while and I think I'm overdue." She looked up at him boldly.

"Um, well, I feel like I can't say no, but, uh, I'm not sure that I should say yes." He looked at her without speaking for a heartbeat. "Okay, yes, what the hell. You're right; I'm not your doctor anymore. And that'd be nice. Where would you like to go?" Now it was his turn to redden a little.

"You know, I've always really liked The Elephant Walk. Do you know it?"

Dr. Litton chuckled.

"I do know it, dark and secretive as it is. And I know that it's favored by lovers, not so much by people who recently had a doctor-patient relationship. I don't think that's really a first-date kind of place." He scratched his head.

Julene was surprised at what kept coming out of her mouth. This audacity was not really true to her form. But perhaps she was reinventing herself a little, now her art was out of the box.

"Well, we could skip the first few dates, if you like." Now they were both just flirting; his eyebrows betrayed him and her cheeks betrayed her.

"You know, Julene, I don't want to say your hormones are speaking out of school. I mean, maybe you're always a ravishing beauty ready to tear men apart."

Julene grinned at him.

"But if you don't quiet down, then my hormones will start talking back and I don't think they'd take no for an answer." He paused to let that sink in. "And I'm still not sure if that's appropriate, right now."

Julene let her eyebrows do the talking while she took some inconspicuous deep breaths.

"Okay, well then I'll let you think of somewhere that is appropriate. I'm free most evenings this week, so let me know."

She smiled before turning and walking away, stupefied at her own daring. But so pleased. Claude 'tsk tsk'ed all the way down the stairs.

"Just as well we are meeting with Ursula Litton this evening. It sounds like you will need proper clothes for dating, too. Perhaps she will be recommending things for you to wear on a date with her brother?"

Julene was on a high and wanted to keep going; to keep walking and do some shopping and take in the sights and be inspired, but Claude was adamant he had promised her parents he would encourage rest at every opportunity, and it had already been a busy day.

"We really should have had you back at home by now, as it is. But these things cannot be helped; being in the early stages of greatness does take its toll."

He spied a sign for an antique book dealer as they walked toward the mall in the center of town. He saw it as an excellent opportunity to find some treasures and he knew shops such as these usually had big, overly-stuffed armchairs for whiling away the hours.

She woke with a bit of a snort and took a moment to remember where she was. The room was only softly lit with occasional small spotlights highlighting some of the shelves. It took more than a moment to get herself out of that over-stuffed chair, but she was glad of the rest. Claude had quite a package under his arm so he must not have minded the break, either.

They stopped at a café on the corner in order for Julene to refresh herself and grab a drink before meeting the inimitable Ms. Litton, who, Claude assured her, was universally adored and respected for her flawless taste.

"I told you, she is *Ms. A La Mode*."

They bustled into one of the stores in the mall and went upstairs to a corridor and were shown into one of the private dressing rooms. It was a very white room with contemporary lines and simple mirrors. And there she was. Ursula was a mere human, even after everything Claude had said about her. She looked fabulous, but understated; Julene had anticipated a woman with a louder personality. She introduced herself like a queen and congratulated Julene on her work for the hospital.

"Wow, news travels fast . . ."

"Well, I just got off the phone with my brother. He's a doctor there and he told me about the art opportunity for you and for other artists. That will be an amazing phase in your career."

She was so sincere and genuine, Julene was surprised she could have withstood the requisite of speculation and gossip by the social-climbing set. And yet. She'd organized multiple private fitting rooms with staff on hand to assist with dressing, and becking and calling in general, in a spendy clothing boutique in which Julene never would have set foot before. She was commanding, to say the least. Julene loved her.

When she later saw herself in the mirrors, her internal monologue consisted entirely in platitudes to Ursula's talents. Julene looked amazing. She'd never seen herself dressed this way. She was surprised, but also in love. She only turned down two outfits because they were just too low-cut for her comfort. But everything felt so comfortable at the same time as stylish and sort of sexy as hell, in spite of or even because of the swell of her belly in the clothes.

Julene was ready to go when Ursula interrupted.

"Oh no, we aren't finished yet."

"Good grief! I already have new underpants. I can't imagine what there is left."

"Don't even get me started on the proper lingerie for pregnant mamas. No. Tonight we are going to work a teeny bit on make-up since you now have a career in the public eye to perpetuate and because you will literally be under any number of spotlights at any given time. You need to look as bold on the outside, under those spotlights, as you are on the inside. Now sit."

Ursula had a few pictures she flashed to a waiting make-up artist who swept in with a veritable bandolier of creams and powders and pencils and brushes. It certainly didn't take as long as Julene expected and she was pleased to find she would take home the pictures with application tips so she could recreate the same look every time. She was shown how to do the major applications a few times and felt confident afterward that she would manage it at home. Ursula sent her and Claude away with assurances, and also a request to be gentle with her brother.

In the cab on the drive home, Julene thought to ask Claude how long he would be staying with her and was apologetic she hadn't already made up some space for him.

"Oh, no Julene. Don't worry about me. You have so much going on right now that I'm going to get in trouble with your physicians as well as your parents. I am booked into the hotel apartments not far from you and around the corner from The ArtCaf." The taxi arrived at her house. "Give me a ring when you get yourself organized tomorrow. But don't make it before lunch. Now get some rest." And he "toodaloo"ed as the car drove into the night.

Julene managed to get inside without dropping any of her bags or slamming them into the door as she pushed it shut behind her. She dumped it all by the door and went straight to the bathroom. It was her intention to take off the make-up and collapse in bed but once in front of the mirror, her reflection had her strutting around and she ended up pulling out some of the new clothes and looking in awe at them all over again. She did manage to wipe off the make-up and get into bed gracefully, mostly, eventually, but she would regret not putting anything away in the morning when she would almost topple over the heap of boxes and shoes on the carpet.

She did manage to sleep in the next morning. Julene allowed herself a drink and a visit to the bathroom, this time walking back on the other side of the bed so as to avoid the pile, before going back to sleep.

It was after lunch when she woke again and immediately called Claude before being told to "go back to bed, if that's what suits you." It didn't, since it was nearly two o'clock, so she ate one of the ready-made meals Janet had left the other day—or was it only yesterday?—and fixed the same to start again in the slow cooker for later. Then she got right to work in the studio, only stopping for tea breaks and more bowls of stewy- or soupy-goodness.

Julene assumed the days before the art exhibit would all be like this and was very happy with that prospect. But would she end up staying awake all night since she had slept all day? It wouldn't be the worst thing in the world if that was her routine for a while. At least it would help her stay in the moment during the exhibit. Cath had assured her and Claude that evenings were the best times for trendy and prominent soirees. So, staying up all night was definitely an option.

She checked the clock and then got right back to it, paint on her cheeks and hair, oily rags everywhere. In another hour she stopped for more tea. After mixing a slightly different hue, her phone rang. She had missed a few calls from her parents so she carefully put down the brush and wiped her hands on a supposedly clean rag before picking up the phone. Perhaps what she really needed was a Bluetooth headset so she wouldn't have to touch the phone at all.

"Hello?"

"Hi, Julene, it's Darcy Litton."

Julene's cheeks burned.

"Oh, Darcy, hi. Ha, it feels kind of weird to call you by your first name."

"Well, yeah. Since, as you pointed out, I'm not your primary doctor anymore, and you've been invited to tender on the art project, I think it's okay to be on a first name basis."

"Oh, well, now you mention it, because of the art tender, will us going out be seen as preferential treatment?"

"I'm not actually involved in that project; I think it'll be okay." He cleared his throat. "So, I'd like to take you up on that date, if the offer still stands. Are you available tonight? I know it's short notice but I've had a few appointments cancel, so, I thought tonight."

Julene looked at herself in a mirror and was shocked with how much of everything she'd managed to waste on herself, rather than the page or canvas which had been the center of her attention.

There were smudges on her cheeks as well as drips on her dark hair, and she seemed to have touched her neck at one point with almost an entire hand smeared in paint.

"Hello?"

"Yes, I'm here. Sorry, I just realized how much paint I have to wash off before I could think about coming out. Did you decide on somewhere respectable to be seen with me?" *Don't think of shower gels; don't think of shower gels.*

"Yes, actually. Since we're both in North Adelaide, I thought we'd just go to The Lion. How does that sound?"

It sounded good and she agreed to meet him there in an hour. She couldn't waste any more time on the phone. Julene ran straight into the bathroom.

There was a bottle of baby oil, which she used generously to scrub the paint off her skin. It was the easiest to get hold of after-hours if one was taken by a fit of inspiration while the art stores were closed, apparently, but she would never use that stuff on her baby. She thought about trying some of the make-up but looked at her watch and thought better of it. She hastily dressed in a new pair of well-fitting maternity jeans and a striped sweater. One last glance in the mirror, however, showed that her face and hands were still a bit red. She could put that down to the exertion of walking in the cold if he asked. She doubted he'd bring up the issue of exertion, however. Julene chuckled to herself as she grabbed her scarf and coat and walked out the door.

It was almost humid when she walked into the foyer of the pub, it was so crowded. She unwound her red scarf and opened her jacket, having a bit of a look around. She stopped short when she saw Samson sitting at a table with a group of people. She lost her breath and then stepped back, lest he see her. She hadn't thought much about that when she came back from London, and she had been so busy with the art in the meantime that she hadn't given—or allowed herself time to think of him. It was unacceptable if she had to speak to him tonight. She turned and walked back toward the door before he called out her name.

"Julene!" But it wasn't him. "Over here."

Standing there was Dr. Litton, Darcy. Surely it was the lighting that made him look so like Samson. But no. Walking over to his table, she took in the sweep of his dark hair, his eyes, the set of his jaw. Damn him. She sat down and apologized for staring.

"Well, I don't want to say it happens all the time, *again*, but I will if it will cheer you up. You look like you just saw a ghost. And not your favorite ghost, I take it."

She shook her head as she set her navy coat on the back of her chair.

"Not at all. I just, didn't recognize you at first. Now tell me, what are you drinking and why did you change your mind about meeting me?"

A waiter came to the table with a menu and recommended a few things from it. Julene could never make up her mind when eating out and she rarely took a companion's advice. She ordered the chicken burger from the 'specials' menu and a Portergaff. Darcy was particular in his recommendation to the waiter about the correct way of pouring the soda before ordering the same thing for himself.

"As I said earlier, my schedule changed. Also, my sister has told me plenty of times I need to get out more."

"Actually, I met your sister last night. She is amazing! She's like everything good from *How to Win Friends and Influence People*, plus clothes and make-up, in one Calvin Klein package. I love her!"

"Yes, she definitely is. She definitely got all the pizzazz in the family."

"I'm sorry, did you just say pizzazz?"

They laughed and their drinks arrived. They toasted to pizzazz. Their burgers arrived soon after and all talk was briefly interrupted.

"Wow, that was a big burger, so full of pizzazz! I can hardly believe I ate so much pizzazz."

Darcy nearly drowned in his beer from laughing. He nodded and smiled and gestured his acceptance of defeat. Then he gestured to her plate and belly.

"I'm a doctor, I know things. Pizzazz is good for both of you, you can take my word for it." They laughed again; ordered another drink when the waiter came back for the plates. "Seriously, though—"

"Pizzazz." They lost it.

"Stop" he pleaded, laughing. "Since the tender is public, there isn't any conflict of interest in us coming out together, but, I think The Elephant Walk would be taking things a bit too far."

Their eyes met in a moment of silence that seemed to stretch in an otherwise raucous pub.

"Well," she conceded, "I do need my rest. However, since the tender is public, I wonder if there's anything else you can tell me about the project. I haven't had a chance to read through the tender document, yet."

"You mean, besides pizzazz?"

Now they were just being stupid. But it was a nice feeling, to forget everything and be in a moment. Darcy lifted a lock of hair away from her ear and ran his finger over what could only be paint.

"Do you mean to tell me I've had paint on my face the whole time and you never said anything? Bloody hell."

"No. Well, yes. But I didn't see it until just now. I'm sorry. Also, I know it won't come off without some special cream of pizzazz and a lot of scrubbing, so I wasn't going to say anything. It's sort of endearing."

He could barely speak for laughing so hard, and she could barely think straight for all that pizzazz. Of course, if she'd used some of the magic make-up his sister had shown her last night, she would have seen the paint and scrubbed it off. She also might have had more luck with some smoldering eye make-up, rather than just . . .

"Endearing. Not quite the look I was going for."

Darcy shrugged. "Well, it works for me."

"Well, that's something, then. Now, back to the tender."

"Pizzazz." He kept a straight face this time, which made it all the harder for her to.

"Stop that. Are there specific spaces for each piece, or will they just go where they fit? Talk to me about that stuff."

Darcy didn't actually know much about the project. It really had been a case of him being in the right time and place; he was not involved in it at all.

Finally, he stopped talking and she didn't have a mouthful of water. Julene leaned in and kissed him and this time, he didn't resist. He touched his hands to her face but he did eventually pull away. She couldn't help but protest. He gulped some beer.

"I'm sorry, Julene. You're, so beautiful. But, I met someone a few weeks back."

Julene was not sure how to respond so she gulped some water.

"It was sort of a weird thing—weirder than talking about someone else when you're out on a date—and I haven't been able to think of anyone since. Except you, a little bit. I think of her when I see you. You both look very similar. I thought you were her when you first came through the door."

Julene had to laugh.

"Yeah. When I came in and saw you, I thought you were someone else as well. I almost left, actually. But I don't think that's why I asked you out to begin with."

"Oh no? Regale me with all these wondrous qualities I possess which drew your attention." He waved to the waiter again for more beer and water.

"Well, you're dashingly handsome."

He nodded.

"And so modest, as well."

More nodding. He added some finger gestures, keep them coming. Julene ticked off on her fingers.

"Well-educated, gainfully employed, community-oriented."

"Wait, enough of that stuff. Get back to the part where I am good looking. That's where we need more adjectives."

Julene interrupted with a no-no-no finger.

"What we really need right now is some verbs." And she kissed him again.

This time she had her hands on his face and she felt his fingers in her hair. She could feel people staring a bit. *Let them*, she thought, and then she thought no more.

The waiter had left the check while they were otherwise engaged. They each reached for it but Darcy insisted, since he was still adamant he wasn't going to take her to The Elephant Walk.

"This will have to be enough, because further down this path is not where we really want to be, I think."

She thought he was being a bit melodramatic but smiled anyway and rubbed her lips, not quite absently. They walked to the glass door and he held it open for her, a puzzled smile on his face.

"Uh oh. I have a dilemma."

"Oh, and I'm intrigued."

Julene wondered if this was a delaying tactic in case he might actually take her to The Elephant Walk. It was cold and dark, perfect for holding hands and standing together, but Darcy politely kept his distance as they walked along the street.

"And now I must draw out this intrigue because this has been an awesome night and I'm not really ready for it to end, even though it must come to an end soon."

Darcy opened the door of a small café and warmth came out to greet them, but there were no elephants in sight. They ordered enormous hot chocolates which they cupped their hands around and licked the frothy tops off in big, old, wing-back chairs. The lighting, however, was stark and unromantic. Once they were settled, he leaned toward her over the low granite-topped table between them.

"So my dilemma is this: I can't just say goodnight and walk

home and let you go home by yourself—that would be bad manners. But on the other hand, I cannot walk you home because it's cold and you might invite me in, to see your artworks, perhaps."

Julene nodded.

"Perhaps."

"And I'd accept your gracious offer because it's cold and because I don't want to be rude and because I do want to see your artworks."

"They are very good, if I do say so myself."

"But then you might kiss me again."

Julene nodded again, eyebrows raised as though it was a good idea he had given her.

"The thought had crossed my mind."

Darcy leaned forward to put his vat of hot chocolate on the table. He took her drink out of her hands and put it down as well, and held on to those small hands. When he spoke again, his voice was low and quiet, intimate. Goosebumps grew on her arms.

"And then, Julene, I might find myself, after having had a nice long evening of joy and just as much beer, if not more, with my cock deep inside you in the middle of the night." Julene gasped. "Now I'm not saying that would be the wrong thing, because it would feel so right." They both swallowed. "But I would regret it. And even if not straight away, I think you would regret it, too."

Darcy reached one of his hands and placed it on Julene's belly. She wished it were an intimate gesture.

"Where is the father in all this?"

Julene wished she had been drinking beer all night as well.

"He isn't, we don't. We aren't on speaking terms. I don't want to talk about that." She pulled her hands away and picked up her drink. They both settled back into their chairs.

"That's okay, but you need to take care of yourself and that probably includes sorting that out, too, at some point. For your peace of mind, if not his, as well."

"You're quite the tease, aren't you?"

"Well, I don't know about that. I think it was a pretty fair assessment of how the evening would progress in a hypothetical, parallel world."

Julene leaned in and spoke conspiratorially.

"I see. Well in your hypothetical, parallel world, as you call it, when you said *this night has to come to an end*, I would say *I want to come on your end*."

Darcy spat his drink out all over the table. His eyebrows nearly went through the roof.

"Because in that world I can be forthright without worrying about you turning me down."

"I think we should talk about the weather." Darcy reached for the napkin dispenser as though it were a life jacket.

"You started it."

They both drank deeply, avoiding eye contact.

"Well. Have you solved your dilemma? I have to think carefully about how I word my conversations with you, now, don't I?"

"I would appreciate that greatly. And yes. I'm going to call a cab when you finish your drink."

"Very sensible." They both nodded. "You know, this sort of carry-on is not my usual modus operandi. This is out of character for me. Maybe it's the full moon. It looks kind of spooky out there."

They both stared out the window as the enormous moon peered in at them. Darcy sat forward on the big chair.

"Maybe you're right. It was a full moon when I met Janine and it was sort of spooky then, too. Maybe I should check myself into a sanitarium and take a break from the women driving me crazy. I've got to keep my head on straight. I'm a doctor, you know; I'm sort of a big deal."

They chuckled and then Julene had finished her drink.

"None for the road, I suppose." She looked at him and he stood up with her.

"No. But I would like to hear your story when you're ready to share it."

They walked outside together and Darcy waved down a taxi as one drove toward them, and then he said something about a cold shower.

# NINE

Victoria had already left when Samson got up for his morning run. It was so cold out that he almost reconsidered going, but reality would intrude in the form of thoughts of another. So he pushed himself for a bit longer until he warmed up and was blowing steam for the next twenty-five minutes.

Today would be long in terms of the physical work load, and he had one or two calls scheduled for the North Adelaide clients, but he was looking forward to a quiet evening. He'd recently picked up a pencil and began making some sketches of traditional residential facades with a few modern details. He thought they would work out really well on the new properties.

Back at home was a different story, though. Something had gone wrong while he was out running—the house was freezing! He hunted around for an errant window, which he must have missed but they all appeared to be closed and locked. There was, however, a blown fuse on the heater switch outside and it took a while to fix.

After a trip to the hardware store to restock for the days ahead and also grab a handful of things for his own house, the morning was further along than Samson was comfortable with and he worked through lunch yet again. He managed to "ahuh" and "ahum" through one of his scheduled calls and crammed the rest of his lunch into his mouth before the next one. He managed to swallow without throwing up and kept sanding through the duration of the call.

At the end of the day, there was talk of a night out with some of the other workers but he declined in favor of a bigger night out when this job was done. He couldn't afford a repeat of his previous night out with friends, if only so his mind couldn't wander anymore.

Victoria left a few voice mails but didn't show up at his house for a while and that suited him. While he enjoyed her company, such as it was he didn't enjoy *her* as much, if he was being honest with himself, which he rarely was these days. She had a few fun ideas but he was happy to sleep unmolested, most of the time. However, since his previous night out and talk of Julene, he'd unwittingly taken to sleeping on one side of the bed again, notwithstanding sleepovers with Victoria.

When she did show up again, Victoria was earlier in the evening compared to her usual schedule. She was pretty excited about something and had bought wine with her to prove her point. He wondered if she knew wine was not his favorite as she pulled stemmed glasses out of the high cupboard.

"Let me tell you, David, everyone in the hospital is so excited. There's going to be a whole new world of art and decoration in a few months. They've engaged a handful of local artists and there'll be pieces on every floor and ward! It's going to revolutionize the entire place!"

She made it pretty clear how excited she was about the whole thing after she had polished off the majority of one of the bottles. Samson was happy to indulge her but wasn't sure he could handle another bottle's worth of her enthusiasm.

"Here."

Victoria came back into the bedroom as he was buttoning his shirt and dropped a pamphlet of an art exhibit on the bed. He picked it up on his way to the kitchen.

"I'd really like to go to this, together. What do you think?" She called to him from the bathroom.

"I guess, sure."

"No, seriously."

Victoria closed the bathroom door against the sound of flushing water and sat down on one of the stools at the dark granite counter in front of him.

"It's at The ArtCaf in North Adelaide and I think it'll be fun. The board is promoting the event, and the entire series, to all the staff at the hospital. It's going to be massive. The exhibit will be on for a few weeks, but I'd really love to go together to the opening night. Please? Say you'll come with me?"

"Yes, I said yes. Do I have to go to all of them, though?"

She reached across the counter to where he was organizing vegetables and gave his shoulder a squeeze.

"No. I won't hold you to that. Though I'm sure you'd find something you like. But no, one is enough for me. Thanks, love."

*Love?* Over dinner, Samson asked how they had got here. Victoria was unsure of what he meant.

"I mean, how did this happen? The last thing I remember was making out with you in the shower of your apartment downtown and now you're here every other day."

She raised her eyebrows over a forkful of Pad Thai. Samson lifted his hands in mock defeat.

"Hey, I'm not complaining. I don't mind waking up to some slap and tickle in the wee hours but I'm not sure if I'm going to stick around. Some of the guys at work having been talking up job offers interstate and even overseas, and I've been thinking a bit about that, too." He wondered if the penny was dropping. Victoria seemed to be waiting for him to continue. "And I'm not sure if you fit into any of that."

"If I fit into it? Geez, don't pull any punches."

"Hey, I'm sorry but I'd rather have this conversation now than in two months, if I've decided to pack it all in for greener pastures. I know I was in my cups for a while and I don't remember what I might have said to you in the beginning. What I mean is, I don't want to leave you high and dry."

Still, she waited. Samson raised his eyebrows and then turned to busy himself with the dishes from the table.

"I know what you mean, David." She scooted her chair closer after he sat down again and folded her arms around his neck, kissing him as passionately as he felt impassionate. "I think we're okay."

That wasn't really what he wanted to hear but then he stopped thinking about talking.

Victoria turned up earlier than her usual time again the next day and Samson wondered if there was a restaurant booking he'd made and consequently forgotten, else why did she seem to flutter between the two couches in the lounge room like she was waiting for them to go somewhere? Were they going to restaurants, now? Usually they ate at his house if she was there, but sometimes she wanted to go out and he was not unhappy with those very occasional arrangements.

"Did you forget? Tonight is the night of the art exhibit in North Adelaide."

Oh, right. He had forgotten. He bundled himself up in a trendy cardigan and overcoat, complete with scarf and gloves. Victoria was excited as though it were the first time they had gone out together. Perhaps it was.

The gallery was *über*-crowded; it was über-everything. It had changed a lot in the short time since Samson had visited, but he grabbed a beer before he could delve too deeply into that memory. The lighting was dramatic over each piece of artwork and the wait staff were dressed accordingly. Obviously this new artist was the next big thing. There was signage everywhere for the new exhibit as well as the entire Hospital Series as it was loosely termed.

"How is it you haven't heard of her?"

He couldn't place the face of the woman speaking to him but he assumed she was someone he might have met somewhere before, as were many of the people he saw around him. He tried to be polite.

"This sort of thing is new to me. I came here with Victoria."

Samson cast his eyes around the room and found he was interested in many of the pieces. It surprised him to feel like they were something he could identify with. Victoria was dragging him over to the bar for more champagne, evidently. Elbowing their way over to a crowd of her friends, it was apparent the artist was among them, or so Victoria's conversation seemed to indicate. Samson turned around and bumped into a guy he knew from university, Rick Toben. They clapped each other on the back and asked the obvious questions. Samson waved his hand in Victoria's direction when Rick asked about a "lovelier other half" but he was vague about the "half" bit. Rick had his own "other half" to introduce.

"Jan this is David Samson. We went to university together. We haven't seen each other in what, eight years?"

Samson smiled a greeting and shook Jan's hand. He tried to call over Victoria. When she finally turned around, she was talking the ear off one of the wait staff but waved him off to walk slowly over to Samson on her high heels.

"I can't seem to find anywhere to put these down!" She joked loudly about the number of empty champagne glasses she held.

It was at that uncomfortable moment the café owner, Cath Thomas, who was herself a flamboyant woman with an explosion of red hair and a barely there dress of eye-catching green, came over to introduce the artist. Cath Thomas seemed to know Rick and Jan already.

"Everyone, I'd like you to meet my latest and greatest, Julene Somersby."

Samson's eyes nearly popped out of his head. Cath Thomas continued, unaware that his eyes might literally explode from his eye sockets and that his heart had stopped beating.

"As you can tell, the evening so far is going off and it can only get better from here. Julene, I'd like you to meet Janine Harrington, Richard Toben, Dr. Victoria Ashton and—"

"David Samson," Rick finished, and Samson touched Julene's withdrawing hand.

Her eyes sparkled like he'd never seen them—that was his first thought. The next was that she must have found someone pretty quickly after she left him because she was massively pregnant. But she hadn't changed her name. She'd done something to her hair, it was darker than he remembered and far longer. Her black dress clung to her and her belly was accentuated to the point of sensuality; he could hardly take his eyes off her changed body. Samson felt like he was dragging his gaze through wet cement because he could hardly glance away from her. But then his eyes found her face again and he watched her darkly painted lips smile and open to speak. He immediately remembered, couldn't help himself, her doing the same thing before—*No, don't go there*, he told himself, too late. He could see nothing else from then on; he couldn't tear his gaze from her lips. He could hear Victoria in his ear but he could feel Julene in his heart, as though he hadn't lived the past six months until that moment.

He wondered who the father of her baby was. There was no mention or pointing out of a husband or boyfriend. He watched his hand extend toward her belly, watched her take it and shake it, could hear her say they'd met, watched her excuse herself and turn away from him, toward some admirer of her work. Had he even said a word?

There were people crowded all around and he tried to peer past them, to find Julene again but he only caught glimpses of her long hair or her gesturing hands as she spoke to someone else. He stood there, cast in stone, unable to call out or move toward her. He saw Victoria head over in the same direction and wanted to go with her, use her as his *open sesame* to get through the wall of people Julene had around her, but he couldn't move.

On the way home in the taxi, Victoria could only irritate him, touching him where he wanted to be touched but he could not stand it. The smell of her perfume was too much, her smile so empty, her words like breaking glass. Later in bed— her lovemaking was too frenzied and he could have been anyone. She was like an animal. After he came, he regretted her. Victoria pretty much passed out after that but Samson lay awake until early, not knowing what he was thinking; he felt lost.

Eventually, he drifted into a listless sleep, feeling the urge to toss and turn but he remained motionless, awestruck by the dream running across the movie-screen of his mind.

*He was locked out of the art gallery and through a cloud he saw Julene in a sheer black dress, beckoning him toward her. The crowds fell away and he was by her side, his hands on either side of her round belly. Her dark lips were smiling at him. His erection touching her belly.*

Samson sat bolt upright in bed; Victoria didn't stir. The baby was his! He jumped out of bed and grabbed his heavy robe, his feet finding their respective slippers and he rushed out of his dark room and straight into the lamp.

"Fucking goddamn it!"

He had hit his face and stubbed his toe particularly hard, and Julene was having his baby.

# TEN

It was the day of the exhibit and Julene had woken at the very reasonable time of 11:15 a.m. She felt rested. She felt excited and inspired. After a long and drawn out breakfast, which consisted of every food group and then some, Julene stayed in the studio until the alarm called her attention to the fact that it was time. It was time for another meal and then time to employ those make-up skills.

Claude had been sending her continuous messages throughout the day to update her on his meetings with the hospital people and others interested in speaking to her; he would meet her at The Art-Caf due to a late meeting. Julene wondered if he had met someone interesting during his short time here. She was feeling pretty interesting herself. Not only was she feeling like a legitimate, working *artiste*, she was also feeling kind of amazing and ready to put on one of those sexy-as-hell outfits Ursula had assured her would be perfect. She hadn't heard from Darcy, except for a text wishing her well for tonight, but that was okay. She didn't want to be distracted from the reality that tonight she was an exhibiting artist. For real.

She sashayed around the house in her shoes to make sure they were comfortable enough and that she wouldn't topple over. There were definitely higher than she was used to, but she loved what they did for her legs. Julene heard the taxi honk outside and she grabbed her bag and turquoise coat.

She was fashionably late for her own soiree. Cath appeared at the door to welcome her and greatly approved of her timing.

"Honestly, you couldn't have timed it better. You *want* to arrive when the place is buzzing, that's the best memory, right there. Otherwise you come in and there are a handful of people who hear the door open and they turn and stare at you. Mind you, about one hundred people turned up at the same time tonight, so, win-win."

They walked as she talked, and Julene was overwhelmed at how wonderful everything looked.

Cath continued, "The promotion at the hospital must have been huge! This exhibit is enormous already on the first night, which is great for my business, by the way. But everyone is already talking about the next one, and the next one, and I've no doubt the entire series will be a record breaker."

Cath kissed her cheek and walked her over to where a number of wait staff were milling around so she could discreetly get everything she wanted. For a while, she was too nervous to eat, but that didn't last long.

Claude arrived and made a beeline for her. His movements were fast and wide; he was ecstatic and kept hugging her. He was almost as much the center of attention as her artworks were. He seemed to have met all the principle art personages in the room before tonight and introduced her to someone new every time she turned around.

She circulated with a smile on her face and with a glass of water in her hand. There were people everywhere and she was glad to see so many of her friends there, as well. There were also people who introduced themselves as working at the hospital, or just people who had come to the latest exhibit at The ArtCaf. Claude introduced her to the other artists who would be taking part in the hospital tender; for the first time she was able to talk the talk with other artists and not feel like she was a pretender to the stage. There were occasional speeches and constant introductions. Cath was immodest but still so gracious, and everyone loved her. It was an amazing evening until she came literally face to face with David Samson.

It was definitely him this time and not Darcy. She thought she'd spied Darcy a few times but perhaps it had been Samson each time. Cath was introducing her to some of her friends and he was there.

"Everyone, I'd like you to meet my latest and greatest, Julene Somersby."

Julene still blushed a little when Cath introduced her but this time she blanched. She held her hand out to steady herself; they must have thought she was offering it for the introduction. Cath's voice faded into a cartoon-like 'wah-wah' until her head cleared. ". . . David Samson." His hand came toward her and she shook it before turning away.

For a moment she wondered if he had also put his hand out to steady himself, too, but she dismissed the thought. Maybe he didn't recognize her, maybe he was ignoring her, maybe he didn't want to acknowledge her, maybe he . . . Fuck him. It was her night and she would not go over everything in her head like she had all those months ago. This was her night and her moment. She resolutely dismissed him from her mind and turned away. The rest of the night was a blur of light and color and music, food and faces and wondering if he was still there and which of the women he left with.

It was time for her to go. Claude had already made his good-byes and left with a small group to parts unknown. There were still people milling around and even people still arriving for a late night tête-à-tête. She'd already said her profuse thanks to Cath and her staff and was planning on slipping out discreetly, but Cath caught her hand on the door.

"Oh no, lady. This was such an amazing night and I don't believe for a second that you're done, yet. We'd love for you to join us for a late night something. Please."

Cath introduced her to her boyfriend and a few other friends, including Ursula Litton. Cath wouldn't take no for an answer. They ended up at The Elephant Walk after all but it wasn't the same as what Julene had originally wanted. That was okay, though. They enjoyed low lighting and impertinent conversation and great desserts. When they did leave, the crowd walked Julene home and headed off to someone else's house. They were adamant she join them but she resolutely declined.

"Hey, don't make me plead pregnancy to get out of this."

They laughed and bid her good night.

It was late but Julene, of course, could not sleep. She was, however, enormously glad to take off her shoes. She wasn't ready to take off the amazing dress or make-up so she climbed onto the couch with some pillows under her ankles and listened to music through the wired speakers in the ceiling above her.

She woke up in the same position some hours later, the lights still on, and realized her house was an awful mess of shoes and clothes strewn all over; parched paint pots and brushes in glasses of water were absolutely everywhere, too. Her parents were arriving tomorrow and, though they knew she was living the artistic dream, she knew they'd be quietly appalled at the mess that had exploded around her. She'd have to think about that later.

Julene awoke, this time properly in bed, to the sound of bustling and water gurgling in the kitchen. Janet peeked around the corner as Julene trudged down the polished hardwood hallway.

"Oh, awake now, are we?" She tut-tutted as Julene dragged her robe around her shoulders over the fabulous dress. "Lucky we talked about this last week or your parents would arrive and you'd never hear the end of it."

"Yes, you're right. Thank goodness for reminding you to remind me to get organized."

Her parents weren't going to be staying at her house, but they'd certainly visit every day at any inconvenient time and catch her unawares in torn clothes and with paint in her hair. The least she could do was clear a path for them through the house. They were very proud of her artwork but weren't all that keen on the artistic process.

Julene hobbled to the bathroom and showered until she was properly awake. She made a mental list of what she should do before her parents arrived while she dressed but found them in the lounge room when she went out to talk to Janet. Hugs all round, and tea and cookies, and then Janet left them to themselves.

"My darling!"

Her mother was so happy and amazed at how well Julene looked, and she thought her dad must have been philosophical about her being (confirmed as no longer a virgin) up and about, rather than bed-ridden and waited on, hand and foot. He conceded that she did, in fact, look like a goddess. They were glad to hear she'd been resting and eating well; she left out any other medical advice she had received before that. They unloaded presents and then went out for a walk and more tea and to take in the sights. They were staying in the same complex as Claude and all met in his little suite for yet more tea later in the afternoon.

Julene left them to it and took a wander down the street by herself. She had yet to run a breeze through her memories of last night, never mind seeing Samson again. She ran into a few friends and while Julene couldn't possibly fit in more tea and snacks, she was relieved to sit on the grass in the square and catch up. After their communal squeals died down, Julene could hear her friends congratulating her on a wonderful event.

"Julene, it was amazing!"

"Oh my gosh I'm so happy for you!"

"It was so professional! Did you know it was going to be like that?"

"Not really. I know Claude and Cath Thomas talked about a few things while I was busy scarfing down snacks, but I never knew it would be like that. I never knew *I* could be like that. It was a dream come true."

"You were gorgeous-"

"And so calm! I saw you while a couple of people introduced

themselves from the University and I was looking at your face wondering how you could keep it together."

"I wasn't feeling calm on the inside, let me tell you. I was so nervous I'm just glad I didn't have an accident!" They lost their composure at that, until Julene begged them not to make her laugh too hard.

"I've been reading a bit and I am petrified I'm going to piss my pants when I laugh or cough or something."

"I think that's meant to be after the birth."

"Start doing your vag exercises now, and that'll help."

"What?"

"Exercise your vagina, woman!"

"Yeah! But not *necessarily* the same way you did seven months ago."

"What? How do I-"

"You have to pick up flower petals with your butt and your vagina at the same time, and hold them."

"Right, or if you can't find any bloody flower petals in your underpants, stop peeing when you're in the middle of it on the loo. Same deal."

"Seriously, I said stop making me laugh!"

"Okay, then let's plan your baby shower."

Squeals reigned with fun ideas a close second, shot into the conversation with the same velocity as a bullets from a gun.

They settled it then and there for the day after next; her mother would be pleased about that.

She brought her friends back to Claude's place and they stayed for an hour or so, enjoying the tea and snacks Claude and her parents had brought with them from London. At some point, her parents decided they'd better relinquish Claude's suite and headed up to their own.

Claude came out with Julene and her friends for another walk, this time the sky shadowed with clouds and blown leaves.

"Claude, do you want to come to the baby shower? We've had a few great artistic ideas."

"Thank you, ladies, but I really thought it would just be for Julene and her lady friends."

Julene's friends looked at each other uncertainly before replying.

"Well, we just thought since you're visiting from overseas, you might like to hang out."

"And there seriously is, an artistic element to the party."

"Well, again, thank you ladies but I think I must gratefully decline." He kissed Julene on both cheeks before bidding them all adieu to go and meet some of his new friends.

Her friends giggled after he'd left. Julene did a pretty good imitation of his accent and then teased her friends about inviting him.

"Why would you invite a man?"

"Well, isn't he, uh."

"Oh come one, he's, artistic."

Julene laughed at her friends.

"You guys are ridiculous. Claude is Claude and he's a guy and I thought baby showers were all either tea and sandwiches or boobs out and whatever else at the other end of the spectrum."

"Well, we're not having tea and sandwiches, so it's best that he's not coming."

"He does seem a little bit, um, bitchy sometimes. How do you guys get on?"

Julene laughed again.

"Yeah, he can be a bit moody sometimes, but he's honest and encouraging in almost everything I do. I feel really lucky to have him on my side."

"Yes, honey, but who is *at* your side? I thought I saw Samson last night."

Julene nodded.

"So did I," but she would say no more on the matter.

Julene didn't get a chance to do more than eat a rudely early breakfast the following day, as her parents wanted her with them to explore the city again. At lunch they talked about plans for her dad because her mother would be attending the baby shower and apparently, men wouldn't enjoy the party as much. That had Julene concerned, but her mother had talked to her friends yesterday about their plans and would have been less interested if there was something improper going on. She put it out of her mind as they did a slow walking tour of the outskirts of the city, taking in the sandstone building facades and well-lit manicured gardens on their way back from dinner.

On the day of the much-anticipated baby shower, Julene slept late and woke to a slate grey sky. But she was Adelaide born and bred and adored slate, so. She let her mother and friends into the house at lunch time when she heard their punctual knocks and they weren't alone. They introduced Sally, Melanie, and Tania, each of whom was a masseuse. Julene wondered what the plural term of masseuse was.

All of Julene's friends visited at one point or another during the afternoon, even Cath and Ursula. The heating was turned way up and they were all walking around in sarongs and singlets or bras. Everyone enjoyed a massage, though not to the extent Julene did. She was lavished with attention, every muscle pummeled and pressed. She was pleased to look around when she could open her eyes and see her friends having a hand or foot massage, or their neck rubbed.

Each guest had brought with them a plate of food or a bottle of something, all decorated or arranged with pink or blue, diapers or bottles or pacifiers. After some lively games, Sally, Melanie and Tania pulled out some pots and brushes, and set to work painting Julene's belly, the top of her breasts, arms, hands, legs, and feet with henna. Julene listened as Melanie briefly explained a bit of the history involved with Henna while the feather-light cones dipped and skipped over her skin.

"It's called Mehndi, traditionally, and women in areas of the Middle East have been applying designs to their pregnant bellies for centuries. It's for luck and to guide them safely through childbirth and beyond with their babies."

Sally and Tania bent over and around each other to finish a design on a different part of Julene's body and to help a few of her friends finish off their designs. The rest of the party were painted here and there as well, and took turns with the brushes on themselves and each other, and each painted a small symbol somewhere on Julene. They were ready to do her face when the doorbell rang again. Everyone agreed Julene must answer the door since she was decorated so beautifully and they waited with bated breath to see the response of the visitor.

# ELEVEN

Samson poured scotch, drank it down immediately, and poured another. He sat back in the deep, brown chair, the drink in his hand caught mid-air as his thoughts ran away from him. His child. *His child.* He drank.

He cast his mind back to thoughts of children. He'd been talking to a friend a while back who had been looking at schools for his own kids; Samson had seen a little of that reality and decided he wanted it at some point, but how had this happened now? He tried to think about when it would have happened; had it been an accident? They'd always been careful because they were both very busy with their careers; how had this happened? And why hadn't she told him? He was sitting stock still in his chair, the standing lamp a blur in the corner, with another drink mid-air when Victoria came out of the bedroom, clearly just showered and finalizing her dress.

"David, what are you doing out here?"

He wasn't sure how to answer that question.

"I couldn't sleep. Are you heading off? What time is it?" He turned his bleary gaze to the clock in the corner but couldn't make it out.

"It's early. My shift starts in a bit but I want to get home first and freshen up properly." She kissed him on his cheek and left.

"Okay, bye," he said quietly. He sat there for a long time.

The phone eventually roused him. He came awake slowly and

fumbled into the bedroom in the dark. The phone was on the bedside table.

"Hello?"

He was late for an early morning meeting that he had insisted the client hold at their house; it was regarding a natural lighting issue he wanted to make a point about at the time the lighting mattered.

"Yeah, sorry, I've had major plumbing issues this morning, but I'm not far away now."

He dropped the robe on the floor, pulled his work clothes on over whatever else he was wearing, and hoped there wouldn't be any cops on the road.

Not everyone had stayed since he hadn't shown up but there were a couple of contractors present and Samson was able to make his point, even though his mind was very firmly elsewhere. He also made a point of apologizing and sending out notes on the lighting outcome, which, he assured the homeowner, he would follow up on with those who hadn't stuck around. He was glad to leave after that.

He found himself in Moose's driveway, the truck engine still idling. Moose was knocking on the window, his head at an angle.

"You alright, mate?"

Slowly, Samson turned off the engine and got out of the truck. He stood against the closed door.

"It's my baby. It's mine."

"Who?"

"Julene. She's pregnant."

"What? Are you sure? How do you know? When did you see her?"

"Last night. Victoria took me to an art show in North Adelaide. The artist; it was her, it was Julene." Samson took a breath, remembering. "She was gorgeous. Breathtaking. And enormous. I mean fucking huge, you know? Like you could put your finger on her belly and she'd explode." He finally turned to face his friend.

"Seriously? Are you ok, mate?"

Samson nodded slowly.

"I had a dream and when I woke up . . . it's my baby. It has to be. It's mine."

"Wait, you had a dream? That's what you're basing all of this on? I think we need more logic in this equation." He took a step back from the truck and beckoned Samson toward the house.

Samson allowed himself to be led inside and he sat down at the kitchen counter.

"You stink, by the way. Have you been drinking already?"

Samson looked around and seemed to realize where he was. He checked his watch and walked absently into the bathroom. Moose gestured for him to sit at the table when he came back down the hall. Moose washed his hands in the kitchen sink and then gestured for him to start talking.

"I did have a few in the middle of the night after I woke up and I guess I spilt one. That's a real shit, actually, I just had a meeting with a client and a bunch of contractors. That I was late to, incidentally. I'll have to clear the air on that, I guess. Bloody hell."

Moose had been squeezing oranges and there was a jug of tea on the counter already. Samson drank what was placed in front of him without comment. Moose opened his laptop and started perusing the local scene.

"So let me get this straight. Julene is one of the artists who are going to be contributing artworks to the hospital invigoration project. She had her first exhibit last night and you went with Victoria. And she's pregnant." Moose cleared his throat behind a fist, his eyes on the computer screen. "Wow, look at that."

Moose's words were punctuated by slight nods by Samson and at that last, he pulled the screen around to look at a few 'out and about' pictures. She looked even more amazing than he remembered, and perhaps not quite as ready to explode.

"It says here she's seven and a half months pregnant. Okay."

They both drank deeply of their tea. The orange juice ended up being too tart.

"I should go round there. I should talk to her. Let her know."

"Let her know what? I think she already knows she's pregnant."

"No, I mean, let her know I know it's mine."

"You mean, ask her if it's yours."

"No. I *know* it's mine. She needs to know that, and that I want to help." He stopped talking; he drank off the tart orange juice and felt his face pucker briefly. "I've got to let her know, I want her back."

There wasn't much to say after that, and Samson had other stuff to take care of before he could dash off declaring his intentions. Moose watched Samson walk back to his car, waving uncertainly as he closed the door.

A long list of items ran through his mind but when he got stuck in traffic and bowed his head against the steering wheel, he realized he needed a shower. He also had a reputation to uphold in his still-young business, and he couldn't just go rushing off because his heart had suddenly burst back into life.

Samson went back to his client's house to apologize and explain. He left out no detail and his client sympathized but conveyed the usual reprimand. Samson made more calls as he drove home to replace his boozy clothes and set off for the next jobsite after scrounging some gum from the cupboard. He could barely concentrate during the day and he hit almost all of his fingers at one time or another with an ill-aimed hammer. He set off for a coffee break, knocking back an extra shot at the café before bringing back two trays carrying drinks for all and sundry. As soon as he'd finished what needed doing and checked in with a few other guys, he headed home and was preparing to go to Julene's house. A million things were running through his mind and he found himself staring into nothing as often as knowing what he was doing or what he was going to say to her.

As he finished in the bathroom he heard the front door close and his heart sank. Samson didn't want to have any conversations with Victoria right now, or frankly, ever again. If Julene rejected him outright, he still wouldn't want to be with Victoria anymore. Wrapping the towel around himself, he walked out into the kitchen. She was there, uncorking a bottle of wine.

"Hi there." She admired his dripping chest and turned to face him.

Samson held his hands up in front of himself as he took a few steps in her direction. As he opened his mouth to speak her phone buzzed and she rummaged for it in her small, blue leather bag.

"Oh shit, I've got to go. I'm sorry I can't stay, I really wanted to hang out here after our big night last night."

Victoria quaffed the half glass she'd poured and then kissed him lightly, trailing her fingers over his chest as she walked away. She called out her good-byes and he heard the door open and close. Samson was glad of the easy escape but knew it would only be worse when he did eventually speak to her.

In the bedroom, he couldn't decide what to wear which was confusing because he usually didn't care one way or the other. His wardrobe contained the usual suspects in varying but similar color palettes. And yet. He took a few steps back and stared at the clothes on hangers in front of him and tried to think of what he would say when she answered the door. What if there was someone else there with her, a man in the background? Just because she'd apparently been alone at her exhibit, didn't mean there wasn't someone else in her life. It was a painful imaginary blow and he sat down on his bed as though hit. His mind tormented him with possible scenarios, things he would say to her, what she would say to him, that this other person might come to the door and what that person would say as he put his arm around Julene. Samson shook his head, trying to clear away what could only be a worst case scenario and lay back on the bed, his hands in his hair, trying to massage his brain into a kinder frame of mind.

Samson sat up and yawned, looking around at the clothes on

the bed and still wondering what he could wear to make the best impression. Checking his watch, he found it was morning, though, the next morning, and he'd slept through his opportunity to call across town. He was running out of courage for spontaneity. He sighed and got dressed in his running gear and cursed his way around the oval until he'd lost count of the number of laps. What was stopping him, really, from running over there right now? But no, he had to think this through properly.

A short shower before changing into work clothes, an ignored message from Victoria, and a toasted bagel in his gob saw him heading out the door for work and numerous attempts—though less dangerous, today—at keeping his mind on the job. It was a good few hours before he could take it no longer and headed home to get ready. It was now or never. He barely glanced at the clothes he pulled out of the wardrobe.

It took him no time at all and no real thought to get to her house and he parked in the spot that his car used to dominate before he traded up for the blue pickup truck; it could have been yesterday. There were so many cars on the sides of the road, though, he wondered if there was a street fair happening just around the corner. There was rarely this much traffic on the side streets.

Getting out, he smoothed his wavy hair—to no avail—and patted the flowers against his chest. He took a deep breath and all but ran to her door before he could lose his nerve. He blew it all out right in her face as she opened the door. He gasped immediately. She was naked. They both took a step back from the door. He could hear laughter from behind her and figured he'd found the street party, though he couldn't tell for sure because he couldn't take his eyes off Julene standing in front of him. She wasn't actually naked, just barely dressed, with drawings or tattoos all over her skin. He could think of nothing at all to say to her. He stepped forward and offered the flowers. She took them and closed the door in his face.

Speechless. He stood there, waiting, because he didn't know

what else to do. Samson heard a bit of a commotion inside but no one opened the door. He turned and strolled back to the road, waiting for inspiration to hit him or for her to open the door again. It was an older lady that came out eventually, also not entirely dressed but pulling a coat over her shoulders as she walked toward him.

"Hello David. I don't suppose you remember me very well? I'm Julene's mother, Caroline Somersby. I'm sure we met a few years ago."

They shook hands and Samson felt absurd.

"I didn't know." He could think of nothing else to say.

"I know. I'm sorry. We tried to convince her to speak to you about it but she felt pretty strongly about your break up. And then we were so busy in London the whole time so her father and I let it drop." So she'd been in London.

"I haven't seen her for so long, and then at the exhibit, I saw her. I thought she must have been with someone else. It broke my heart." The clouds also broke and Samson felt a bit of warmth on his back. He took it for encouragement.

"I'm sorry. It sounded like you broke hers, too. Have you talked to her about that at all?"

Samson felt like hanging his head, hearing all this common sense as though he were being chastised at school. He squinted against the sky, instead, leaning against his truck.

"She wouldn't take my calls. And then I never saw her. I wanted to give her some space but she wasn't around. I didn't know she went away." He felt like he was talking to his grandmother, spilling his worries. "I know I could have done more. What's she doing in there?" He nodded toward the house.

Caroline explained about the henna baby shower, that they weren't naked. She showed him her tank top under her grey coat, the henna painted on her arms and hands and throat. He was dying to see Julene, to see her properly painted, but he wasn't sure she would see him.

"Why don't you wait a bit and I'll see if she'll come out. Don't leave unless I wave to you through the curtains, okay?"

He took a deep breath and nodded.

When nothing happened immediately, Samson pulled his phone out of his pocket and doodled a bit so he didn't feel like such a fool standing there. Eventually he saw heads peering at him through the curtains and felt like a fourteen-year-old boy again, come to call on his first girlfriend after a sleepover or something. The door slowly opened and his heart leapt at the thought of her, at the sight of her. He stood up quickly and nearly swooned. He waited for her to come to him, lest he scare her off if she didn't want to talk, but she spoke first.

"Hello."

"Hi." He waited. They both did.

"What are you doing here?"

Samson wanted to convey his surprise and his concern but what spilled out was a bit of a mess.

"I love you. I'm sorry, I mean, you're pregnant! And I was like, wow, she's huge. And you were naked. But then your mother showed me her chest. No. No!" He scowled.

Julene laughed. That was something but he'd lost his chance at a first impression.

"Julene, I'm sorry! I'm sorry for what happened."

He reached out for her but she stepped back, her arms crossed. She shook her head slightly, dislodging silent tears.

"I'm sorry. I am sorry. You never gave me a chance to explain."

She nodded but didn't relax her arms or her frown.

"I know. I saw you; I saw it happen." She shook her head, seemed to be angry at her tears. Dark hair from her ponytail swishing onto her shoulder. "I heard you and her. I understand, sort of. But it didn't make it any easier to take. I couldn't talk to you, couldn't look at you without seeing it all over again. And then I found out I was pregnant, and I heard you'd been seeking your respite elsewhere." So many tears. "So I left."

"London."

Julene nodded in reply. She looked squarely at him, waiting. Her arms were still crossed but her expression was no longer blank.

"You're right. About everything. I'll never be able to say I'm sorry enough times for you to understand how much I mean it."

His voice caught a little. He wiped his nose on the back of his hand and took a deep, slow breath. Julene's eyebrows smoothed out momentarily and she opened her mouth as though to speak before closing it. She took a breath.

"You were with someone the other night."

"I was." Samson waited for her to continue but she said nothing else.

They were at an impasse and stood there for a while, squinting at each other and then away, the sun at a bad angle for holding grudges.

"Look, I'll let you get back inside."

Julene nodded.

They both moved at the same time and Samson dropped his keys; they bounced off her knee, falling behind her. Julene stepped back and bent over to pick them up. She inadvertently stepped onto the corner of her robe and it pulled open, the cord hanging limply at her sides as she stood up. Samson gasped again and felt his heart stop. This close, before she wrapped the cloth around herself, he could see the delicate designs in detail all over her swollen stomach, her chest and her throat. She tied the cord resolutely and stood up straight in front of him before handing him the keys, saying goodbye, and going back inside the house.

All the heads disappeared from the window and he turned and leaned against the hood of his truck. He was stunned, breathless. He stood up and was sorting through the key fob when a head appeared at the window again and shook in the negative. He recognized Caroline and stood there with his hands in the air. What did she mean? Then the head disappeared and Julene opened the door again.

"I thought you were leaving?"

"I thought I was." He was happy not to be sure of that.

"Mum says I should talk to you properly, but I don't know how to do that."

Julene walked the short flagstone path and stepped past the invisible protection of the gate. Samson saw her hesitate and then take a few steps more and look at him crossly.

"I feel like I don't know you at all. So much has happened."

He watched while she took small steps in one direction before stopping and changing direction.

"I've been so busy, and I didn't let myself think about you, about anything, and now I don't know what to do."

Julene stopped ambling and looked at him. She took a step toward him. He held his breath. She took a few more steps and then slapped him in the face. It was surprising but not uncalled for. He touched the side of his face and looked at her, waiting for her to speak. Tears streamed down her face but she was quiet. He took a slow step toward her and took her hands. They beat at his chest a few times and then he held them. She wouldn't let him put his arms around her. She pushed him but didn't walk away just yet.

"You weren't there when I needed you." Julene was openly crying now, and her eyes pierced him. "I might have been able to forgive you for what happened at Sean's house. But you gave me no time before you left me! You left me for anybody and nobody. How could you do that?"

She pulled a lace-edged handkerchief out of her pocket and wiped her eyes and nose. He wanted to reach out and touch her face. Slowly, he laid one of his hands on her shoulder and when she didn't shake him off he enfolded her in his arms. He was so relieved when she relaxed and leaned against him, even though she was hitching and sobbing. She finally lifted her head.

"And now you're ruining my baby shower."

"Baby shower, huh?" Julene nodded. "Does the father ever get to go to the baby shower?"

"You mean does the nasty cheater get to go in and take the attention away from the mother-to-be by turning up after a handful of months and making nice with her friends? No chance." It seemed a suitable rebuke.

"Point taken."

Julene stepped away from him and tied her robe tighter. She looked around like she'd just woken up and realized she was having a domestic on the street.

"Um, I don't want to stay out here anymore." Samson eyebrows were hopeful. "But I don't want to you to come in right now." He brightened at her use of the words 'right now'.

"I'd like to see you."

She nodded, absently or uncomfortably, he couldn't tell which. He was hopeful from all she'd said that they had much more to say to each other. It was a good feeling.

"Okay." She took a step away but he touched her hand.

"Tell me. Tell me when or how or what I can do. I can't leave here until I know." He was surprised to find tears pricking his eyes and blinked them back.

"I'll call you."

He shook his head; the blinking hadn't been very effective.

"No. I need to know. I can't go until I know."

Julene was done in at this point.

"I'm going to need a nap. But we could meet for a drink tonight, if you like. Say, at the chocolate shop near your house. Maybe around 5:00 p.m."

Samson could only nod as Julene walked back inside and gently closed the door. Finally he sat in the truck, the doors closed and the key in the ignition. He sat there awhile before driving away.

# TWELVE

The flowers had been put in a vase and were on the table at the back of the room looking a little worse for wear. Julene was quiet and everyone waited for her to set the mood. She'd been outside for ages and her friends weren't sure if she wanted to continue the party. The henna trio had left during the tête-à-tête but everyone else had had another glass or two and another plate of delicious baby-themed snacks. Julene's mother broke the ice.

"Julene, my love, I'd completely forgotten how fucking gorgeous he is."

Everyone gasped, and then laughed. A few of her friends hugged her and offered another glass of juice or sparkling water, another pacifier-shaped fruit popsicle. Julene put on a smile and someone turned up the music.

There were songs with naughty lyrics and a few nursery rhymes in the mix, as well. Julene was able to relax, which relaxed her friends and after a while she put her feet up on the couch.

She woke up to her mother fussing and telling her to get a proper rest in bed but it had already been more than two hours since Samson had left. Julene let her mother shoo her into her bedroom— there was no point arguing. She feigned rest until her mother left.

Julene woke herself up properly with some cold water in the bathroom. She freshened up and put on a change of clothes. There was a new shirt that was quite sheer, a gift from the henna party so she could show off the designs on her skin. It looked great. Julene opted for the eye make-up but not the lipstick; it would only come off on the mug of chocolate, anyway. A green scarf, a grey jacket, a cool new hat. She was ready to go but not ready at all.

The taxi pulled up to the café. Julene paid and peered through the window, wondering if he was there already, wondering if she was crazy. Wondering if he was. There he was, crazy or not, coming over to open the door for her in a dark sweater and extending a hand to help her out of the car. She was inwardly indignant but she really did need his hand. He didn't try to kiss her and she appreciated that. He had staked out a table with a newspaper and a bag or two, and he pulled a chair out for her to sit down at the dark wooden table. All of the tables seemed to be painted or stained in shades of chocolate. Samson waved over a staff member and Julene ordered without seeing the menu. He ordered the same.

"Did you end up having a nap?"

Julene smiled shortly and nodded, told him she'd probably fallen asleep almost straight away after he'd left. He asked about the henna and how long it would stay on. Would it still be there when the baby came?

"No. At least, I hope not. I'm due in five weeks; the henna usually lasts one week, or thereabouts. It was fun for an afternoon but it'll wash or wear off over the next few days, I expect, since I wash a lot in the studio."

Neither of them seemed sure what to say next; Julene tapped her fingers on the table before stopping herself. They couldn't seem to bring up the baby, the birth, the arrangements, the *name*. Julene took a deep breath.

"Mum said I should apologize to you, and I suppose she's right. So, Samson."

She saw his face change when she said his name. He tentatively covered one of her hands with his, until she slowly pulled it away and picked up her mug.

"I'm sorry. I am. I shouldn't have left, I should have told you sooner; I should have told you. Maybe I still wouldn't have told you if you hadn't come over today, or if you hadn't come to the exhibit. I can't imagine how much of a shock it was for you. I'm sorry."

"I'm the one who's sorry, beyond sorry for everything that happened. And I was shocked, for sure, seeing you the other night, more than I've ever been in my life. But after that, after my brain cleared, I was amazed. You were so . . . tender that night."

Julene raised her eyebrows as she sipped.

"Well, that's what I thought, sort of, after I was able to start thinking again. You looked enormous with your belly, like a goddess, maternal. But your hair and make-up were very 'come hither'. It literally blew my mind."

Julene could not smother her smile.

"And I felt awful, seeing you like that, because you weren't mine. But I couldn't figure out who you were with. There was no ring, no boyfriend, no one there with you."

"But you were so certain when you came to the house."

"I was." Samson nodded, remembering. "I had a dream and when I woke up, I just knew. It sounds ridiculous but in the dream the baby was mine and when I woke up the feeling didn't go away. I stayed up the rest of the night thinking about it, about you, about everything that happened, about what I want to happen."

"And what, exactly, is that?" Julene looked doubtfully at him, sitting back in the chair with her arms crossed.

"Um, you've got a chocolate milk moustache. Well, the simple answer is you. I want you to live with me and raise our family together and live happily ever after. I want to take you in my arms again and kiss you and hold you. That's all." Samson nodded into his empty mug.

"That's all." Julene laughed at the absurdity, ignoring the feeling in her stomach when he said the words. "Did you expect I'd just take you back and forget about everything?"

"No. Of course not. But you asked what I wanted, not what I thought would happen." He sighed as he looked up at the ceiling, the chandeliered lights glancing off his dark hair. "If you asked what I thought would happen I would've said that you slap me again and walk away from me again, and never speak to me again, and move back to live near your parents overseas again, and maybe send me a picture postcard or two after I send the alimony." Samson's shoulders slumped as he leaned back in his chair, too.

"That's a pretty extreme alternative. Is there no in-between?"

"I don't know that there is. I don't know anyone who lives in a mythical in-between of being separated from their kids. I know plenty of people do it, but it sounds like hell on earth, frankly."

Their mugs were empty and they couldn't stomach another dramatically rich drink like that again. They fiddled with the napkins and stole glances at each other.

"Would you like to come back to my place?"

Julene was in two minds as to what she should do but in the end, she consented.

Outside, Julene asked where he'd parked. He had walked but could easily flag a cab.

"No, we can walk. I like to walk in the evenings, sometimes."

Julene shoved her hands into her pockets and found a pair of gloves. She pulled them on as they headed toward the trees. The evergreens were dark masses; the trees without their leaves were spidery in the wind. Small stones crunched beneath their shoes as they skirted the edge of the parklands and uncomfortable conversation. Close by the streetlights, the air was teeming with moths and an occasional feasting bat. Julene tried not to cringe when they flew by.

"Do you want help with anything?"

Julene could feel Samson sneaking sideways glances at her as they walked.

"Like what?"

"I don't know. Anything. Dinners or something?"

"I'm okay. Janet comes over once or twice a week and puts a heap of things in the slow cooker so there's always plenty of food."

"Janet? You mean your old neighbor?"

"Yes. She kept in touch with my folks since they moved away, and you know she used to pop in sometimes."

"Oh, I remember." They both laughed.

"Well, she still does. She called me a few times when I was in London to ask me what I wanted her to organize for when I came home. And honestly, I'm glad she did because I was so tired and overwhelmed and I didn't think about shopping or sheets or anything. She'd gone in and tidied up a bit and brought a few things for me. She didn't buy much food, though, so the first afternoon was slim pickings."

They'd arrived at Samson's house and Julene was surprised by how different it looked.

"You know, I just did all the things I always said I was going to. I had time on my hands after I quit the force. I quit my job, by the way."

"I know."

"How do you know?"

"My friends looked you up online while we were talking outside. They found the page for your contracting business."

Samson flipped the light switches as they came through the door and Julene was impressed with the internal updates as well.

"I love these floorboards. It changes the feel of the whole house."

Samson busied himself with the kettle and Julene sat down on one of the long leather couches. There were new cushions to lean into and she was comfortable immediately.

"I hope you don't mind me making myself comfortable over here. I've learned those wooden chairs are no good for me, right now."

"I'm just glad you're talking to me, let alone getting comfortable on the couch." He smiled over at her but she was asleep.

# THIRTEEN

Samson wondered that she could fall asleep so quickly and assumed she was just dozing. He walked through the kitchen and put the cups down loudly on the coffee table, assuming she'd open her eyes and smile at him and he would pass her the cup and their fingers would touch and she would say his name again.

But she didn't wake up. Her breaths were long and deep and some of her long hair was being blown back and forth near the side of her face. He wanted to touch it, to smooth it out, but didn't. He sat on the opposite couch and put his feet up, sipping his tea. When she didn't wake up after a few more minutes, he turned on the TV. It was something he couldn't keep his mind on so he closed his eyes as well.

It was the sound of a key in the door lock that woke him. The TV was on but the sound was a low hum. Samson heard the door open and close, then a few click-clack footsteps. He got up immediately and looked at Julene—still sleeping. He walked down and met Victoria at the hall closet, hanging up her jacket. She was surprised to see him.

"Victoria, I'm sorry but you have to go."

"What? Why?"

"I've met someone, again. From before. I'm sorry. We can't, we can't see each other anymore."

"What? What are you talking about?" She demanded. "When

did this happen? And why are we whispering? Is she *here?*" Her voice rose at the end.

"Yes. She's asleep on the couch."

"That was fast."

"I don't want to explain tonight. I'm sorry. This took me by surprise as well, but this is what I want." He reached into the closet and took her jacket from the hangar.

"And that's it? You're throwing me out?"

"No. I'm saying to you that right now is not the time for an explanation, and I need you to go."

She grabbed her jacket from him and left, her eyebrows knitted. Samson heard her car pulling away and he walked back to the lounge room. Should he turn the lights up? Should he turn the TV off? He boiled the kettle again and made more tea, sipping it on the end of the couch and sneaking glances at Julene while she slept. He leaned closer to peer at her, at her belly, her throat. He wanted to touch her belly, to feel her, but he didn't; he needed to wait until she'd allow it.

"What are you staring at?"

"Shit! When did you wake up?" He laughed at himself.

"When the kettle boiled. Is there enough hot water for me as well?" Julene scooted back to sit more upright, the leather creaking embarrassingly beneath her.

"I can reheat your cup. You were asleep before I brought it over, I think. Do you always fall asleep so quickly?"

He picked up her cup from the table and reheated it in the kitchen. Holding it out to her, their fingers did touch briefly but there was no subsequent make-out session. He stood there awkwardly.

"No, well, yes. I'm usually working all the time in the studio. When I stop, I go to bed. I sleep late and do it all again the next day. It's been great for a late night in town." She looked away in case she was blushing, thinking of her night out with Darcy before the exhibit. "And the exhibit."

"Do you want me to take you home?"

"I don't know." She sipped the tea, avoiding his eyes.

Samson crouched by the side of the couch, resting an elbow on a knee.

"Julene, there's something I should tell you. Well, some*one* I should to tell you about."

She nodded.

"I know. I saw a scarf by the front door."

"Her name is—"

"I don't need to know her name; it's none of my business."

"I *want* it to be your business. I want you know I've nothing to hide, and I don't want to give you any reason to push me away again. I've been spending time with someone but it's not serious. It's over."

"Just like that. Since, what, yesterday?"

"Actually, since I saw you at the exhibit. The very moment."

Samson's voice was low and he was desperate to kiss her. It was a physical thing. The leather creaked as he sat down at the end of the couch near her feet. He turned and looked in her eyes. She held her hand out for his.

"Do you want to feel?"

His face relaxed into a burgeoning smile and Samson turned his whole body toward her, easing closer on the edge of the couch. She guided both of his hands to different spots on her belly and waited. He jumped back.

"Oh! That was it! I felt it!"

And he gingerly put his hands back, waiting, feeling the warmth and the tickle of her long hair against the side of his fingers. Samson tried to ignore it, the feeling, the tickle, the gravity of everything, to no avail. He turned his hand and twisted the lock of hair in his fingers, feeling how smooth it was. It was very dark against his hand. His eyes followed the lock to her face and a tear fell down her cheek.

"Hey, hey." His voice was soft.

"We've been so stupid," she whispered, wiping away tears.

Julene put her hand behind Samson's neck and pulled their faces together in a kiss. His eyes widened in astonishment but then he put his arms around her shoulders and kissed her in return. God, he had missed her. He ran one of his hands over her hair, there seemed to be more of it than before. It felt glorious against his skin. He put his hand on her neck and felt the warmth and her pulse; it was fast. His breath quickened as Julene put both of her arms around his neck and pulled him down. He pulled away after another indulgent moment, but her breathing was fast, too, and her jacket had fallen open; he could see the swell of her breasts and the henna patterns in the sheer top she had on underneath. She pulled him back down.

"No." He gulped. "No. You'll regret me and I couldn't stand that. And I have to get up early in the morning."

"No way. Did you really just say that? When did you get so old?"

She laughed and it was almost like it used to be, her laughing at him, him kissing her quiet, but he didn't do that this time. He pulled away.

"God knows I want you but I want you to be happy about it. And I don't think you would be. I mean, just last week you hated my guts, if you even thought of me at all. And yesterday you didn't want to talk to me. I'll wait for tomorrow."

Samson took the tea cups into the kitchen and began turning off lights. He could hear Julene getting up off the couch and deliberately stayed in the kitchen with the counter between them as she walked into the bathroom. He went to the linen cupboard and brought out a few extra pillows and blankets and laid them on the couch.

"Oh." She smiled at him. "You're not going to offer me the bed?"

"They're for me. I'll stay out here and you can," his words trailed off as his eyes trailed quickly over her body and then to his feet before he turned away. He tried to clear his throat quietly. "I'll stay out here."

Julene put her hand on the side of her belly.

"Clem. That's what I've been thinking for the name. Clement for a boy and Clementine for a girl."

"In my dream, the baby was a girl."

"Mine too."

He wished her goodnight and watched her walk to his bedroom. Samson sat down slowly on the couch and heard the bedroom door close.

# FOURTEEN

Julene thought she'd be up all night thinking about everything, but she slept soundly—notwithstanding the pee breaks—and only woke when she heard school kids on the path outside. She opened her eyes and took a moment to remember everything, not entirely sure about what she was doing.

Before, she would have never seen Samson again after what had happened. But now, pregnant, she had to stop being naïve and be open to forgiveness and compromise. To be brutally honest he hadn't cheated on her, he'd gone about his business after she'd left him. She couldn't hold him entirely responsible for the fiasco at Sean's house, either. She'd seen how Linda and her friends had been teasing Samson about being a cop. Julene had turned a blind eye to Linda's flagrant flirting, instead letting Samson ignore it without any jealous input from her. And things had been fine until she'd gone to discreetly heave her guts up in a bathroom away from the patio, coming back much later to the scene of the two of them. He'd clearly been set up; she had overreacted; he hadn't waited for her to come around. Maybe he thought she wouldn't and perhaps he'd been right. But having a baby changed her perspective and she had to be far more objective about the situation, which really meant making excuses so she could be nice to him, or more than nice. He obviously wanted to be (more than) nice to her.

Julene got into a steamy shower and continued her internal monologue until spasms gripped her belly.

"Ow! If those are Braxton hicks, I'm not ready to know about the real thing."

They subsided eventually. She dressed in her clothes from last night and was gathering her things to leave when her phone rang. It was Claude.

"Julene! Where are you? Are you at the hospital?"

"No, Claude I'm fine. I'm just, uh, out right now. I'm on my way home. What's going on?"

"Well, I had a meeting with Cath Thomas from The ArtCaf this morning, you, well it was informal, but she told me that many of your pieces are sold!"

He went on to tell her exactly which ones and at which prices had been offered. She was flabbergasted.

"You simply have to come home straight away so we can talk about the hospital piece. I will wait at the other café around the corner. Call me as soon as you can."

Though Claude was in a hurry, Julene was intent on walking home. It sounded like a long journey but in reality, it was merely three miles, maybe an hour and a half. It would be heavenly to walk through the parks and stretch her aching body and mind. She ignored a few more calls from Claude as she walked and instead listened to the birds and the rustle of the wind through the branches overhead, the cars in the distance, the chatter of people not far away.

She walked into the café and, after listening to Claude's exclamations about how long she'd taken, they walked back to Julene's house together. Claude had paperwork to endorse the sale of the artworks and more paperwork about another submission at another public building. Julene had to assume that she'd need an assistant of some kind after Claude went back to London—he was awfully up to date and she'd feel his absence if she couldn't keep organized somehow. Claude set to making lunch while Julene changed into some clothes appropriate for painting. They ate a hasty meal and then retired to the studio—Julene to render life in watercolor, and Claude to bear witness and to peruse the newspaper.

Julene worked until she was finished with the canvas. Her arms ached and her back and feet were sore. Claude was asleep; someone else had been burning the candle at both ends, apparently. She made an enormous pot of tea and had a mouthful of food then returned to the studio, setting a cup of tea on a shelf for Claude as well. She stacked another canvas on the easel and set to work again. She'd previously been working with dark oils or pastels; the watercolors were like a breath of fresh air and she used the foliage from the walk home to inspire her brush.

It was time to dress for dinner with her parents when Claude finally snorted himself awake. He exclaimed over the painting she had realized while he was asleep.

"Julene, you're a marvel. I needn't worry that your work will suffer after I've left."

"On the contrary. I know you'll be calling and texting and emailing at all hours to keep my nose to the grindstone."

"Julene, there are few people I have worked with that are so familiar with the grindstone as yourself. You are like a woman possessed. Your hands seem incapable of imperfectly completing the tasks set by your imagination."

That was all very well but her father would be annoyed if he was kept from his dinner. She washed and changed and Claude took a few pictures of her work and they set off to meet her parents for dinner, coats and scarves against the cold for the walk to another of the local restaurants.

After her father had a good amount of stroganoff in his belly, he was ready to slow his eating and participate in some polite dinner conversation. Her mother, however, had other plans as she dabbed her mouth with a white linen napkin.

"So, Julene, how did your date with David Samson go?"

Her father's eyebrows got a little wiggly. She glanced at him before answering her mother.

"Good. It was good. Thank you, Mum." Her own eyebrows danced around meaningfully. "We went to a café by the parklands and we talked. I apologized to him as you suggested, and he did, too. I think we're somewhat on good terms now and can talk about moving forward."

Her father's eyebrows started dancing again.

"Slowly."

"Good. That's good. Of course, don't rush into a wedding just yet," someone at the table choked. "But I'm glad things are better. Now, onto a new topic. You know what I want to do tomorrow? Visit some of the wineries. I'd love to get out to McLaren Vale. Who's in?"

Julene politely excused herself from the long day, happy that Claude would accompany them, leaving her free to sleep, instead.

And sleep she did. She stayed up into the night painting and slept until nearly noon. In a drawer beside her bed, there was an old scarf that had seen better days which she used to wrap around the top of her head, tamping down the raging bed hair and hopefully keeping it out of her face better than the elastics she'd been using recently. Otherwise she'd have to start working in a shower cap.

Julene consumed a goodish-sized bowl of something Janet had prepared and then went straight to the studio. She was mid-stroke when she felt a drop on her shoulder. Looking slowly up, Julene saw that there was some water staining on the ceiling and wondered how long it had been there. Of course, it could have been there since she'd come back from London—and probably bright pink— and she still might not have noticed until now. The drip came again and again, steadily now.

"Damn it!"

Julene couldn't decide: should she finish her current canvas or abandon it to move and cover everything else? The drip splashed into a bit of a puddle and she awkwardly pushed and pulled the easel as far from the drip as she could. It wasn't very far. She pulled her phone out of the back of her pants and called Samson, her heart pounding as she dialed his number.

"Hello, Julene? What's wrong?" He sounded alarmed.

"Um, well something, yes, is wrong, but it's not the end of the world. Why do you sound so anxious?"

"Seriously?"

"Yes."

"Well, I didn't think you'd call for a while, let along the next day, so I assume something must be wrong. Is there something wrong?"

"Yes. There's a leak in the ceiling, which means, I guess, that there's a leak in the roof. It's in my studio. Can you help?"

"I'm already on the way."

# FIFTEEN

Samson hadn't slept well the past few nights. If it weren't for his long days of physical labor, he'd feel like an insomniac. As it was, he'd had dreams that had him tossing and turning, waking up, unable to settle down to deep sleep. His body was working long hours during the day, but since he'd seen Julene his mind was working overtime now, too.

He'd been about to leave for another job when Julene called. He'd jumped into the truck as soon as he saw her name on the phone display, anticipating a problem or else why would she call him so soon? He was relieved when he ended the call and rescheduled his client as he was driving through town.

He took a moment to compose himself before knocking on her door.

Julene looked amazing to him when she opened it. Her face was flushed, her hair disheveled under some sort of head wrap, paint smeared here and there on her skin. Her sleeves were rolled up so her arms were bare from the elbows down; her shirt was taut across her chest and belly. She held what looked like a stained apron in one of her hands; there was paint on one of her feet. He was in love again.

She smiled tentatively up at him and stepped back so he could come in.

Samson looked around as she closed the door. It was mostly as he remembered it—brown-stained floorboards, cream-colored walls, bold red in the kitchen—but he felt like a foreigner.

Julene told him to go on through to the back room while she washed her hands again. Once there, he spotted the stain on the ceiling and watched a few slow drips, but only barely; he was too taken with the canvases to focus on anything else. There were small paintings hanging from the picture rail with barely an inch between the edges, medium-size frames were nestled in the racks, and a number of large frames in various states were leaning against the walls.

"Wow, I love what you've done with the place," he said over his shoulder as Julene walked up behind him.

She swatted his arm and moved past him to close the lids of some paint bottles. She gathered up a handful of brushes and took them through to the laundry.

"So get to work already," she called, "or I'll have to assume you're a spy. Or a critic."

It was a tough to concentrate, but with the ladder unfolded from the bed of the truck and the wind picking up as he scooted around on the roof, he did his best to push away thoughts of the woman inside the house beneath him.

It wasn't hard to find the leak; there were quite a few broken branches and even a limb or two collected together in one of the valleys. The roof was pretty old and a few cracks in the corrugated iron had let in a bit of water here and there, but that was it. He'd never been so happy to come inside and give a homeowner the bad news.

"It'll be straightforward to fix the outside, but I'll need to get into the crawl space in the ceiling to assess the damage. Where's the manhole again?"

As soon as he was inside, the dust had him sneezing. He took a moment to wipe his face—which was hard in his cramped position. He could hear Julene moving in the room below and his earliest memories of her bubbled up.

Samson had worshipped her in school—obviously not as privately as he'd thought back then, given Joey's comments when they'd been out—and he'd been heartbroken when she moved away. After working for a few years at various jobs, he'd decided to go back to university. She'd moved back to town around the same time and enrolled in some classes at the same campus. Oh, how he had inwardly rejoiced. He was more experienced by then, so he'd been able to speak to her properly, without getting tongue-tied or shy. They had become fast friends and, eventually, fast lovers.

On that first day, her hair had been tousled by the wind as she tried to carry a large stack of books and a few other supplies from the bookshop. Seeing her today was just as thrilling as it had been nearly seven years ago. Of course, he had far less room to be excited about it at the moment.

He rubbed his eyes to clear his vision of dust and crawled through to where the inside of the roof was damaged. On closer inspection, he saw that quite a bit of water had seeped through the damaged roof and into the beams and ceiling plaster. He measured how far the beams were from the intersecting walls and then hurried back out the way he came so he wouldn't forget the numbers. He found a scrap of receipt on the floor of the studio and scribbled the measurements down, then stood back to contemplate the ceiling.

"What's the verdict, then?" Julene had quietly come up behind him, and he jumped at the sound of her voice. She laughed at him. "Penny for your thoughts?"

"Um, no. So like I said, the damage on the roof is not that bad, but the weather won't help it to dry, and if it's left much longer, the ceiling will start to mold. I'm going to head out and grab some new pieces of iron to repair it. You'll need to move everything out of the studio so I can take down the ceiling plaster and get some fans in here before I replace it all."

"Oh. That's quite the production. Is this something I should make a claim on insurance for?"

Samson shook his head and turned toward her in the doorway. "No. You asked me to help, and I will. Do you need anything else while I'm out? Otherwise I'll come straight back."

She didn't need anything, so he hurried off, intent on getting back in time to finish before dark and perhaps share dinner with her afterward. He sent her a message that he could bring back dinner unless she had other plans. He tried not to think too far ahead when he read her short reply and stopped off at a local butcher on the way back to her place.

He'd had the corrugated panels pre-cut at the store to expedite the process, so the roof was fixed in plenty of time before dark. He ended up moving most of the paintings himself, Julene directing him where to move and stack them all. He tore his shirt on the corner of the drawing table, and soon after that knocked into a water pot balanced precariously on one end of an easel, spilling that all over himself as well. Not quite the impression he had wanted to make. As he finished emptying the room, Julene came out from the kitchen and watched him work, smiling at the mess he'd made of himself.

"Now you look like me."

She laughed as he took the glass of water she offered, and as he took a sip she wiped a smudge of paint on his forehead. He looked at his tattered shirt and wiped a blotch of damp plaster dust from his arm onto hers.

"A work of art."

Their eyes held and he froze, wanting to make sure it was okay to kiss her. Julene stood on tiptoe and leaned her face into his, putting her hand on his chest. His skin burned where she touched him and the feel of her lips on his own was heavenly. They stood transfixed.

Samson broke away first.

"Let me get the, the meat."

Julene caught her breath.

"I mean, I left the meat from the butcher, in the truck."

Julene stepped away from him with a small smile on her face.

"Let me get that. Why don't you take a shower? You're filthy. Go on." She stood there looking at him, gesturing for him to step into the bathroom.

"Go on yourself." He nodded to the front door.

"I'll meet you back here, then."

Samson grinned and nodded. He stepped into the bathroom and heard the front door open and close, and felt a breath of cold sneak under the bathroom door. He turned on the shower and the water ran muddy for a while. There must have been more muck in his hair than he knew. He let the water cool down considerably before he turned it off. He still had to get through dinner, and he thought his head might explode if he couldn't calm down.

Stepping onto the bathmat, Samson realized he didn't have a towel and wondered how to proceed, but then he spied one hanging on the doorknob. He grabbed it up and inhaled, trying not to get too sentimental about the fabric softener she still used. He stepped out of the bathroom with the towel around him. He was sure she'd thrown out any of his clothes that might have been left around from before, and he didn't fancy making dinner in the towel—but he wouldn't let his mind go further than that.

"Ah, Julene? About my clothes?"

He couldn't hear her anywhere and wouldn't presume to go looking through the house. He went back into the studio and took another look at the ceiling. And then he swore, because he'd forgotten to bring back a heater or fan to dry it out. He tried to remember if Julene had these things. Maybe they could concentrate the central air by closing the door; would that be enough? He turned toward the kitchen and the spare cabinets there. He thought he could take a look inside those for a heater or fan or such without worrying about looking like a snoop if Julene found him with his head inside. And if she did, no harm done. It would surely be better than having had his head up his ass for the past six months.

# SIXTEEN

Julene tried to close the door quietly but the wind grabbed it from her and threw it closed with a bang. Samson stood up like a jack in the box.

"Oh! What are you doing over there?"

"Julene! Woah, you startled me, again. I called out before but I guess you were busy. I don't have any clean clothes and as much as the heat can be turned up, I don't fancy having only this towel on all night."

Julene barely managed to hide her smirk.

"I don't suppose you have a painting smock or something I could fit into, do you?"

He leaned back against the wall, affecting a Mills and Boon pose with a smoldering look in his eyes. She grinned back at him and shook her head. She took a slow step toward him, butterflies competing for room in her belly. Samson's smile faltered.

"Seriously, I need some clothes."

She took a few more steps and lifted her hand from behind her back. She held a T-shirt and some loose pants but she wouldn't give them to him.

"Julene, don't be ridiculous. Give me the clothes."

But she refused and took a step back every time he advanced, grinning the whole time.

"Seriously, I don't feel comfortable dropping the towel just yet."

"Mmm, sounds like you are throwing *in* the towel. How typical."

Samson's eyes and mouth opened in surprise. "That was a low blow."

Now she had caught him unawares, and stepped close to him.

"Not as low as the towel."

And she tugged, the towel falling onto the floor. Their eyes met. Julene took a step closer until her belly touched his. Movement in her belly had them break their gaze. Samson gently put his hand on her and waited. They both felt it again and let out their breaths. Samson reached around with his other hand and grasped the clothes Julene held behind her back but she wouldn't let them go. She moved her face so she could keep looking into his eyes, her mouth waiting for his. Finally, finally, he held his hand on the small of her back and leaned in to kiss her. She stood on tiptoes to get more of him and he wrestled the clothes out of her hand. He stepped back as he unfolded them, holding her gaze as he stepped into the pants. Julene sat on the navy couch, smoothing her hands over the corduroy as she watched him.

"That was excruciating, you know that? And did you even get the, the meat from the butcher out of the truck?" He said it fast so he could keep a straight face without swallowing too loudly as he pulled the shirt over his head.

"Of course I did. You took bloody ages in the shower. It's in the bottom of the fridge. I ended up walking around to a friend's house on the next block and borrowing those from her husband. They were all ears as to who they were for."

"Oh. And what did you tell them?"

"Nothing. I kept them in suspense, just as you've kept *me* in suspense."

"How have I *possibly* kept you in suspense? I've been falling all over myself to help you in any way I can, without overstepping any boundaries. And now you're telling your friends stories about a random guy for the night?"

"Who said anything about random?"

"Oh." Samson sat in one of the dining chairs. "Well, I, assumed, you know, since you haven't been able to keep your hands off me, that there wasn't anyone else on the scene."

"Uh huh. That's quite the assumption. You obviously don't know, then, that pregnancy can bewitch a woman."

"Bewitch?" He sounded doubtful.

"Spicy hormones. It's the spice of my life, right now."

Samson reddened and stood up from the chair. Julene followed him to the kitchen and closed the fridge he had opened. Her eyes told him she meant business and he held his ground. She kissed him on tiptoe, at an awkward angle because of her belly. She found the step-stool with her foot and moved it noisily closer to where she was standing. She stepped up and gingerly sat on the counter and he moved slowly to stand between her knees. He looked at her breasts, quite close to his face, now. He kissed her neck, her chin, and finally her mouth.

"Well." He stopped short and stood up straight. "I can't take advantage of a woman who isn't in her right mind. Especially since you might be seeing other random guys. Or not random."

Julene smiled, smelling him—clean but still a little brawny. Oh, she'd missed him. And now she had him in front of her, she wondered how she'd lived so long without him by her side. Her throat tightened with emotion as her hands moved to his shoulders.

"Don't leave me again."

He looked in her eyes and then kissed her fully, a hand in her hair, the other against her back, pressing her to him for a sweet moment.

"Okay, can we eat now?"

"No. Remember I said 'spicy'? That's totally a thing. So no, we can't eat now."

She slid down off the counter, against his body, and led him by the hand to the bedroom. He grabbed an apple from the bowl on the table and ate it in seven bites before reaching the bed.

# SEVENTEEN

Samson woke customarily early and, wearing the same clothes from last night, he ran all the way home. He'd thought about driving but wanted the invigoration of the cold. He took his time, thinking over the events of the evening as his feet moved along, grinning the whole way. Coming up to his driveway, he saw Victoria stepping out of the front door. He wondered when he was supposed to have called her for that explanation.

"Where have you been?"

She seemed to have forgotten his last words to her.

"Hey, Victoria. I've been out at some jobs and seeing . . . people. What are you doing here?"

"I waited for you. I came over last night and you weren't here. So I left, but I really wanted to see you. I came back this morning and you still weren't here. Can we talk now?"

It was as good a time as any. He nodded and unlocked the door she had just closed. Inside he asked her for the key she used; she didn't look happy about handing it back. In the kitchen, Samson put the kettle on and raided the fridge, switched the stove on, and dropped a pan onto the gas burner. Victoria sat down on one of the stools and watched him. Finally, he stopped procrastinating and turned to her.

"Victoria, do you remember last week or whenever it was, I started to talk about where you fit into the scheme of things?"

She nodded absently, her eyebrows raised.

"Well, I didn't really *have* a scheme of things, but I do now."

Minimal response.

"Victoria, I never asked what your situation was before we met and I don't remember if you asked about mine."

"It didn't matter to me. It still doesn't."

Samson nodded impatiently.

"Okay, well it needs to matter now. I'd recently broken off with someone and we stopped talking and she moved away. And now she's back in town," more nodding, "and we're getting back together."

Victoria looked crushed.

"When did this happen?"

"I also mentioned it the other night when you came in late."

"But, I thought we were good."

Samson poured eggs and milk and all the vegetables he had found in the fridge into the pan.

"We were okay."

"Just okay?"

"We were okay. I was aloof and you didn't seem to mind. It was convenient and we had fun. But I wasn't even that nice to you. I don't think I was awful, but that's not really cool either."

"I thought you were cool. I thought *we* were cool. We were just starting to go out sometimes."

"I'm sorry, Victoria."

He set to work mixing and flipping and swishing the pan. He pulled a plate out of the cupboard and turned off the stove. He was almost surprised to see her still sitting at the counter when he looked up. He asked her if she wanted some eggs, too.

"No."

Her eyebrows were creased but that was it, she seemed to have spent her conversation. She said good-bye and click-clacked out the front door. Samson sighed in relief. He wolfed down the eggs, relieved, as well, that he didn't have to share them. He grabbed a change of clothes plus his work clothes and a bag to stuff them all in. He made a phone call as he locked the front door because he'd be late again, but he couldn't care much about that today. With the bag strapped but bouncing the whole time, Samson ran north through town and paused at the front door, huffing a few times before he let himself back in.

Julene was still sleeping; her arms were thrown out of the blankets. He showered and dressed for work, leaving a heartfelt note before walking quietly down the hall to the front door. Just before he closed it behind him, he had an idea and checked his watch.

Samson felt cumbersome in his work clothes; he really should have waited until later but he was a fool in love again. He ran a few blocks into the commercial district, and then ran farther and farther. He'd forgotten where all of the flower vendors were on this side of the city. Why hadn't he just driven, he wondered. He eventually found one and all but cleaned them out, taking as long tying everything up for the run back as the run had taken in the first place. He galumphed all the way, only dropping one or two bouquets as he went. People would occasionally laugh at him as he passed, but he received as many hollers of encouragement as not.

When he returned to the house, people were out and about freely on the street, getting ready for work or heading to the bus for school. Samson struggled inside, loaded down as he was, and set about leaving bouquets of flowers on every surface and in every container he could find. Most of what he initially found had been used for brushes and still stank a bit of the brush cleaner, but he found some tall glasses and mason jars, too. The kitchen counter, the table, the side table, window sills, the bathroom sink, he placed a make-shift vase full of pink blooms on each of them and sprinkled extra petals all over the bed. He was in no danger of being interrupted because Julene was deep in her pregnant-lady-snores. He couldn't look at her for too long. He would stay all day, and he had to get to work eventually.

When he did finally get behind the wheel of his truck, he had to keep reminding himself to slow down. He was in no hurry for a speeding ticket, though he felt like he could probably have talked his way out of it at this point.

People commented on his upbeat mood the entire day. Some jerk on the job site even said they thought he was someone else because they'd never seen him so animated. He joked about the joys of love and its effects on the complexion. Ho, ho; he was a barrel of laughs.

He was driven yet diverted all day. As much as he could focus on the job and work through any opportunity for a break, at any moment something would remind him of the night before, or of something she had said, or the curve of her changing body. Samson was a wreck, frankly, and said as much when he made his escape from the house he was working on. He wanted to rush right over to Julene's house but went, instead, to the rental shop for a large heater and fan. He was overdue in replacing the small fan he had eventually found in a cupboard in her laundry. He also chose some larger tools he'd need to fix the ceiling.

After he arrived and squeezed his truck into a questionably-sized parking spot, he hauled the big machines out of the back. Samson had them at the front step before knocking and waiting for her to come to the door. He kept waiting. It was a bit of an anti-climax. Samson had wanted to see her come out of the front door with a big cheesy smile to mirror his own from the flowers he had left that morning. He looked up at the wind-blown clouds in the sky and laughed to himself. He knew where she kept a spare key, or assumed she still did, but didn't want to go in without her. As it was, he turned and saw her walking down the street.

He stepped out onto the path and waved. Julene's face lit up and she quickened her step, though it had changed to a bit of a waddle, even since the art exhibit which was only last week. Samson had wanted to kiss her over the threshold but he settled for at the garden gate. She was farther away than he thought so he sat on the brick pillar by the gate and, when she finally made it home, he was at the perfect height for her to kiss him, her belly squarely resting in his lap.

"I got off work as early as I could. I wanted to bring over the heater and the fan."

"Thank you for my flowers. It was a lovely thing to wake up to. I only woke up an hour ago."

"I dare say you'll get a shock when the baby comes, because I hear you never get *any* rest."

"Indeed." More kissing.

"Shall we go inside?"

"No."

But they did because it started raining. Samson brought in the appliances and positioned them in the studio, closing the door behind him when he was done.

"There now. It's sort of noisy, but there isn't much to be done. If you can leave the door closed, it'll help dry the ceiling out that much faster. Hey."

Julene had her arms around him and was pulling his shirt out of his waistband. She smiled and nodded when he made his perfunctory denials, all the while unbuttoning her blouse. She reached up and covered his mouth with her own, pinning him against the couch so he sat down against it.

"Ah, this is the 'spicy' that you spoke of yesterday."

"Mmm, no more talking."

And that became routine; Julene sleeping until late and Samson heading off to work early; he going over to "visit" during his midday break and then heading out again for supplies or afternoon work and she working on her own projects.

It was a bit annoying for Julene. Since the studio was out of action, she had to carefully set up and put away each individual piece, rather than working hell for leather all at once and worrying about the clean up after the fact. Samson was thinking about that one afternoon on his way back across town, after doing a brief clean up and putting a load of clothes in the washing machine at his own house. He didn't stay at Julene's house every night, but she said she preferred it when he did. He'd also been thinking about their living situation when the baby arrived. Neither had brought up moving in together—they hadn't been doing much talking at all. That was fine, super fine, actually, but it was not a realistic play in their current situation. Samson made a call while driving and renegotiated the traffic.

# EIGHTEEN

Julene woke up on the couch after what should have been a little rest, but it was getting dark when she looked outside. She wondered if Samson would bring dinner or if they would whip something up. Since he'd been coming over, the food Janet had been making didn't last half as long. Janet was also less likely to come over now she knew Samson was back on the scene, and Julene was supposed to be making her own food, which she really ought to have done a month ago instead of letting someone basically wait on her.

She shuffled past the furniture crowding the lounge room and hall and held her ear to the door of the studio. The noise was muffled but still quite loud. She wondered when the ceiling would be properly dry. Samson had said this past week of rain didn't help, but she hoped it wouldn't be much longer. She had been thinking about fitting in baby furniture somewhere. She wondered about fitting in Samson permanently, too.

The kettle was boiling when he knocked on the front door before walking in to greet her. She immediately perked up and her concern over space gave way to concern about clothing. He commented about the 'spice' before lifting her skirt as she walked backward to the bedroom.

"You know," she said between passionate kisses, "the spice will give way to . . . tiredness and disinterest . . . so you should . . . kiss me . . . etcetera . . . while you can."

He certainly did, but later they were interrupted by the crash of a falling rack, which had been stacked on top of the file drawer. It startled them both and they made breathless comments about tidying the lounge room, later.

Dinner was Bolognese and a mountain of pasta cooked by Samson. They were sitting at the dining table—the one space in the small house that didn't seem heaped high with things that belonged elsewhere—when Samson shared his thoughts with Julene about their pressing concerns of space.

"I think we should move in together."

Julene looked at him mid-twirl of her fork and spoon. "Elaborate."

"You should move in with me, like now, tonight. And I should convert this entire place into a studio and office for you. I mean, I'm working on the studio as it is, or will be when the ceiling is finally dry, which, incidentally, I think will be tomorrow."

Samson paused to eat most of what was left on his plate while Julene gaped. It was an interesting idea, for sure.

"I could knock down a wall here or there, you could have a separate room or space for a particular art form. Maintain the kitchen but change the lounge and dining to maybe a small gallery or exhibition space, reception area. There are options. But time is ticking."

He pointed his fork at her belly, and then loaded it up again and demolished the rest of his plate.

"You're right. I don't have a lot of space here right now, but when the studio is back in order it will be different. But then there'll be the baby stuff."

"That's what I mean, Julene. It'll be cramped, regardless, but I want us to be together and this is one option." Samson refilled his plate. "You don't want to take too long to make a decision, but we can sleep on it."

"I don't want to sleep."

But they did go to bed and later discussed options for furniture and bits and pieces if they did, indeed, move her into his house.

"I'm open to alternatives, but I can't think of what they could be so close to your due date."

Samson looked up at the ceiling in the bedroom, watching the lights travel across the darkness as cars occasionally drove past.

"There's what, three weeks left? That's zero hour, in my mind."

The sheets started moving again and Julene didn't answer him.

"I'm starting to wonder if I'm just a convenient concubine for you, missy. Are you even listening to me?"

In the morning, Samson woke up to Julene gripping his arm tightly. He gasped.

"What is it? Is it the baby?"

She nodded.

"Holy shit, what do we do?"

"Nothing. It's okay, but it . . . hurts like shit. I just want you with me."

She grimaced and tried to breathe through the pain. Samson jumped up and ran back and forth between the end of the bed and the door.

"Tell me what to do!"

"You can start by calming the fuck down. Ah. Get one of the rice bags from the drawer in the kitchen and—whooo—warm it up in the microwave. Now!"

Samson ran into the kitchen, bumping into things as he went. He was back after the interminable microwave beeps and she managed to roll over for him to place the rice bag under her lower back.

"Call the doctor. Please. The number is, in my phone."

She kicked her feet a bit, the blankets falling on the floor, and then she fell back against the pillow, exhausted and apparently pain-free.

"That's it? Do I still call them?"

She laughed at him.

"Yes. The pains will come again. Just call."

He gave her the handset after he had asked some bumbling questions and she added a few comments before hanging up, relieved.

"So, it's probably nothing, or at least, not the real thing, but I should stay in bed and keep an eye on the time in between. What are you going to do?"

"What do you mean? My wife might be having a baby today. I can't go to work!"

"Wife, huh?"

"What? Oh, it was another idea I was going to run past you at some point."

"So . . . romantic." Julene grimaced and held her breath again.

After another ten excruciating minutes, the pain subsided and did not return. Julene convinced a hesitant fiancé to go to work, if only so he could pay for the lavish wedding she teased him with. He kissed her passionately so she really didn't want him to leave, but he did leave and she settled back for a rest. She phoned her parents after a short nap and they came over, surprised to see everything higgledy-piggledy. They had a peep in the studio but quickly closed the door again. The noise was considerable. They were just as concerned as Samson had been about the contractions but, having been through it themselves, they were a bit more resigned to the inevitable. They stayed for a while but were obviously bored, so Julene suggested they hit the town and bring her back something nice.

"Animal, vegetable, or mineral?"

"Let your own tastes dictate."

She blew them kisses and was relieved when they were gone. Julene tried dozing on the couch for a while but the pains were not distinct, so she gingerly got up from the couch and had a bit of a walk around. She ventured back to the bedroom for some slightly heavier duty underwear, lest the baby decided sooner was preferable, and then walked unsteadily back to the kitchen. A glance inside the fridge showed she wasn't really hungry but probably bored.

Julene pulled a few pieces of paper from the drawers and sidled the easel to a better angle for drawing, setting to work doing just that. She had whipped out a decent sketch of her body in profile and then filled in some details of what was going on inside her belly, adding shading here and there, some pigment on the sides, even some watercolors very haphazardly, and it was beautiful. But it was hers, to be framed and hung, rather than considered and sold. She thought it might be something special for Samson. He called soon after she'd finished the sketch and she told him not to worry, the next few weeks could very well be exactly the same as that morning.

"All the more reason to make a decision quickly about how we're going to organize our living situation."

Julene knew he was right and as soon as she hung up, she started cramming things in bags and boxes. The art equipment was first, of course. There were some key clothing pieces that went straight into her bag, above and beyond all others, and then there were the universal items, and a few special ones, too, like the nice dresses chosen by Ursula and a handful of jewelry. By the time Samson came over for a late lunch, Julene had packed two bags, plus her three large suitcases, and five boxes. Samson was surprised, to say the least.

"My love, this is way more methodical than I anticipated. Luckily, there isn't much else in the back of the truck right now. Let's get these stowed straight away."

"Oh, wait!" Julene reached out her hand as he turned around, concerned. "Say 'my love' again."

He did; she kissed him; it took longer to stow her belongings than he had anticipated.

"So, one of my many concerns is that all of this 'spice' will bring things on sooner than they otherwise would be."

Julene kissed his arm before pushing herself off the bed.

"I do not share your concerns, lover. The universe will pull the baby out whenever the time suits."

"You know, I don't like the sound of that." Samson watched her move past the end of the bed and open the sliding door of the wardrobe.

"I don't either, but I'm pretty sure that's what it's going to feel like. And besides, I'm not picking up on any of your 'please-no-don't-make-me-fuck-you-again' signals."

She raised her eyebrows as she slowly and ceremoniously draped a thin robe over her skin. He grinned at her. He hopped off the bed and came and put his arms around her, holding her firmly against his body.

"Julene, I love you." He held her face with his large hands and looked into her eyes, trying to convey how deeply he felt with his eyes alone.

"Yes," she said, "you loved me pretty hard just now." And she laughed at his surprised eyes. "I love you. I. Love. You. Now kiss me again."

It was all fun and games until someone had to go back to work. After Samson left, Julene threw on an apron over her robe and did a few more belly sketches, this time detailing them in pastels, each one of a different hue. As she washed her fingers in the bathroom, she started to think seriously about the hospital piece and what sort of color scheme she should work in. She had some preferences right now but she wondered if the colors would change when she decided on the subject matter, and also if the colors would change as she got closer to giving birth, or after the baby came. She rifled through some loose papers, looking for the tender document and read through the details. After reading them thoroughly for possibly the first time, she shot off an email as to her preference for the location of her contribution, copying Claude. She thought a large canvas or series of canvases of the same as she had sketched out earlier today would be perfect.

# NINETEEN

Back at work post lunch time love-in, the only thing that could keep Samson's mind on the job was the thought that the sooner he finished, the sooner he could get back to Julene. He'd hastily unpacked the truck at home before scooting back to the jobsite for a few more hours. This was his final job before starting on the studio at Julene's house. He wanted to be able to concentrate on it and finish as soon as possible. Now, depending on how she reacted to the plans the architect had drawn up for him, it might take longer than she wanted but he was confident it would bring an outcome she approved of.

Moose called as he was getting into his car and with all of every-thing going on, Samson realized he hadn't updated his friend. He negotiated late afternoon traffic to get to the local and bought a bottle of champagne before heading over to tell him the good news. He burst into the house singing as though he were already drunk.

"What's all this?"

Samson finished his song with an arm around his friend's shoul-der, the other arm with the bottle in the air, punctuating his song.

"I told you, man. The baby is mine. And due in three weeks!" He waltzed off around the house, bellowing at the top of his lungs, the champagne bottle still held aloft.

"Seriously? Wow, wow!" Moose sat down on the black couch and waved Samson over so they could uncork the bottle. "So I guess you've been pretty busy that you couldn't give me the good news before now."

"Sorry, man. It was weird there with Victoria, and then speaking to Julene for the first time in so long. It was, full on and, well, you saw me that morning. I've dropped a few balls of late."

"Dude, don't even worry about it. Cheers." The cork popped.

They drank from the bottle and sang at the top of their lungs. There was some spillage but the majority of the bubbles ended up in bellies. Moose robbed the refrigerator of any and all snacks and they became sentimental over soft cheese and water crackers.

"And that's it, all is forgiven?"

Samson nodded and wiped at something in his eye.

"She apologized, she accepted my apology. She kissed me, I sort of asked her to marry me, she's moving in, we're having the baby. It's amazing." They ate in silence until Samson's phone buzzed. "It's Julene! Oh. She said she just woke up and is going out with her friends."

Moose laughed at him.

"It's not the end of the world, mate. You can still go over there and see her later. It sounds like she's up 'til all hours, anyway."

"Yeah, she is. But the thing is, she's been having contractions. She says they aren't the real deal but *they could be*, any time now. And I've already missed so much."

They were quiet for a moment, until Moose slapped him on the back.

"Off you go then." They both stood up and hugged for a moment, awkward and not caring about it. "Give her my good wishes. And let me know if you need anything. *Either* of you."

Samson left and drove across town. He was too late to be going back to the jobsite and he was too distracted now. He thought about going across town packing a few more things for his *fiancé*, but he still didn't want to go into her house while she wasn't there. It seemed silly considering everything they were going through together, but it was precisely because of everything he wanted to respect her privacy. As it was, she would be moving into his house soon—tonight, if he had a say in the matter—but he wasn't going to go rummaging through her things while she was out.

He pulled the truck up to the curb at home, but Samson checked the rear-view mirror and pulled away. He'd just had another an idea.

He drove until he finally found a carpark in the city center. He rarely went into the city, or at least he hadn't been there recently, but he knew it was the place to go for fine jewelry. He ambled past a few shops and saw his reflection in the glass shop fronts. Who was that guy? And what was he looking for?

Samson watched other people as he walked along and asked himself the same questions about them. He came up mostly with the same answers: just a guy; works in an office, or at the train station or the ice-cream store; found a woman he loves and he's going pop the question. Tonight.

Samson turned a corner and walked to one of the estate jewelers. He didn't know her ring size, of course, he hadn't thought of such a thing, even as he'd been thinking of them as husband and wife. Perusing the sparkling showcases, Samson saw a few nice settings but wasn't sure they were exactly right. He mentioned his concern to a willing salesperson and was ushered through to a smaller office.

"We have a few extra special ring settings in another cabinet."

The saleswoman opened a box lined with black velvet and pulled out a velvet ring holder that she placed on the top of the glass, and then she opened the cabinet behind her. Samson could see over her shoulder that the cabinet contained a dozen or so rings, many of which looked like pieces of Jupiter. She placed them on the velvet ring holder.

"Oh, wow. They're amazing." Samson lifted a few of them and watched them sparkle under the lights. The tiny price tags winked off his eyes, almost blinding him, too. "I'm not sure about the prices, though. They look like very special pieces."

"Oh they are. And if nothing else, they're something to think about if our other selections aren't quite what you're looking for."

Samson touched a few more of the spendy rings and though they were completely amazing, he felt like they weren't quite right. His wallet breathed a sigh of relief as he left. There was another store on the other side of the mall and he sauntered over there. He took his time, scrutinizing every facet of every ring that caught his eye. Julene had never worn much jewelry so he wasn't completely sure what her style would be; he had to be judicious.

And then he found it. He felt it as soon as he saw it, the one she would love above all others. He didn't take his eyes off it as he waved his hand around. He probably looked mad, waving his hand around while staring at the shelf. But, of course, the salespeople knew he was going to buy something, they had plenty of experience with people who had that certain look and there was someone shadowing him the whole time, waiting for him to find the compliment to his heart. A salesman came over immediately.

"This is the one. This is it. What size is it? I don't know her size." Samson looked up in concern.

"Not to worry, sir. The ring can be resized during the day if it's not the right fit. Let's take a closer look."

"What is that? What do you call that?"

"This is sometimes referred to as a 'halo', since these diamonds surround the center stone, and that's a cushion cut diamond. A very nice choice, sir."

Samson picked up the ring and turned it around, wondering at how fragile it looked against his large fingers.

"Will it break?" Of course it would not. "And are you sure this is a diamond? Do diamonds come in this faint yellow?" They absolutely did. "How much is it?" It was absurdly priced, of course it was, but his taste was impeccable and the rest would take care of itself.

The ring was paid for, boxed, bagged, tightly held. Samson walked out of the shop so light on his feet—and his wallet—that he thought he might fly back to Julene's house. He'd wait for her in the front garden so he might kneel among the fairy roses and present the ring to her there. He started toward the carpark but got waylaid by a crowd. He held the bag tightly, just in case. They were just teenagers, though, not watching where they were going. Perhaps they were in love, too. Perhaps they would pull their pants up and brush their hair out of their eyes and be fruitful pillars of society. He laughed and then bumped into another group, but this was Julene.

"Hi!" They both said, grinning at each other. He kissed her.

Julene's friends crowded around them and made a few jokes and a few admiring comments, too. They hadn't seen Samson up close for a long time. Julene insisted on introducing them to "her fiancé." They laughed until Samson wouldn't let go of Julene's hand and got down on knee. Everyone gasped and backed up a few steps. Other people walking through the mall peeked over shoulders and made a bigger circle, which drew a bigger crowd, again.

"I love you, Julene."

She lost her breath with a smile.

"I've loved you since you first came to high school."

Now she gasped. She'd never known that.

"I was heartbroken when you left and you can't imagine how my life changed when you came back. I never want to lose you. I never want to hurt you. I will use this ring as a manacle to bind myself to you, always. Will you marry me?"

The crowd cheered as she said yes and after sliding the stunning ring onto her finger to her delight, he stood and kissed her. Their kiss was so long and drawn out that the crowd had dispersed by the time Julene pulled away.

"Take me home."

"I certainly won't say no to that."

"Seriously, my belly is killing me right now."

He waved to her friends who had taken to sitting on a bench, waiting to see if they would undress each other in the mall or not, and talked to her about deep breathing while they walked toward the carpark.

"Look, Julene, unless there's anything else you need at home, I'm driving straight back to my house. Let's get you settled tonight."

She nodded tightly as he drove onto the street. They arrived shortly and he eased her out of the truck, though her pain had improved by that point. Walking through the door, Julene saw her bags and boxes and was excited, even in the midst of her discomfort, that all of her things were unpacked and ready for her to go through.

"I wasn't sure where you'd want everything but you should have enough space to do a few things."

He was right, there was enough space and there was enough paper and paints and brushes; she would make the rest work.

"I can't think of anything else I need from home, for a while, at least."

"Well, we can go back anytime and I'm ready to start working on the studio probably tomorrow afternoon. I'll be finished at Peter's house by noon, I'd say. After that I'm all yours, m'lady."

"That's what I like to hear. I do have a request, if it's not too much to ask."

"Anything, my love."

"Take off your clothes."

He raised his eyebrows.

"You did say anything."

"I did, I surely did. Your wish is my command."

Samson tore off his shirt and settled onto the couch beside her, searching for her waistband beneath the cotton blanket she'd snuggled under.

"You know, reading up on this stuff a little bit has me thinking that you're taking this 'spicy business' a bit too far. What are your thoughts on the matter?"

"I don't think too much." She let her hands do the talking.

"Maybe you're thinking in brush strokes or pencil lines. I'd like to know."

"Seriously, I don't think too much. I think about you and then I stop thinking. Not thinking helps me, relax. So stop talking."

He also let his hands do the talking and no one was thinking much of anything until later.

"Seriously. What's going on with all this 'spice'? The books say you should hate me by now and be eager to have the baby out, already." Samson stroked the hair off her forehead and traced the curve of her jaw with the other hand.

"Seriously, does a ring mean all-access passes to my inner thoughts?" She teased him.

"Manacle. I said manacle and I meant it." He drew her hand up to his face and kissed each finger.

"Well then, you should know all the sex helps me relax. Semen is meant to soften the cervix but other people say it won't happen if your body isn't ready, so I just figure, let's get it on until it doesn't feel right. Okie dokie?"

"Uh huh, except I'm starting to feel more protective and less interested in boning until we pass out all the time, especially with the contractions coming on. And I'm worried about hurting you."

Julene turned to look at him and moved her arm to drape over his waist.

"Every man's dream, to have a cock big enough that he might hurt the baby." They both laughed. "Seriously, let's see about that."

"Julene, no. I mean it, I'm worried about hurting you."

"I know you are and I appreciate your concern, but there are other aspects of you I'm appreciating right now."

She shushed him with her fingers on his mouth and she sat up at the end of the couch with the light behind her. She look intently down at him, waiting.

"Come here," she whispered.

"You're not going to let me get my breath back?"

"I'm waiting for you to get your breadth back. But you have to come here because I can't move."

He laughed at her and liked seeing the flash of her new ring as she brushed some hair out of her face. She pulled him as close as her belly would allow.

The next day dawned early for both of them. Samson was used to rising early but Julene was worn out from a night of restlessness. Samson went for a run and Julene went back to bed. He took his run across town to Julene's house and had a walk around, thinking things through. He did a quick run past where her parents were staying and saw lights on in what he assumed was their apartment so he took a chance and knocked lightly on the door. They were surprised to see him but welcomed him nonetheless. He made quite the impression on Julene's father.

"I'm pleased to meet you. We've both heard quite a lot about you."

"I'm sorry that it probably wasn't all good recently. But I'm here to assure you that my intentions are to honor Julene, and I officially proposed to her last night."

Both Caroline and Trevor Somersby gasped.

"I had planned on calling or visiting you last night after I bought the ring but I literally bumped into Julene and her friends in the mall after I came out of the store, and I couldn't hold myself back."

They were very happy for him and Trevor, especially, was relieved. Caroline couldn't help but ask if they had discussed the wedding at all? Samson's eyebrows belied his outward calm.

"No. Julene was having a few more contractions when we got home. I've moved her into my place on the other side of town so I can work on her place, starting today. You've probably seen the ceiling, but I went and saw an architect and Julene's going to look over the sketches to update the house. I'm converting it into a full-time studio."

Caroline was very interested in what the layout would be but Samson suggested she give Julene a call later, because he'd be working on the ceiling and she'd probably speak to the architect before he got home.

"Oh, Trevor, we should go over there later. That way we can see how she's feeling and have a look at the sketches."

Trevor didn't mind the idea of checking out what sort of work Samson had done on his house and then making up his mind about the man, even though he would never say as much to Julene.

Samson jetted back home and jumped into the shower. He microwaved some vegetables for breakfast before heading to the hardware for supplies. The locals had just begun to emerge when he arrived at Julene's house and took the plaster pieces inside. He'd had them cut to size at the store so the neighbors wouldn't be bothered by the noise of a saw.

The ceiling took longer than he'd anticipated but he was happy with the result. After that, Samson had to hurry to catch up at Peter's house. He wouldn't make it home like he wanted, so he called to check in with Julene. She was overjoyed that the studio was back in business but had yet to speak to the architect.

"Shall we go and speak to him this afternoon?"

"Yes. Let's do that. I've seen the sketches but I feel like they aren't quite right, or not exactly what I envisaged when you mentioned the idea to me initially. Should I just meet you there after you call them?"

"No, I'll come and get you. It'll give me a chance to have a quick shower, as well."

If he'd thought things through in a bit more detail that morning, he would have been clean and well-dressed to talk to Julene's parents rather than the architect, but he'd only had the idea of visiting Julene's parents well after he'd left the house. Damn it, making a good impression on her father had weighed heavily on him whenever he had taken a breather during the day. In any event, the meeting had gone as well as possible, or so he thought, and he called the architect on the drive home.

Julene called out to him from the bedroom after he closed the front door.

"Are you okay? What are you doing in here?"

Turned out, she was waiting for him and would they have time before they had to go?

"Good grief, woman, you'll wear me out and then I won't be of any use to you after the baby comes."

"Honestly, I don't know that you'll be of any use after the baby comes, anyway. You simply don't have the lactation capabilities."

Samson was indignant. "I'll be able to hold the baby, after she's finished nursing while you take a rest. Or something."

"Yes or something. Bring your 'or something' over here."

Samson was still in two minds but his body would not deny his would-be wife.

"I love that you love me enough to love me."

He nodded.

"I do love you, and I do love loving you. But I also want to love the baby and I don't think I can love you any more. I'm really nervous about all of this loving. And we're going to be late if you don't stop loving me back, lover." He did kiss her again, though.

They jumped into the shower and fought over more love before getting into Samson's truck and heading the short distance to the architect's office. Julene thought they could have walked but Samson reminded her she'd used all of the walking time for loving.

"Touché."

There was street parking in front of the simple, glass-fronted building and they were met by the principal architect when they entered the office. Rivers Jacobson was glad to be able to accommodate them. They'd secured the last appointment of the day. Actually, they'd secured an appointment after hours because the architect had heard great things about David Samson Inc. and was keen to work with him. It also didn't hurt that he was involved with the new local celeb Julene Somersby, and he wondered if he might collaborate with her on some projects, as well. It was a fortuitous meeting for all.

Rivers had drawn up a few more sketches for them to look at and enlarged copies were hanging on the large magnetized white-board which doubled as one of the conference room walls. Samson was happy to sit back with a glass of water while Julene talked to Rivers about ceiling details. Rivers assured her they could adapt the design to incorporate whatever she wanted. He agreed to send updated sketches tomorrow.

"Thank you, Rivers, so much for making time for us tonight."

"Not at all. It's been my pleasure to meet both of you. I'm off now to go and pick up my wife and see your exhibit at The ArtCaf tonight. We've both heard great things."

"Thank you. I was really happy with the write up in the news-paper. And the opening night over there was magnificent. Cath Thomas, the owner, she's just wonderful."

"Are you going to the reception at the river restaurant for the next featured artist in the series?"

"Oh, that's right. I've almost forgotten what day it is. Things have been, I would say, hectic, for us lately." Julene looked at Sam-son with a sly smile.

"To say the least." He said no more.

"I'd love to go, though. I know social engagements will be harder to coordinate in a few short weeks."

"Speaking of which," said Samson, "we'd better get out of your hair so you can head off."

They both thanked Rivers and left the office, walking a short way down the street to where the truck was parked. It was dark, save for the street lights which the few remaining cars were parked beneath. Samson suggested they go out and celebrate.

"I'm not dressed for going out."

Samson laughed at her as he held open the passenger door.

"You are *the* local celebrity artist, right now. People will be looking to you what to wear. Besides, you're as gorgeous as ever."

Julene poo-pooed him when he hopped behind the wheel. She tried to smooth her hair in the mirror.

"I suppose it doesn't matter, anyway. In a few weeks I won't be able to leave the house at all or without milk or vomit stains on me. You're right; this'll be fine. But," she punctuated her words with finger pokes, "I am going to get dressed up to the nines for the next exhibit, which I think Rivers mentioned is the day after tomorrow. So you'll have to wear something snazzy, too."

"Why? Nobody will care what I'm wearing. No one will even be looking at me."

"Don't be ridiculous. If I'm the *artiste de jour*, then everyone will want to know who you are and what you do and where you go and if you can start working on their houses, too."

"Hey, you're right! Proposing to you will be the best thing to ever happen to my career!"

They both laughed and then argued about where they should go. Julene didn't want to go somewhere upscale in deference to her stay-at-home clothes, while Samson argued in favor of the rich rags.

"Celebrities are the ones who made lounge pants trendy in the first place."

She scoffed; they compromised. Samson rang an upscale establishment and asked for a quiet table away from any melee. He was happy to report that they could oblige and he managed to find a parking spot right by the front door.

Walking past the outdoor seating and through the unassuming front door was a slow affair, which drew more attention than Julene was happy with and she gave Samson some meaningful looks. He kept his smile small in return. The maître de led them to a corner table, away from the vibrant bar. Julene was still fussing with the napkin when Ursula Litton floated over to them and issued an invitation to join her table. Samson deferred to Julene, who looked interested but uncomfortable.

"I'm sorry, I can see I've caught you both unawares. Give me a wave later on, though, I want you to meet a few of my friends."

She waved at them and floated back to her table. Julene smiled over in that direction and Ursula's friends waved at her, including one of the Directors at the School of Art, the Dean of the Arts program at the university whom she'd met at the opening night of her own exhibit, and two of the other artists involved in the hospital tender.

"Good lord, what a night to be caught out in these shitty rags."

"I'm sorry I didn't suggest you change before we went to meet Rivers. I figured you were comfortable with what you were wearing, because going to his office also counted as going out, I thought?" Samson waved his hands at her, *forget about it already.* "Now, we came out to celebrate, so shall we do just that?"

A waiter appeared at that opportune moment and Samson asked for a recommendation on champagne or other bubbling, non-alcoholic celebratory beverages. Julene interrupted.

"I'll be fine with a half glass mixed with juice or similar. Thank you."

The waiter nodded and came back with a petite bottle of something pretty and brandished a pair of flutes. The table was furnished with some complimentary appetizers and a small jug of cranberry juice and the waiter poured their drinks and slipped away.

"My love, let us raise a toast to you."

Julene opened her mouth to speak.

"Uh uh. I propose this toast to your enquiring mind, not your interrupting words; to your enormous and fruitful belly, and your enormous and loving heart; to our future together—all three of us— and to inviting new friends to join us in what promises to be an exciting evening, even in sweatpants."

Samson clinked his glass against Julene's and drank off a goodly mouthful. Then he winked at her and beckoned over the waiter. A moment later, Ursula's party brought their drinking glasses over while the wait staff joined tables together, and they sat and Ursula introduced everyone.

"So what brings everyone out tonight?" Samson asked after Ursula ordered a round of her favorite appetizers to share. He wasn't sure if it was the woman from the University or the Art School who replied.

"We were actually just across the road when we saw Ursula outside."

"And Paul and I know Ursula from way back," chimed in one of the artists.

"It was Ursula who pushed me to submit some of my art ten years ago," volunteered Paul.

The appetizers arrived and everyone dug in, but Samson was unsure of the dates.

"I know bacon is good for everything, but wrapping around dates? I'm not convinced."

"They're gastronomic gold," Ursula assured him. They were, of course, and Samson's head nearly exploded. "And what brought you both out tonight?"

Samson looked over at his fiancé but she was mid-sip with a coveted date on her fork.

"We had a meeting with the architect whose working on the studio this evening."

"I really loved the sketches he'd drawn up."

"Which architect?"

"Rivers Jacobson. His office is over on Greenhill."

"I've seen his work."

"And he was off tonight to go and see Julene's. He and his wife were going to the exhibit right after we left."

Paul admitted that he had been to the exhibit twice and he and his wife were very impressed by her work. He pulled out a business card and asked for one of hers.

"You know, I don't have any with me tonight." She looked over at Samson for help.

"So, Ursula," he said, redirecting everyone's attention. "Do you know anyone to recommend, or, dare I ask, have experience yourself with wedding planning?"

Ursula quickly looked to Julene's finger and exclaimed.

"Wow! Congratulations again, you two. That *is new*, isn't it? I didn't miss that important detail when I dressed you for the exhibit did I? Well then, yes, I do have experience but talk to me later about dates as to whether or not I can help." She looked at her watch. "But in the meantime, we'd better be off. We'll let you enjoy your dinner in peace."

Everyone said good-bye and Ursula and company left their congratulations and best wishes again.

"See? They didn't even notice your sweatpants."

# TWENTY

Julene managed to sleep in the next day but it wasn't very late. She took it to mean her body was counting down to zero hour and zero sleep. She sighed and got out of bed, showered and scavenged some leftovers from the fridge. But she was still hungry afterward and couldn't easily remember where everything was stored and didn't fancy rummaging around.

She walked from one room to the next and back again, unsure of what she should be doing. She tried to find a new place for some of the furniture so as to make space for painting, but she felt like painting something enormous and the other bedroom was already full of standard home office furniture as well as some of her studio furniture and older paintings. She sighed and sat down instead to sketch out some designs for the ceiling of the studio.

Julene wondered if she should do the ceilings the same in each of the rooms or variations on a theme. She opened an e-mail from Rivers Jacobson and was astonished with the sketches he'd sent, as well as a walk-through of what the finished product would look like. It was very exciting. She sent through her ceiling design sketches and thought that she'd better get to work on the hospital project so she could afford the renovation

Her parents visited in the overcast afternoon and after her dad had wandered around, obviously sizing up the work Samson had done in each room, he was able to relax onto one of the long leather couches. She and her mother spent time talking about the baby, when the wedding might be, and what her mother wanted to include in it, as well as job opportunities for them in the future.

"Don't be coy," Trevor gently admonished his wife. "Your mother has received an offer in South America, and it sounds perfect."

"It is pretty exciting," her mother admitted.

"That *does* sound exciting. And so does the prospect of visiting. The art and architecture over there are phenomenal, or so I've heard. And speaking of which, Dad, can you move some of this furniture around for me?"

Of course, what ended up happening was *all* of the furniture got moved around and pushed to the periphery of the room. He poked around a little bit more while Julene and her mother brought out the easels. Her parents bid her farewell and she'd barely moved her hair out of her face before she started throwing the paint around. Luckily, her dad had found some drop cloths before they left.

Upon finishing, she called Claude and asked him to visit. He taxied over immediately and was hardly through the front door when she asked him about business cards.

"Where are the ones I gave you?"

"Umm."

"Julene, I picked them up from the printer the day after I arrived. Okay, let me think when and where that was. Ah, I remember. I was on my way out to meet some new friends and I put them in a large envelope with a note and pushed it through the mail slot at your house. You must have picked it up at some point or you would have fallen over it. So. You tell me where they are."

He walked past her into the lounge room and stood before the canvas with his critical eye. Julene was thinking out loud.

"Hmmm. I'll send Samson a message right now, he's over there reworking the whole house."

The phone buzzed a few times and then she filled Claude in on the renovation and about her new fiancé. He was beyond thrilled about it all. She showed him the ceiling sketches and the walk-through from the architect and he danced around her, arms in the air. She laughed and they talked about the hospital project and about Julene's dinner the previous evening.

"Oh, I will give them a call shortly," Claude said as he paced around the easel in the middle of the room. "I heard on the grape-vine the School of Art is going to be having their own exhibit, including students, obviously, as well as local artistes, but we will need to register in advance. That will be great, too. But what we need to do today, before you have your baby," he looked pointedly at her belly, "is to organize an accountant because there might be tax implications or something along those lines. I know it will be different than what has been my own experience in England, but I also know you are a little bit forgetful on the legalese, so to speak."

Julene nodded, characteristically unconcerned.

"Yes, exactly. So expect a call from someone tomorrow, I dare say. And, finally, I have tentatively scheduled my flight home. I feel like your career is settling well and after your little cherub is born, I think there will be nothing more for me to assist with."

As Claude put his hands on her arms, Julene's hormones kicked in and she started crying. She pushed aside her vagrant dark hair and thanked Claude for being a wonderful friend and an amazing colleague. And then she shooed him off so she could get back to work by suggesting he head over to her house on the other side of town and see the work for himself. He eagerly agreed and was off in a swirl of dark silk and wool. Julene took a moment on the leather couch now pushed against the far wall, to consider what life would soon be like: a newborn, an artistic apartment, no parents or Claude, a husband.

After varnishing one of the paintings from the other room, Julene changed into some acceptably clean street clothes and went for a walk. The air was exceedingly fresh due to an impending storm, but the color in the sky was breathtaking. She didn't mind the wind whipping her hair in and out of her eyes almost constantly. There were the usual shops along the road—cafés, a stationary store and more cafes—but Julene walked into the electronics store. She'd gotten enough looks recently to confirm her need for greater organization and prompts for the same.

"You mean calendar or task reminders?"

Julene had ambled around the store until she'd found the smart phones desk. And yes, she needed a phone that was smart and better at remembering things than she was. There was a dizzying array of options but she chose one in particular because, "My fiancé has the same brand." There were plenty of things to customize and the customer service rep was able to show her the main features she was keen on. She walked home and sent Samson an appointment invitation for the art exhibit at the river restaurant for the following night. He called her almost immediately.

"Hey! Did you get a new phone? I thought someone must have been impersonating you before I saw your 'spicy message'. So yes! I accept your invitation."

He told her he'd be home soon and that he had other news to share, but no, he would not elaborate over the phone.

At the house, Julene was reclining on the leather couch and Samson was taken aback at the change in the furniture situation when he came inside. He changed his work clothes for black cotton pants and a thin grey sweater.

"So, what's a babymoon?"

Samson poured two glasses of water and sat down on the floor next to the couch.

"It's like a honeymoon before the baby comes. I even thought of a great place we could go that's far enough away to feel secluded, but with a few shops and really nice restaurants close by, and still close enough to home for a quick trip if we need to get back. Like, for birth, or something."

He kissed her jaw and smoothed the fabric of her blouse over her belly. He felt a returning push from the inside.

"Well, it sounds nice but when would we go? It would have to be soon but I feel like there's a few things going on right now."

"Yeah." Samson looked up at the ceiling with what might have been a feeling of being overwhelmed. "I spoke to Claude at your house today. I brought the business cards, too. And I think we could go soon, maybe in two or three days. I can check with my friend who owns the house but I think it would work out perfectly. Please say yes."

He kissed her jaw again, this time running his hands through her long hair.

"Yes, but only if you keep doing that."

"Are you telling me," he whispered as he ran his hands slowly through her hair again, "that if I do this when I'm asking you things, you'll always say 'yes'?"

"Mmmm, no comment."

She stopped his next question in her usual fashion but then she sat back onto the couch, clutching her belly. Samson didn't feel quite so panicked now as he had when he'd first witnessed Julene's contractions. This time, he grabbed the rice pillow from the kitchen counter—though it was hard to find straight away because it was almost the exact same color as the dark granite—and heated it up. He also poured some warm water on a flannel washcloth and brought them both over to her. But he could only do so much. He called her doctor, just to be on the safe side. After that, Samson quietly timed the pains but they never made it to the five-minute mark and they stopped after an hour. A whole hour, come to nothing. He suggested they set up camp in the bedroom since the lounge room was now more of a work space than anything else.

"You don't mind, do you, that I had Mum and Dad move things around?"

"Not at all. Besides, now I know I could massage your scalp and ask you to move it all back and you'd say yes."

The next morning after some extra rest—by then it was almost afternoon—Julene retouched and varnished a few older paintings and then gave herself the rest of the afternoon off to get ready for the art exhibit on the river. She'd chosen a sleeveless dress even though it was mightily close to the heart of winter and no one would even see her arms under one of the super cool new jackets Ursula had short-listed. She was going all out tonight, since she had to assume it was her last hurrah—make-up, cool shoes, a fabulous dress and a bit of perfume here and there for an added bonus. She sniffed: a tease, yes, alluring, not overpowering. Perfect.

Samson walked in just then, loudly admiring her before bestowing kisses and more kisses.

"Also, I have this." He showed off an economy-sized pack of rice pillows he'd picked up across town. "Let's take a few tonight, just in case."

He asked what she thought of that while he stripped off in the bathroom.

"I think I'll need a bigger bag."

"You'll need a bigger bag anyway, because you want to take some of your business cards with you as well as your very important, super cool, new phone. You'll have heaps of follow ups to put in there. You need to carry it with you *all the time*, otherwise you might as well not have it."

"Oh, love, chastise me again."

Julene had walked down the hall and was leaning against the doorjamb of the bathroom. He stepped out of the shower and she stepped forward, running her painted nails along his waist. She had only kissed him twice, however, before her belly stopped her in her tracks. But she would breathe through it tonight because it might well be her last, if these contractions were anything to go by.

Samson held the towel against his face, his expression concerned.

"Julene, maybe we shouldn't go. We can stay home, watch TV on the couch, and suck on ice chips in anticipation of the big day, if you like. It's all very busy in there of late." He gestured vaguely to her belly.

Julene punched his arm and went to sit on the long leather couch. Samson called after her.

"These things keep coming more and more and then who knows, maybe it would be go-time when we're in the middle of something. I don't know if that's the kind of publicity you want."

"I want to go tonight, but after, we should go on that babymoon."

"Great! Okay, let me make a call and then I can pack when we get home tonight."

Samson came out dressed in charcoal and handed Julene a scarf of hers that was the same color. It was striking against her red and black dress.

"Whose place is it, by the way? And where?"

"A friend of mine I went to university with, Rick Toben. I bumped into him at your exhibit and I've spoken to him a few times on the phone since then. He mentioned that he's going overseas for a few weeks. He was looking for a house sitter or something. Anyway, I thought it'd be perfect. It's up in the hills."

On the drive over to the river and the restaurant on the bank, Samson talked about a few things people had mentioned to him about their wives and birth stories.

"So, toward the end they have a hospital bag with them that they take everywhere, so if it all starts while they're out, they're okay. Do you have one of those?"

Julene shook her head. "I'm not really worried about stuff, you know?"

"Well, then I guess I've been doing the worrying for both us. And the research, by the sounds of things. When we get back, let's pack a few things in a bag, if only to put my mind at rest. Pack whatever clothes you want, or socks, or lip balm, or clothes for the baby, underwear, pads, nursing bras, nursing pads. What else did it say? I read a whole bunch of them online today."

Julene looked across the cab of the truck at her fiancé, the lights moving across his earnest face as they drove. She wondered why she'd ever been so stupid to deny herself his company. He was a rock, and she had been an idiot.

"When, exactly, have you been doing all of this research? Not at my house, I hope. I've not been paying you top dollar to be dawdling your days away on the Internet."

"Top dollar, you say? I've also been pulling extra hours for my employer and she expects physical favors as well!"

"I suppose I could put a few things together and have it in the truck if we went somewhere, or something like that."

"Yes, *something like that* would be great."

"Seriously, though, when have you been looking all of that up?"

"Usually at night. I haven't been sleeping so well. I'm getting a bit anxious. You wanting sex all the time isn't helping either, by the way."

Julene just smirked. They found a carpark and hopped out. Julene stepped down with the hand Samson offered her and then gently pushed him back against the truck and kissed him passionately. Eventually his hand slid up under her dress to the cool skin at the top of her tights and she gasped.

"There now. Let me pass, madam. Lest I set my hands on you again in this cold night air and startle the baby right out of you."

Julene grumbled her dissatisfaction as they walked into the restaurant. Samson immediately grabbed a glass of cold water and used it to ward off Julene's advances, else he pour it over her entirely to cool her off. She headed for a touring plate of hors-d'oeuvres but stayed close to him all night, because he was awesome and because he was hers. And because he was carrying her bag that had the extra rice pillows.

They explored the length of the restaurant and viewed all of the paintings. The restaurant itself had glass walls so each painting was displayed on discreet easels in clusters under directed lighting. It was a fantastic effect, which highlighted the artworks in different ways, and Julene felt honored to be in company with people who could produce works such as these. However, she couldn't stand up with them much longer.

Samson found a free table and they sat, enjoying some spicy canapés and similarly spicy dialogue. After the canapés, however, Samson retreated to the kitchen to have the rice pillows warmed up. He'd just sat down and put his hand on Julene's lower back when the directors of the Adelaide School of Art and the Adelaide University Art Department asked to join them. They were happy to oblige. Everyone was curious to know when Julene's baby was due and surprised when she informed them it was so close. Julene was asked some polite questions, including if she was carrying a hospital-ready bag around with her, just in case; Samson could not hide his satisfaction.

As one person excused themselves and left the table, two more came to introduce themselves and sat down, and so on until Julene and Samson had met and swapped cards with each of the seven other artists involved in the project, as well as their friends or significant others by the end of the night.

The contractions had been light and eventually subsided. Julene was able to enjoy herself properly for the remainder of the evening and had another walk around to each of the paintings. After a while, Samson asked if she was ready to head out. She nodded but then spied Darcy under one of the lights and wanted to introduce the two of them. Julene waved at the doctor and walked over to speak to him, a small smile on her face.

"Darcy, hi. It's nice to see you again."

He said the same and held out his hand to Samson.

"Samson, this is Dr. Darcy Litton, Ursula's brother. He was my doctor when I first got back from London. Darcy, this is my fiancé, David Samson."

They exchanged pleasantries and stood there looking at each other. They were about the same height, both with dark hair. They had similar shaped faces and both were broad. Darcy commented first.

"You kind of look like me." He glanced at Julene surreptitiously; she ignored the look.

"No, *you* kind of look like *me*." They both laughed. "I think I've got a few more grey hairs than you, though."

"Perhaps it's the lighting." They laughed again and then Darcy looked around and waved his hand. "I just dropped in after work. I tagged along with one of my colleagues; she's around here somewhere. She's enthralled and is really looking forward to the exhibits for the rest of the artists in the series. Oh, here she comes."

It was Victoria, and Samson's face fell. Darcy made the introduction and Victoria was excited to see Julene again, after having met her at The ArtCaf exhibit. She was less enthusiastic to "meet" Samson, and was confused when he was introduced as Julene's fiancé. Samson made their excuses and good-byes and they left.

Away from the lit walkway, it was quite dark as they walked to the truck and Julene shivered inside her turquoise coat. She jammed on the heating as soon as Samson had the key in the ignition. He was quiet on the drive and Julene credited it to an anxious mind compiling lists of what she should pack in her hospital bag and what they should take on their babymoon. But it was unlike him not to talk at all.

"Penny for yours?"

"I was thinking about that doctor. He really did look a lot like me."

"Yeah, right." Julene looked out the window lest her awkward grin give her away.

"Have you thought about driving again? Or getting another car?"

"What? No. Well, yes, a little bit? I figured I'd get a baby carrier of some kind. You know, I've seen some of the hippies carrying around their babies, or even some toddlers, and it looks amazing. I wasn't going to look closely into getting another car and I've enjoyed not having one. But you know me."

"Yeah. You're not really worried about it."

At home, Samson packed a small bag for their trip to the hills and harried Julene until her hospital bag was packed, too. Her appointment with the accountant was first thing in the morning and Samson wanted to leave town afterward. He would go over early—"even earlier than usual?"—to her house and pick her up after the appointment and hightail it out of town.

It was tough waking up so early compared to her usual routine but Julene was excited about the meeting so she could get everything in order before Claude flew back to London. And yes, she assured Samson, she was excited about the babymoon as well.

The receptionist in the wood-paneled office was very attentive to Julene while she waited to meet the accountant. After she'd replied to his question about strollers, he was full of information about baby slings, baby carriers, wearable folding fabric wrap carriers, and even which fabrics worked best.

"Oh, my wife swears by the wraps and carriers. We live pretty centrally in our area so we rarely use the stroller, and were thinking, actually, of selling it and just hiring one when we travel. And when I'm with the baby, it's an amazing feeling—once I get the thing on properly, of course—to be able to wear the baby, too." He laughed to himself. "I've got some of my friends into baby wearing and they love it. And we get free drinks sometimes if we go out as a group and we're all wearing our kids. If we were single dads, it'd be the best pick-up opportunity ever."

He laughed with her and showed her into the boardroom when the accountant was ready. After the meeting, Julene came out and heard him filling Samson in on the local baby-wearing groups. He wished them well as they left.

"So how'd it go?" Samson asked as they walked into the crisp air and the meager light peering through the cloud cover.

"It was really good. They've had a couple of artists as clients before, but not currently. So they did some research on how exactly to handle things for tax and the house in North Adelaide and different entities and, stuff." She shrugged. "It's going to be great. But not as great as getting out of town, I think."

# TWENTY-ONE

Samson listened to Julene talk about the way the baby felt inside her as it moved and he wondered if it would be a boy or a girl. He wondered if it would look like a Clem when it came out, or if it would grow into the moniker over time. Would Clem look like him? Would he feel a connection immediately, given he'd missed the majority of the pregnancy? He glanced over at Julene, smiling at him, talking about what she wanted for dinner, and wondering if there was a spa nearby, if the bed would be comfortable. He was glad she'd agreed to take off for a few days; she'd been working pretty hard lately.

"Did you just say 'pretty hard'?"

"What? No I didn't."

"I think you did. Sounds like a Freudian slip."

"No, I guess I was thinking out loud. My actual thought was that you'd been working pretty hard lately, and it's a good thing you've given yourself some time off."

She was unconvinced.

"I didn't realize I wasn't allowed to work while we're here. I brought paper and pencils for sketching."

Samson slowed the car and turned off the main road.

"Looks like we're here. See the house, down there behind those trees."

The driveway was long and the sweeping views were fantastic, as was the garden, which shielded the house from the neighbors, far off on the other side.

"Oh, it's lovely here. This would have been perfect for painting!"

"Maybe another time. Today, it's the perfect spot for relaxing. Maybe a massage, yoga, preternatural tea-drinking experiences, all of that Zen stuff."

"What about other stuff?"

"I'm not making any promises."

He helped her out and hefted their bag from the bed of the truck.

"Do I bring in the hospital bag?"

"No. Leave it in there because if we have to go, we don't want to have to find it inside the house. It stays in the truck."

"Yes, sir."

They were impressed by the pale yellow rendered stone of the house with the wrap-around verandah and accompanying gardens. They settled themselves in the master bedroom with its low, minimalist bedframe and dark feature wall, and took a long nap. Julene slept much longer than Samson and he busied himself in the kitchen and then with the TV remote until she woke up.

In the evening, they walked the cobbled brick sidewalks to a local restaurant for a signature schnitzel dinner and peered through the windows of shops nearby afterward. They would walk there the next day to investigate properly.

"Julene, look in this window. They have baby slings and carriers."

"And that beanie! Oh, I want that. Let's get that tomorrow."

And they did walk back the next day for brunch, for shopping, and for dinner again in the evening. Samson used some avocado oil he found in the pantry to give Julene a foot rub morning and night, and then he used it on the salad at lunch time. He found an acoustic guitar in the lounge room coat cupboard and strummed it a few times, remembering tunes from his days in a high school band.

"That was before you moved to town. There were six of us, way too many players. We all wanted to do it but couldn't organize ourselves properly. Then we all got girlfriends and quit."

He strummed through a few songs and then put it away again.

"Do you have a guitar at home? You sound pretty good and it's nice to listen to."

"I'm sure it is when you're lying on a thick carpet all spread-eagled. I don't know that you'll think the same when the baby hasn't slept for hours and I've come home fresh-faced and enthusiastic for your company. You might just as likely smack me with it than listen to the stingle-stangle of the chords."

Samson crawled over beside her and ran his hands over her hair, gently brushing his fingers through. He thought she was dozing but her hands sprang up around his shoulders and she kissed him quickly, pinning him against the couch.

"Gotcha."

She moved her knee against his thigh, her shirt open and falling back off her shoulders.

"This carpet might have seen better days."

"I don't mind what the carpet sees."

She slowly worked her way up to her knees, taking time to lift her belly off the floor. Unbuttoning Samson's chambray shirt was also slow going because she was leaning over in order to get to the buttons. She didn't really want to bust open his shirt, even though it sounded so good in the novels her friends were reading. The fire had warmed them, so putting her hands inside Samson's shirt only gave him a few goose bumps. She licked his lips a little. He reached up to undo her bra.

"Oh no, please don't. These things are so heavy, it sort of hurts to have them out." But she moved his fingers over her breasts and the fabric of the bra; they weren't completely off limits.

The fire burned low but they didn't notice. Sweat beaded on Julene's forehead and on Samson's back. He whispered to her.

"I think the fire is burning my ass."

"I'm burning up, too, but it's not because of the fire."

She ran her hands over his shoulders and hard biceps. He ran his hands over her breasts and round belly. They moved together on the rug, holding hands, kissing, whispering, breathing.

Time at the house flew by. It was beautiful in the sun even though it was still very cold. They walked up and back a few times a day to the restaurant and bought a few things in the shops, including three different baby wraps. The lady in the store showed both of them in great detail how to wrap and they left feeling pretty confident. Driving home, however, down the steep road into the city when they could least afford the distraction, they joked that they wouldn't remember about the wraps when it came time to use it on their own.

Samson went back to working on Julene's house the day after they got back and Julene went right back into painting. Claude was leaving the house as Samson was coming home days later, and Claude told him briefly that Julene had finished the work for the hospital before waving and walking away down the street. Samson opened his mouth to reply but frowned instead. He lifted his own hand to wave, too late, and went inside.

"I just saw Claude. You sent the hospital pieces off without showing me?"

"Yes. But I did make something special for you, which I think will hold you over until the unveiling next week."

Julene lifted a drop cloth off a side table; underneath was a navy box. She waved at it with her hand, rather than bending over to present it to him. Opening it, he gasped.

"Julene! This is gorgeous. This is perfect. Thank you!" He beamed at her and took the framed sketch completely out of the box. "My very own Julene Somersby original. This is priceless. This is amazing." He put it down and hugged her. "I love it."

Samson picked it up again and began wandering along the walls, trying to find the perfect spot to hang it while watching out for misplaced furniture. Right near where the dining table had been before Julene's parents pushed it back into the corner, right there was the perfect spot—just the right amount of indirect light, line of sight from the kitchen and hallway, the last thing before heading down the hall for bed at night. Julene lifted her feet onto the arm of the couch, sighing in relief.

"So, the hospital piece will be a surprise for you as well."

"Yes. And that's what, next week? Baby Clem is cutting it fine for show time, I have to say." He pulled a pre-made bowl of dinner out of the fridge.

"Hey, when did you make that?"

"This morning before I left. Do you want some?"

Julene declined. She raised her eyebrows as she looked up at the white ceiling with its simple plaster ceiling rose and bold crown molding.

"I should shoot for the unveiling as my last public appearance. What do you say?"

"I say you'd better get your parents and Claude over to North Adelaide soon, before the baby comes. It's really close, Julene. You'll have to decide what you call it."

"What do you mean?"

"The Julene Somersby Studio; Studio Julene; Studio Somersby; Somersby Studio. That sort of thing."

"Not Samson?"

"Well, no. That's my name, like Madonna. And the art is yours. You've become known by your name, you should keep it for the art, even if you decide to change it after the wedding."

Samson had wolfed down the food in record time and left the

bowl in the sink. He wiped his hands on a linen napkin as he walked to the couch.

"Speaking of which, I know my mother will want to know if we've decided on any details, so might we talk about it?"

"We could practice for the wedding night, if you like." He wiggled his eyebrows and threw the napkin towards the kitchen.

"I would like, but Baby Clem doesn't feel right about it so much, anymore. The day has come when I'm sort of desperate to be done."

She looked up at him and he laughed.

"You were so dismissive that this day would come, and now here you are," he said, reaching down to her.

Julene put her arms around his shoulders.

"We could keep kissing and see where it leads us."

Samson agreed. "We can keep kissing until my head explodes."

He picked her up gingerly and carried her to the bedroom, laying her down on her left side and scooting in beside her. They kissed and kissed, their heavy breaths steaming the windows where the drapes weren't quite closed, but Samson's head did not explode. He did take matters into his own hands at one point and then Julene fell asleep on his chest.

Samson lay for as long as he could. It was heavenly to feel her completely relaxed and he tried to forget the previous six months altogether. But everywhere he looked he saw a bachelor pad with embarrassing touches of ex-girlfriend hiding beneath the new dressings of his fiancé: a book Victoria had given him beside a stack of art magazines received in the mail and carted over from Julene's house; a throw cushion bought somewhere and gifted to him to "liven up the couch"; a couple of CDs he didn't recognize on the wall unit behind the couch. He didn't want to see those things anymore. He figured on speaking to a real estate agent in the morning. He was asleep pretty quickly after that.

# TWENTY-TWO

When Julene opened her eyes, she didn't move, merely lay there and contemplated her belly. What was the baby doing inside? Did she feel anything going on down below? She practiced her pelvic floor movements and then had to get up to visit the bathroom. After a bit of coffee and toast, she changed out of her pajamas, flicked on the radio, and scrolled through the news on her fandangled new phone. Julene loitered near the kitchen but didn't go over and look through her paintings. She didn't want a break from it, per se; she'd just had one. But after finishing the hospital art pieces, she was at a bit of an artistic loose end.

She pulled on her heavy navy coat and a pair of boots and closed the door behind her. It was a short walk through the parklands and it was nice to be outside. The sky looked like it might rain but she kept walking. Leaves were shaking and falling as Julene passed through the shrubbery that bordered the edge of the city. She reached the outskirts pretty quickly and pushed on through to the mall, passing the spot where she had literally bumped into Samson and he had proposed to her. She bought an ice cream and sauntered on past the book shop. She couldn't think where she wanted to go in particular so she kept walking. She kept a slow pace so she felt fine and wondered if the constant movement was keeping the contractions at bay or if it would bring them on like hellfire when she finally sat down somewhere.

Julene walked until she was standing outside her house in North Adelaide and assumed it had been her intention from the start. She stood catching her breath by the gate and listened to the workers inside calling to each other. Samson came out with a large bin between his hands, dust on his arms and neck, speaking over his shoulder until he dropped the bin and noticed her. His eyes widened.

"Julene! Are you okay? What are you doing here?" He almost ran to the gate, looking at her belly as he did and then seeing her calm. "Did you walk here? Good for you." He smiled and kissed her, but didn't move aside.

"Can I come in and see?"

"Uh, no. No, I'd like you to wait until I present it to you. Tomorrow, I think, around one o'clock."

"Oh. Well, I might go around to The ArtCaf for a bit. Can you pick me up on your way?"

"I've got a better idea. How about I tidy myself up when I'm done and then we can go back to The Elephant Walk. I still need at least another hour, though."

Julene's face lit up with the idea and she kissed him good-bye. He went back inside immediately and she watched him go. It was nice to watch him go. She tried to see past him into the house as he walked through the door but he turned and closed it after him, smiling at her as he did so. She consoled herself with the thought that it must be fantastic inside, picturing the ceiling roses she had designed. She looked forward to a menu sampler at The ArtCaf as she walked away, and was in anticipation of what graced the walls inside.

The clouds above were almost as pregnant as she was; their waters broke and Julene hoped it wasn't an omen. She tried to hurry around the corner but Baby Clem would have none of it and Julene settled back into her customary shuffle. Her hair was damp when she walked inside but the heaters were on and she felt the difference immediately.

The waiter remembered her from the exhibit and was happy to fill her in on the details of the current exhibit as well as the menu specials as she unwound her scarf and hung the navy coat on the opposite chair. There was plenty of reading material at the surrounding tables so Julene had little problem waiting for Samson to be done. At one point Cath Thomas came out and shared a pot of tea with her and Julene updated her on the renovation.

"Wow, that sounds like it's gone through really quickly. That's fantastic."

"I was lucky there wasn't a lot of damage inside the ceiling and there were no structural walls to be moved around. It's primarily aesthetic so the permits were easy. But the finish is a surprise, apparently, and I'm not allowed in until lunch time tomorrow. I think he's up to something."

"It does sound like he's up to something, but I bet it's something sweet. That babymoon was a sweet idea."

It was another half hour or so before Samson finally walked in, looking every inch of his six feet and two in some well-turned out cords and a dark zip-up cardigan. He held out his hand for her and she stood up to meet him, feeling more than usually short standing next to him with her big belly and flat shoes.

"You're usually wearing slouchier pants or a bigger sweater, or something."

"Yeah, I guess. I found these pants at the back of my closet the other day and thought I should stand around intimidating people more often."

They ambled the few grey and damp blocks to The Elephant Walk and Julene was excited when they arrived, though she wasn't sure Samson would fit into a booth. She was right but the waitress took them to the end seat and it was really only half a booth so Samson was able to stretch out his legs a little bit. He communicated with the waitress via his eyebrows and she smiled and left. Samson didn't waste any time before putting his hands all over her and making low, animal noises. She could barely contain her amusement.

"What are you doing?"

"I know you always liked coming here and from what I recall, this is mostly what we did when we weren't eating."

That was true. Eventually they ordered some sort of dessert and something else but Julene didn't pay attention to the food. She felt like a newly-minted high school senior, making out with the hot guy from the back row of her English class. Except now, she'd gone all the way.

Hot and heavy in the back row decided corduroy was no good for his manhood and suggested they go home. She was happy to acquiesce. The cool night air was shocking to Mr. and Mrs. Corduroy after the humidity of dessert and the drive home was rather subdued.

After walking through the front door and pouring a glass of water for each of them, Samson stepped over to his painting to admire it in the evening light. When he turned around he saw Julene striking the same pose and stepped over to her.

"I thought you said you were finally done with me? And since when did you become a model for life drawing?"

She merely smiled at him.

He drew her to him and down the hall to the bedroom where they made a nest on the bed but it wasn't long before Samson came out to the kitchen to heat up the rice pillows. He brought back a cup of crushed ice, as well.

"What's that for?"

"Haven't you read anything about giving birth?"

"I don't think I need to because you keep telling me all the good stuff."

Samson couldn't quite muster a sigh of frustration.

"Sometimes you don't want to or aren't allowed to eat or drink, but ice chips will hydrate you. You know, during the birth."

She took a mouthful and then settled back, in obvious pain.

"Julene, it can't be far away now, surely. This could be it. We're going to meet our baby. God, I love you."

"I love you, but I need you to not talk anymore."

Samson intimated that now it might really be happening, this is more of what he had heard about. He was expecting swearing next. Julene tried to muster a laugh but fell short.

"Julene, this is poor timing—"

"Then please stop talking."

"I need to be candid with you." He started twisting the blanket in his large hands. "I think talking to you while you're already cursing my name is as good a time as any." Samson took her grunt for consensus. "The other day when you were sleeping, someone came here."

Julene unscrewed her eyes.

"It was, uh, the woman I'd been seeing before the art exhibit."

"Ow. You mean, *at* the art exhibit, don't you?" She grimaced.

He nodded.

"Is it Victoria? The doctor who was, ouch, with Darcy at the river restaurant the other night?"

He nodded again.

"Damn it. I thought she looked pissed. It's 'cause she's jealous. I can't blame her; you're fucking gorgeous. OW! Okay." She looked at him, waiting for him to continue. "I'm assuming," Julene took a few moments to breathe through the worst of the pain before continuing, "there's more to your story. Unless you're waiting for me to tell you the names and addresses of all the people whose hearts I broke after you broke mine." She arched her eyebrow even as her back arched a little.

"I broke it off with her when she came over that night when you were sleeping on the couch."

"What? OW! For fuck sake, OW! But you told me it was from"— she took her hands away from her belly to make quotation marks in the air—"the moment you saw me. Dude, what the hell?"

Samson gave her a long look and then went to reheat the rice pillows. He took his sweet time out there. She gave him no time when he came back into the room.

"Seriously, what the hell?" The pain had subsided enough for her to move around and sit up, and she watched him closely as he sat on the edge of the bed.

"In my heart, I decided as soon as I saw you, but I was only able to talk to her about it that night when you were here."

"But that was, what, three or four days later? How does that happen?"

He met Julene's eyes but had no answer.

"I'm telling you this because she'll probably be at the hospital unveiling next week. She's apparently super keen about all of the art exhibitions."

"Oh, you don't say."

"I don't know that she'd say anything to you, but I don't know that she wouldn't say anything to me, either. I don't know if she'll make a scene."

Julene eyed him as he ran his hands through his dark hair and paced the room.

"I suppose it doesn't make much of a difference now. Come back to bed, why don't you."

Samson looked over at her from his position near the window.

"I didn't mean to hurt her, but I honestly didn't feel like we weren't really, involved except . . ."

"For physically. Yeah, right. Whatever."

"What? I'm just being honest with you. I don't want to hide things from you. I can't help it if she thought she had more than she did. I tried to talk to her about, stuff, I was never misleading with her. I can't help it if she got more involved than I did."

"No, I suppose not, but you can't help it if that's still no fucking excuse, either."

Samson looked sorry but not as though he really knew why.

"So, do you think she will scratch my eyes out, or something?"

"I don't know. No, I don't think so, but if she's upset then, like I said, she might say something to me. I don't know if she'd make a scene. I'm guessing not since she also works there, but who knows. She likes a drink and maybe that would make her talk. Look, let's assume the best and not talk about this anymore. I don't want you to be stressed or anything about this. I'm sorry."

Julene wondered if he was really sorry or just really sorry he'd brought it up.

# TWENTY-
# THREE

It was early. Samson was feeling a bit anxious about his schedule. He wanted to fit a few more work things in but he wanted to be available at the drop of a hat for Julene if Baby Clem decided it was time. He felt like pacing but wanted to be fiddling around on his computer with his contacts and business cards at hand, but he didn't want to be tapping away and writing notes and talking to himself in the study while Julene was sleeping in the next room. He didn't want to risk waking her because she was probably still pissed with how he'd expressed himself and the state of affairs with Victoria last night. He pulled on his shoes and left the house instead.

Samson started his customary run but then instead of running around the oval or his neighborhood, or even to North Adelaide and back again, he ran all the way to the bay. He'd never run that far before and it was intimidating with the traffic so close to him, heading in all directions, on the highway mere feet from where he was pushing the pavement. When he finally made it to a café on the water, huffing and puffing outside before being seated at a table by the window, he made plenty of calls.

The view to the beating waves was amazing. Samson devoured a gourmet omelet and rich coffee before walking back the way he'd come. After a while he started running again and made it back to town before he felt like he would be sick or fall apart. At that point he had to call Moose to come and collect him, he couldn't take another step even though he might have been only half a mile from home.

"Good lord, man, what have you done to yourself? You're positively fading away."

Samson smiled at his friend and crammed himself into the passenger side of the small green Mazda.

"Running's a thing for me now. Ever since Julene left me, I ran to avoid thinking. And now I run so I can avoid thinking about what I've got to lose. She's gonna drop the baby any day now."

"Yeah, I've been waiting for the good news every time I get a message or phone call. How's it all going?"

"Oh man, it's great, just great. Literally fantastic. But last night I talked to her about Victoria and she was a bit annoyed at me. Or something."

"Why'd you do that?"

"Well, Victoria works at the hospital where Julene's artwork is being installed in a few days. I thought I had to bring it up because we're going to the unveiling, and what if Victoria said something next time? I kinda think she didn't the other night only because she was caught off guard. That'd be shitty timing, especially since we're in this good place together. It's almost like we were never apart, except for missing most of the pregnancy." Samson shrugged. "I didn't want to hide anything."

"Well, good luck with that. Hey, there she is."

They'd arrived at Samson's house and Julene was outside, having gone to buy the newspaper. She was surprised to see him in Moose's car as much as he was surprised to see her out of bed. Julene gave Moose the hero's welcome. They hadn't seen each other since before she went overseas and, to his eyes as well, she looked full to bursting. She invited him inside for tea or coffee but he declined on account of having to go to work.

"It's a tough life, mate. Thanks again."

Moose said something about a treadmill and then waved and drove away.

"How are you this morning?"

Julene put her arms around him and her head against his chest.

"I'm good. I'm glad you told me about Victoria, eventually. I'm sure it'll be fine. Now come inside and make me some breakfast."

"What? I'm out bringing home the bacon and you just got out of bed. You should be making my breakfast, and baking me cupcakes and cracking open beers upon my return."

"You're not returning from the coal mines, or anything. Anyway, need I remind you that you're still in my employ? Get your ass back to my worksite and finish my house."

She smacked his ass. He wrapped his arms around her and kissed her passionately.

"You're right, today is the big reveal."

He kissed her cheek and then sprinted for the shower. On his way out the door, he reminded her of their one o'clock appointment and suggested she dress up a bit, since it was the official handover of the project and the unofficial opening of her artistic residence.

There was really only the clean up to take care of, now. Samson had invited Claude and Julene's parents to come and help finalize everything. He'd already purchased a few pieces of furniture and would pick up the rest of the art equipment and furniture from his house but otherwise, it was merely a cushion here or there on the decorative sofas, filling a cabinet with *über* trendy water glasses and matching pitchers, or repositioning a vase around the window that was needed.

Samson wanted Julene to dress up because her parents had thought it would be a good idea to invite Julene's friends as well, and then Claude had decided that an hour afterward would be a great time to invite some of the local art community, too. So after confirming the timing with everyone else, Claude had collaborated with Cath from The ArtCaf again, used the same guest list from the exhibit, and added extra names for the grand opening today. He would go with Samson and choose which of Julene's paintings and sketches would hang in the new gallery, not to mention the furniture.

In the end, Julene hadn't been able to decide on a name for the gallery but had chosen "Julene Somersby, Art Studio and Gallery" for signage. There would be sparklers in the yard today but the sign wouldn't be delivered until the following week.

Everyone was gathered and ready, every speck of dust swept, every inch of window and flat surface buffed and polished. Samson and Claude drove across town to wait inconspicuously at the other end of the street. When they saw Julene get into a taxi cab, Samson moved the truck to the house and they brought out the chosen artworks and furniture. One of Julene's friends had asked to catch a ride in the cab with her—as instructed by Samson—so he and Claude would have a bit of extra time to get back and get everything hung up. Luckily, Julene's friend was characteristically melodramatic and it was not unusual for her to want to stop somewhere to pick something up on the way. It ended up being a bamboo plant for luck.

It seemed like forever until Julene finally walked through the door but the expression on her face proved how worthwhile all the work had been. Her face positively shone when she saw how the floorboards had been reworked, the luster of the newly painted red walls, the updated lighting and, of course, the ceiling roses. She would have rushed over to him but she settled for a slow walk and threw her arms around him with tears in her eyes.

"This is amazing, just amazing!" She wiped her eyes carefully. "I never imagined how wonderful this would turn out. Thank you so much!"

He was thrilled with her response and he ushered her around to see every corner of every room. The doorbell called them back to front of house and Julene opened the door to Cath Thomas. She brought in some covered trays of hors-d'oeuvres and placed them on the polished table before heading out again.

Claude clapped his hands and made a small speech about how supportive Julene's parents and friends had been to her since her return from overseas. He looked at his watch and then announced the official opening to the public would start in fifteen minutes and suggested they raise a toast before Julene's public arrived. Toasts to opportunities, artwork, supportive networks, and happy futures were drunk and then there was a knock at the door and Julene opened it to a veritable flood of people who 'ooo'ed and 'aah'ed over the interior of the gallery as well as the pieces gracing the walls. It wasn't long, however, before Julene found Samson in the kitchen, hopeful he had some rice pillows stashed close by. He was already taking one out of the small microwave on her old fabulous red countertop.

"I saw you massaging the small of your back and grabbed these."

He put his arms around her and kissed her slowly, holding the small heated pad against her as he did. A few people poked their heads into the room but smiled and left immediately. Julene didn't mind staying in the kitchen for a bit, reheating the rice a few times and slowly sipping water. Samson came back in a few times to check on her and Claude popped in to speak to her as well, but she stood up, announcing herself feeling better and wanting to circulate.

"Oh good, I wanted to let you know I've had a few calls and still more people are wanting to come over, including a journalist and photographer from the newspaper."

Julene marveled over it all.

"They will be here in about twenty minutes, but I thought that afterward you could go. I'd be happy to stay until it all winds down."

The team from the newspaper came earlier than she expected and stayed only a short time. They were really only taking notes for the

Out and About section but assured her she'd receive a call soon for an in-depth interview.

Julene gave her unequivocal thanks to Claude and her parents, said her farewells to the last of her friends, and went home with Samson. She managed a few words of praise and pride, and gratitude, but fell asleep before she could suggest other ways to celebrate. Pains woke her after Samson had very carefully brought her inside and she remembered her celebratory thoughts to him between contractions. He appreciated the thought but suggested she focus on the task at hand. His hands were especially busy massaging the small of her back and then he was running back and forth from the kitchen to her bedside while the pains were waning.

"I don't know how much longer I can live like this. Perhaps I should go and see the doctor tomorrow, and see if there's any actual business going on. Maybe we can schedule a caesarian and get this over with." She was only half joking.

"My love, you have to do what's right for your body, but I'm pretty sure husbands everywhere have suggested that nature will have what nature wants." He ducked. "Right before husbands have things thrown at their heads." He lay down behind her where he figured he would be out of the line of fire.

"The next exhibit is in just a few days. I can make it that far, can't I?"

"Take it one day at a time. But maybe you should see the doctor. When's your next appointment? Do you want me to come with you?"

Samson pushed her hair out of his face as she nodded her head at the wall.

"Wait, what did you say?"

Julene turned her head and spoke to the ceiling.

"I said, it's a shame you've been so busy or you could have come to the other appointments."

"I wasn't sure you wanted me to, since I wasn't there for the rest of the pregnancy."

She turned toward him, slowly, with a certain look.

"You can make up for it now. I'm going to."

"Make up for what?"

She inched herself up on an elbow and kissed him passionately, working her way down to his pants with her other hand. It was the corduroys again. There was nothing for it but to try to remove them, slowly with one hand, which really only hastened his interest in the whole endeavor. His breathing was labored.

"Julene, I had a dream about this, you know."

"I'm sure you did."

He laughed throatily.

"Seriously, I had a dream after your exhibit in North Adelaide. Not in bed though." He sat up and unbuttoned her blouse and helped her remove her arms from the sleeves. Then he eased aside the fabric of her skirt with fingers as slow as her own.

"Were you doing this?"

She looked at him through low lashes. He tried vainly to swallow before taking a swig from her cup of ice. He answered breathlessly in the negative.

"Was I doing this?" Another negative. "What happened, then?"

He smiled with his eyes closed.

"Well, uh, I saw you, through, the window," he was having trouble concentrating on his story. "I saw your belly and it looked like you would drop the baby right then and there, and then, I was, hey!"

Julene giggled.

"And then I was inside standing next to you, and then I touched you, like this."

She giggled again, and they both stopped talking.

# TWENTY-FOUR

Julene was frustrated after her OB appointment because basically, nothing was going on. Sure, there were contractions but they weren't having the desired effect and she would just have to suffer on through to the end.

After negotiating the carpark at the Memorial Hospital, Samson was keen to drop into a café but Julene couldn't bear the thought of eating anything; he bought coffee in a to-go cup as they walked through the mall. They also checked the start times at the cinema but Julene had a twinge and couldn't bear the thought of sitting still for that long.

"We could go home and you could make it up to me again, if you like." Samson had a twinkle in his eye but was really only teasing.

"Yes, I'm sure you are but I'm not feeling very sorry for you, all of a sudden." Julene's smile faded as Victoria walked toward them, her small bag held forcefully against her hip.

"Excuse me for interrupting but can we talk?" She looked meaningfully at Samson and then back at Julene.

"Um. Please, don't mind me. I might get a drink, after all."

Samson objected. "You know, I'd rather not do this right now."

"Actually, Samson, I think I would rather you *do* do it now." *And get it over with*, Julene thought. "I'm going to take a load off over there."

She could hear them talking in low voices as soon as she stepped away. Frankly, she was happy to be able to sit down, though she hoped this wouldn't take too long. Baby Clem must have gone to sleep because Julene couldn't feel any of the customary round-house kicks to her bladder anymore. She placed a drink order and then sat down at one of the grey metal outdoor tables to watch her fiancé, letting her turquoise coat fall open, though she was feeling a distinct chill and wondered if it was only in her mind.

Julene made no attempt to hide that she was watching, she thought she had a right to since they were far enough away to have the privacy Victoria wished for. Julene could see her speaking heatedly and Samson responding gently, or at least, without much physical response. Victoria attempted to touch him but Samson shook his head, again speaking reservedly. He gestured in both of their directions a few times and used some small placating hand movements but didn't seem to get worked up. Victoria, on the other hand, looked alternately hurt and angry, sad and indignant. Finally, she looked at her watch and then walked away from him. He waited a minute before walking over to the seat beside Julene, ordering another coffee when the waiter came with an offer to refill the teapot.

"Sorry."

"Don't be. She's taking more initiative than I did."

"Yeah, well."

They sat in silence while Samson fidgeted.

"Is this something we'll be dealing with for the foreseeable future?"

"I don't know. I don't think so. I said the same things as before and she did, too."

They finished their drinks silently without looking at each other.

As things continued physically in the same fashion, there was nothing to do but carry on and simply wait for the baby. Julene encouraged Samson to get back to work and while he encouraged her not to work, she was keen to do a few sketches and then head over to her new studio.

It was a fantastic feeling to be working in a proper studio in a professional gallery. She had yet to post hours for the gallery, however, and would have to talk to Claude about that. She thought about what else she'd have to speak to Claude about before he flew back to London and jotted occasional notes between wiping of hands or washing of brushes. Julene didn't realize how long she'd been there until Samson came in anxious because she hadn't answered her phone. It was tucked in the bottom of her bag, of course, and had been left in the kitchen.

"It's late, didn't you notice? And you probably haven't eaten all day," Samson admonished her.

"I've eaten a little. But you're right, it's late and I didn't notice. I've been here since, noon I think, and I haven't had any contractions and I was just working along. What's going on?"

"Well, nothing, I was just worried when I didn't hear from you." He kissed the side of her forehead. "The unveiling is tomorrow, I thought you might like to get some rest."

"Actually, I'd really like to keep working."

Samson raised his eyebrows when he saw the wrappings from some energy bars in the trash and then shook his head at her emphatically.

"Okay, dinner and *then* keep working."

Julene did her best impression of puppy dog eyes.

"I didn't think I'd be able to stand around so much, and this is so relaxing, and it takes my mind off my impending doom."

"Okay, but dinner first."

Samson helped her clean up and then he locked up. They walked a few blocks and slipped into the Lion Hotel, which was unusually quiet. Darcy had walked in behind them and greeted them in the foyer.

"Oh hey. Look, Julene. It's that guy who looks like me." The two of them laughed and shook hands while Julene forced a smiled.

"Are you guys meeting anyone or do you want to share a table?"

Julene wanted to think of a reason to avoid staring at the two of them seated together but Samson was oblivious and insisted. After a rectangular plate of stuffed mushrooms arrived, he and Darcy got to talking about how they'd met their significant others.

"Actually, we only met recently but I haven't stopped thinking of her since. I met Julene for dinner here a while back, you know, before you were on the scene, of course," he and Samson laughed and Julene blushed into her mug of tea. "I said the same thing to her then. It was a weird meeting, one of those fateful moments you don't really believe in until it hits you like a freight train. What about you two?"

"Well, it's pretty simply, really. Julene moved to town in high school and I fell in love right away. We were sort of in the same circles but never friends. She moved away and I thought I'd die. It was pathetic. A few years later, she moved back to town and we caught up at university and it finally grew from there."

They talked about university and people they'd known in common. Samson's friend's name was brought up.

"Rick Toben? Yeah, I knew him. He wasn't a friend of mine, though. We never really got on."

"Oh. I knew him a bit and we played the occasional rugby game, went out on a few guys' weekends together. I really liked him. I saw him recently, actually, at Julene's art exhibit here in town."

Darcy turned the conversation.

"But tell me about the wedding. I see a nicely polished rock here on this hand, have you made plans for the big day?"

"My parents are keen for us to do just that, and we keep starting a conversation but I've been having contractions, so we haven't made any decisions."

"Must be soon, then. Your due date is almost nigh, isn't it?"

"They've been happening for a while. Samson is philosophical about it all, but he can afford to be."

Samson's face said otherwise.

"Oh yeah, it's got no bearing on me whatsoever." They laughed. "But besides all *that*, everything is going really well and we finished the renovation of Julene's house into a gallery and studio, and she gifted me with an original sketch which is hanging on the wall at home. You should come and see it." Samson drained his beer. "I think we'd better get home but you should come and hang out, Darcy. I've got a few nice bottles on the shelf at home, too. What do you say?"

Darcy turned and spoke to Julene.

"He is as cool as he is good-looking."

Coming home was a nice feeling for Julene. She really had wanted to work a few more hours in the studio but she couldn't argue with being home instead now that she was drowsy from dinner. She immediately took off her shoes and heated some rice pillows. Darcy knocked and came in not long after she was settled on the leather couch. Samson had a few bottles already on the kitchen counter.

"Good man. Are any of them open already? They're all worthy of a nip, that's for sure." Darcy picked up one of the bottles to read the label. "Is this a special edition? I must have missed it."

"Then that's what we'll start with." Samson poured a finger on ice in two glasses.

"And this must be the sketch. You're right, it's magnificent." He stood there a full five minutes, inspecting and admiring.

"Hey, that's a self-portrait as I'm sure you're aware. Eyes off."

Darcy laughed and turned away, avoiding her eyes.

As soon as the heat had faded out of the rice packs, Julene wished them both a good night. She lay staring at the ceiling, listening to their low voices. She tossed and turned before falling into an equally restless sleep. She dreamt that Samson delivered her baby but Darcy had fathered it; she couldn't remember which baby was hers when she went to the nursery, and then she went to the hospital art exhibit and everyone asked where her baby was but she didn't know.

Julene woke up with a start and relief washed through her when she realized it was a dream. She threw off the covers and gingerly walked to the bathroom, careful to step loudly so she wouldn't sneak up on the men in the lounge room. She needn't have bothered—she could hear a sports review program on TV.

# TWENTY-FIVE

Samson also had trouble sleeping when he finally got into bed. He lay staring at the ceiling for what felt like hours until he also got up for a drink and then fell into a fitful sleep. He dreamed he couldn't find Julene anywhere and then when he did, he couldn't get to her because Victoria was always in his face trying to talk to him. Then he was at the hospital for the art unveiling and saw Julene having her baby in a spot-lit corner, surrounded by strangers. He woke up with a start, sitting bolt upright, a shooting pain in his arm. He looked down and saw Julene's hand gripping his forearm. She was breathing deeply with her eyes wide.

"Is this it?"

She nodded and then shook her head, and then nodded again.

Samson bolted for the kitchen. After he'd heated the rice pillows in the microwave and drank hastily from the faucet, he ran back to the bedroom and quickly got dressed. Julene hadn't moved on the bed and Samson looked at her now, in between finding things to throw into a bag for himself. He stepped into the hall and threw the bag; it skidded to a stop at the front door. Julene stared at him when he came back into the bedroom, breathing deeply all the while. He crawled onto the bed and stroked her hair.

"This was a bad idea, this whole baby thing. I've changed my mind. I don't want to do it." She smiled at him and kissed his hand.

"Are you ready to hop in the truck?"

She nodded shortly.

"Yes, let's hop. Then you can skip and I'll do a backflip, and we can run away and join the circus and forget all about this birth plan nonsense."

"What else do we need?"

"I don't even care, at this point. Nothing can be as painful as this. You can slow down as we get to the hospital and I'll jump out the open door. Tuck and roll."

Samson assured her he would bear that in mind, depending on the traffic.

It was later in the morning than he'd thought, though it didn't make a difference to the amount of sleep he hadn't had. There was quite a bit of traffic as a consequence, the early morning commuters heading to all points of the compass.

Samson left the truck in the drop off zone of the Memorial Hospital and walked Julene inside, heedless to the bags and sweaters and drink bottles rattling together on his arms as people walked by them. A nurse came and assisted them with their check-in and then they cruised slowly up in the elevator to the ward. Samson put on a brave face but he didn't feel calm or philosophical anymore because Julene had become more pained and agitated with every passing moment. The contractions were also coming more frequently with less time in between than when he had started timing them in the truck.

"Excuse me, sir, is that your vehicle parked in the drop off zone?"

Samson nodded distractedly while pouring a drink for Julene from the clear jug on the white bedside table; she hadn't said a word since their arrival.

"You'll need to move it. The parking inspectors are pretty particular, even at this early hour. There's a parking lot just around the corner, you can see it over there, through this window."

"Are there no valets? I've missed almost her entire pregnancy, I don't want to move the truck only to find my kid comes when I'm not here."

The nurse shook her head and then made some notes on the clipboard hanging near the door before leaving the room. Samson took a few things out of the bag for Julene and then smoothed her hair while she breathed through another contraction.

"Do you want to get in bed? The nurse said I have to move the truck but I don't want to leave you. But I don't want to have to go and do it later, either, when you really really need to be swearing at me. What should I do? Julene?"

She looked through frantic eyes at him.

"There's no time! I think the baby's coming now!"

"Are you sure? You sound so calm about everything."

That got him a smile and he pressed the call button a few panicky times.

"What do you want me to do? I want to put my arms around you, or hold you or something. Talk to me, I don't want to stand here stupidly any more than I already am." He was all but wringing his hands.

Julene shushed him with a look and took his hand in hers whilst leaning against the bed and held it against her belly. Samson was shocked at the movement he felt there. And then Julene's water broke and he fainted.

He opened his eyes. Julene was calling his name. He expected to see her lying next to him in bed before he remembered they were in hospital! Nurses were milling around and then filing out of the room. Julene was wrapped loosely in white sheets and a pink blanket, leaning back on a mound of flaccid, white pillows.

"My love, you missed it."

"What happened?"

"You fainted." But she didn't look at him as she spoke; she only had eyes for the bundle in her arms.

Samson scrambled from the armchair where someone had dragged and/or dumped his useless body to where she rested in bed.

"The baby? I missed the baby? I missed it all. Julene, I'm so sorry." His vision kaleidoscope as his eyes teared. He tried in vain to blink them clear; he did not want to miss another second.

A nurse came to help Julene wrap Baby Clem in a thin white blanket, and Samson still didn't know if Clem was Clement or Clementine. He didn't even care at that point. Julene handed him the bundle and his tears spilled over.

"Daddy, meet Baby Clem, short for Clementine. No news on a middle name, yet."

Samson's eyes couldn't keep up; he whispered love and encouragement to his daughter, and adoration and devotion to his wife until he could barely speak at all.

A lactation specialist came to assist with nursing and then it wasn't long before Clementine fell asleep. Julene was eager to do the same. The nurse helped Samson to lightly wrap the baby in the blanket, and he held his new baby for an hour and a half while his fiancé slept on and off.

Samson wanted to call Julene's parents and Claude but he daren't take his hands off Clementine. He barely took his eyes off her. But then she started making a bit of noise before outright crying and Julene held out her arms. As soon as they were settled in the bed, Samson took his phone out to make the calls but Julene shook her head to let him know it was okay to wait.

"I had a thought."

"While you were sleeping?" He laid a hand over a blanket-covered knee and wondered at the pair in front of him. Wondered over the miracle of babies, and the fortitude of the women who birth them.

"I thought it would be nice to give Clementine my mother's name, too."

Samson's eyes moved to Julene's and he nodded at the idea, and then did send some timely messages. The replies were immediate. Julene smiled at him when he told her the new namesake would be right over. Samson called Moose next, and then sent messages to a handful of Julene's friends before moving back to the bedside.

Caroline and Trevor arrived with flowers and baby blankets and a handful of teddy bears. Caroline was crying and she walked straight over to look at her beautiful grandchild, whose head was thick with dark hair like both of her parents. Trevor shook hands heartily with Samson and then pulled him into a hug before going over to the bedside as well.

"Well then?" Demanded her mother. Her father was more able to wait for the announcement.

Julene was happy to have kept them in suspense for a few short minutes.

"Clementine, this is Clementine Caroline Samson."

Samson's eyes teared up again and nodded his approval and appreciation of the name before excusing himself for a short while to get a decent coffee while his soon-to-be-parents-in-law cooed over their new grandchild. He was dehydrated and overwhelmed with love and a bit of anxiety as well. Moose met him at the vending machine.

"Dude! Congratulations. Are they both well, sleeping?"

Samson updated Moose on the situation and they shared coffee at a table before walking back to the room. Claude arrived at the same time and was uncharacteristically quiet while Clementine was wrapped in one of the new blankets and handed over to him. He gazed at her for a full minute before declaring her to be a masterpiece. Julene's parents excused themselves for a bit and then there was more room for Moose to squeeze into one of the chairs. Claude stayed a while longer before proclaiming himself overwrought from how wonderful Baby Clementine was, because he would soon be leaving all this beauty behind him to go home to London. It was then Moose's turn to hold the tiny bundle, all the tinier when held in his large hands. He, too, left and then Clementine nursed again before being wrapped for sleep once more.

Samson took Clementine for a walk so Julene could get some proper rest and met Trevor and Caroline along the way.

"David, I'm not sure if Julene told you but we've been looking at moving back overseas and after some phone calls last night, it looks like it'll be sooner than we were anticipating."

Samson could hardly stand to tear his gaze away from the miracle that was his new daughter.

"I think, yes, she mentioned it briefly. She said South America, I think."

"That's right. Originally Caroline was offered a job starting in three months, but the program there has been significantly restructured."

"What we were wondering, David, is if you and Julene—and of course, we realize you've both had plenty going on—well, we'd really like to see you married before we go."

Samson nodded, and then stroked the blanket near Clementine's little face.

"We meant to talk about it in detail but got waylaid every, single, time." His words were punctuated by strokes of Clementine's abundant hair. "Julene mentioned a few times—before, mind you—that she wanted a big wedding, but I'm not sure if that was just teasing. She might want a small wedding now, with Clementine. We spoke briefly to someone about organizing it but didn't get much further than to give her a follow up call."

"We'd be happy to cover most of the costs."

Samson met his soon-to-be father-in-law's gaze.

"I don't want Julene overwhelmed with a wedding if it's not what she really wants." He paused to let that sink in. "Why don't I leave Clementine here with you and I'll head back to Julene's room and see if she's awake."

Caroline and Trevor were eager to spend time with their grandchild and sent Samson off with their assurances. He peeked into the room and saw Julene getting back into bed.

"Hey, my love. Tell me what I can do for you."

She smiled as she pulled the blanket over herself. "Where's Clementine?"

"With your parents around the corner. Shall I call them in?"

Julene shook her head. "I'll be glad of a few more minutes rest. Lay here with me."

He scooted onto the bed beside her and then a nurse came in to check on Julene.

"No funny business, you two."

"Oh, I think her days of funny business are over for a while. And just as well, she ran me ragged."

"You'd be surprised what some people get up to."

The nurse asked Samson to step outside for a few minutes and while he was waiting, he spied Julene's parents walking back to the room, Caroline pushing the little cart and Trevor carrying a protesting bundle of blanket and tiny fists. He held the door open for them when the nurse left.

"Well, sweetheart, we might head out and let you three get some time together. Is there anything you'd like us to bring back for you tomorrow? Anything from the house or the shops? Anything at all."

They were persuaded that nothing more was needed and Samson gave them a distracted wave while he gazed at his family on the bed.

# TWENTY-SIX

Julene and Baby Clem had been home for a few days and everyone was doing as expected, that is, nursing and sleeping and trying for more sleep but usually not. Add in some adoration of the newborn, soreness on Julene's part, and feelings of inadequacy on Samson's, and days passed in a blur. Julene eventually convinced Samson to get some earplugs and try and sleep through the night feeds and he agreed to get some nightlights so Julene wouldn't have to turn on actual lights; maybe he could get some rest and be able to get some work done in the days to come. Julene assured him she also wanted to be able to get some work done, but she was a bit more realistic about when all of that would take place.

"I don't like it either, having to get out of bed and all of that, but I do want to start doing some painting again soon. I thought in a few weeks when I'm feeling better, I should use the wrap and carry Clementine on my back for an hour or two in the afternoons, and throw something together in the studio before coming home again. If we could sleep most of the morning away, I'd be happy with that. What do you think?"

"I think you're too reasonable for someone who is sleep-deprived and supporting the life of another person from your own person. But I guess you're right."

Julene nodded and closed her eyes again, pulling the blanket over Baby Clem in the bed next to theirs, before pulling the blanket over herself.

"But, you need to give yourself time and not rush into things."

"Yes, Dad."

"Dads have authority, you know."

Non-committal noise issued from the vicinity of the pillow. Samson padded out to the kitchen, thick dark socks guarding against the cold floorboards, to catch up on some morning news and make up some meals for the day. Janet had offered to help with her slow cooker and they were happy to accept, but Samson didn't want her coming over first thing in the morning, which she wouldn't hesitate to do if given half a chance. After preparing and covering three different types of salad and making room for them in the fridge, Samson headed back to bed as well.

# TWENTY-
SEVEN

After a week of being home, Julene was ready for Samson to go back to work, "just for a few hours." He was so helpful in many respects and trying to be just as helpful in others, but for that reason he wasn't actually always helpful. He could tell she was trying to let him down gently and telling him to piss off in the most tactful way possible for someone so tired and physically strained. Samson often wanted to sit and spend time with her but Julene really just wanted to go back to bed. One afternoon when Trevor and Caroline were visiting, Julene's mother said as much.

"David, you want to help, of course you do, and you've established such a wonderful routine with the food and the laundry and spending time with the baby in the evening. But I'm sure you want more conversation or fresh air than what you're getting. And Julene needs the opposite. I remember when Julene was born and we brought her home, Trevor was wonderful and then he was insufferable. I was so glad when he went back to work, and she was just four days old."

Trevor nodded and shrugged. "There's only so much I could do."

Samson knew they were right and the following day, when Julene surfaced for a shower, he told her as much. He was surprised when she hugged him tightly.

"No, you're not that bad, but I know you need more and I know I need less, at least for now."

Samson stocked up on earplugs when Julene insisted he leave the house. He made a few calls while he dawdled and arranged to go back to work the next day. It took a few days to get into the swing of things and to stop boring his co-workers with tales of the wonderful things his fiancé and newborn were doing, but he managed.

He went to work early, often jogging beforehand, and then came home for lunch before going back for a long afternoon. The afternoons were longer than he was used to but he accomplished plenty and was more likely to sleep through a wakeful Clementine during the night.

One evening, Samson came home and Julene handed Clementine to him and went for a nap. Her parents were there and brought up the idea of the wedding again.

"Did you talk to Julene about this?"

Trevor answered in the negative.

"Well, when are you thinking? Like I said before, I don't want anything to tire her or stress her out. And I don't know if she wants a big wedding now."

"Like we said before, we'd be happy to contribute heavily to the wedding, and I think if we talk to the right people, we could make it happen regardless of the scale of the thing."

Samson considered what Trevor had said.

"We'd be happy to bring it up with Julene but wanted to defer to you and also, we weren't sure if you'd discussed it recently."

"We haven't but I know you've got it on your mind. Let me mention it to her tomorrow. There's nothing more I want than to walk her down the aisle but Clementine has her own agenda."

Caroline smiled and nodded and they left soon after.

It was actually two days later when Julene brought up the subject of the wedding, rather than the other way around.

"Oh shit, I was supposed to ask you about that yesterday."

"I'm not surprised my parents have been scheming. I *would* like to do it before they go, but it's just so soon."

"So tell me about this lavish wedding you've apparently been planning since you had your first crush. Your mum had some pretty specific input."

Julene blushed and laughed. "Yeah, I can't deny it, I had it all planned out when I saw Jason Bateman for the first time."

Samson raised his eyebrows.

"And don't think I wouldn't think twice about you if he came knocking at my door, because you'd have my footprint burned onto your ass pronto, mister."

"Oh, I've missed you talking about my ass."

She smacked it.

"I'm not sure I want puffed sleeves anymore, though, or sleeves at all, for that matter. We should talk to Ursula. She'll know who can help us, if anyone can."

The following week Ursula met them at a hotel restaurant downtown for lunch, including Baby Clem and Julene's parents. Julene assumed her parents were splurging on the lunch because they had expectations for getting their way with the wedding.

Ursula was delighted that they'd asked her because she knew just the place and a few retailers who would be able to help them out on short notice.

"Do you have ideas on what you want the wedding to look like?"

Clementine woke up noisily which stopped Caroline before she could begin. Julene rearranged her wrap to accommodate nursing and jumped in before her mother.

"Much to everyone's surprise I don't have any crazy demands for a wedding, but I do have some ideas which I wrote down here."

She slid a few sheets of paper across the dark wooden table to Ursula.

"Oh, I love these! As for the dress, I know someone who can help but I wonder if you should go with a simpler gown that can be embellished, and that way it would be finished much more quickly."

Julene nodded around some spinach and feta.

"Okay, so let me get back and I can email you a checklist of things to think about. If you really are set on that date, which is in exactly five weeks, then you have to get back to me tonight on pretty much everything. I know it'll be a lot but I don't want you to be disappointed. And as for the cost—"

"We'll pay for everything," Caroline declared.

"Ah, unless there's anything in particular Samson wants to organize for himself, of course."

Samson appreciated Trevor interjecting; there certainly were a few things for his fiancé he would like to take care of himself.

"Well, that's settled, then. I'd better go, but we'll speak soon." Ursula wished everyone a great day and glided away in her under-stated dress, which reeked of a high-fashion brand that no one at the table would have heard of.

"She really is remarkable." Caroline watched Ursula go.

# TWENTY-EIGHT

There was plenty to do to organize *her wedding*, not to mention needing plenty of rest to take care of her infant and herself. Julene should have known that she wouldn't able to get back to painting as quickly as she would've liked. Speaking to Ursula at lunch had her creative juices flowing but she really had to channel them into the wedding.

The first thing Julene did was throw down a handful of sketches of what she wanted in a wedding dress. Looking over the papers, she was surprised to see they were all mostly the same—variations on a theme.

"That was easy, then."

She had a look through some of her past sketches and paintings and decided on a design similar to what was currently hanging in her gallery across town, and then daubed on some watercolor. It was perfect, or perfect enough for a gathered skirt that people would only glance at anyway. Clementine woke up in the other room and Julene went to soothe her by putting her in the wrap. She felt the familiar pull as her milk let down and Clementine settled into her half-dozing nurse.

"But people won't be looking at me the whole time, will they, baby?"

She sent Ursula scans of the dress sketches and the watercolor design with her fingers crossed and then she hammered out a guest list and crossed off a bunch of other items on the checklist Ursula had sent. Julene wondered how her twelve-year-old self would have reacted to the news that Jason Bateman would have to sit on plain chairs, rather than draped with silk and bows.

The following week, Julene decided she was ready to paint again. Her fingers were tingling from having done a bit of sketching but they were aching for more. Samson was working long afternoons and she'd been having trouble sleeping if she took an afternoon nap; she wondered if she could manage some artwork during that feverish mid-point of the day. What convinced her was finding the other wrap she'd misplaced, the one she really loved from the shop in Hahndorf when they'd gone on the babymoon. It was a blue and green watercolor pattern and it would be ideal for working in the studio. When Clementine woke next, she tied it on and wore it the rest of the evening. It was perfect, and Samson agreed when he came home.

"Frankly, I'm surprised you've held off as long as you have."

"Yes, holding off is not really my forte, is it?"

"I'd say something about holding, but you shouldn't overdo yourself."

"Or *yourself*." She kissed him, with her hands around his neck and her body pressed to his. "Ow. Yes, that still hurts. These boobs are not ready for manhandling, I'm afraid."

"That's a shame," between kisses, "because this man really, really wants to handle them." Samson pushed his fingers through her long hair and massaged her scalp. "You should go and rest a bit, and I'll go and take a cold shower."

Samson wanted to drive her to the studio but Julene insisted on starting her own routine. She caught the bus, saving the walking for warmer weather. After nursing Clementine again, she was ready to get in some serious studio time but had to re-tie the wrap a few times before she was completely comfortable since she was trying Clementine on her back, hoping to avoid paint splashes. The signage looked great outside beside the brick pillar when she peered through the window at it yet again. Then she walked along every wall in the gallery before setting up an easel in the studio at the back of the house.

Samson interrupted her before she knew it.

"Hello! Anyone here?"

Julene set down her brush and wiped off her arms with one of the scratchy terry-cloth rags. She showed him her progress when he found her in the back room.

"Haven't skipped a beat, have you. Are you ready to come home?"

Clementine woke at the sound of her daddy's voice and he toted her around after lifting her from his wife's back. Julene bent herself into a few stretches and then cleaned up properly.

"You know, the renovation worked out so well and I know we're pretty well settled into my place, but I wonder if we should look for something bigger."

"I didn't want to say anything to you but I've been thinking the same thing."

Julene came out to the kitchen and poured water for both of them. Over his glass, Samson suggested the names of real estate agents he'd met through work and wondered if she knew any to add to the list.

"Why do we need a list?"

"We might not like the first person, or the second person might not listen to what we really want, or the third person might not—"

"Okay, I get the picture, the third person might not be our best friend. Are there actual qualifications a realtor should have or just these warm and fuzzies?"

"Pipe down, you, I know what I'm talking about." He wrapped his arm around her while holding Clementine in the other. "Baby Clem agrees with Daddy, so there."

Ursula was able to point them in the direction of some great real estate agents and Samson organized a meeting with one of them for the following day.

"Do we really want to add this to our list of concerns, right now?"

"Remember, Baby Clem agrees with Daddy, so I've got the majority. I'm just going to mention what we're looking for and see what happens from there. I know the wedding is in two weeks, but it sounds like it's all plain sailing. And besides, it'll be good for me to have something to focus on that your parents aren't involved in."

Julene laughed quietly. "Got it."

Samson lay Clementine down in her bed in the bedroom and came back out to and sat beside Julene on the couch.

"How did you feel now about some warm and fuzzy stuff?"

He kissed her neck.

"You know, I don't think I can go all the way with you, I'm getting married soon."

"I won't tell your husband if you don't."

"Okay, good, because he's a big guy and I think he might hurt you."

"That's okay, I can defend myself. Let me show you how big and strong I am."

# TWENTY-NINE

It was after another meeting with another realtor that Samson thought to grab some hot drinks to take home. He went into a café next to the book shop at the plaza. As he walked out the door, drinks in hand, the sun caught him full in the face, making him squint and look away. He paused, blinking, and caught a glimpse of a woman who had him doing a double-take as he started walking.

She walked away and he tentatively followed, a ball of tension in his belly and sweat on his brow from thoughts of that stupid party. Samson rounded a corner and brushed some low-hanging leaves out of his face. He saw Linda grab a cart and push it into the grocery store, the same look on her face as when she had been teasing him that godawful night.

She had a baby in a sling, a very young baby with a head of thick, dark hair very unlike Linda's. He stopped short before backing away, feeling sick, "No," repeatedly coming off his lips. He held the drinks tightly as he walked back to the car. He tried not to think.

When he got home Julene pointed out he'd spilled coffee on his shirt. He stayed quiet and pottered around the house for a little while, not really doing anything and occasionally jumping when she went up to him.

"Not getting cold feet, are you?"

She laughed and handed him the baby. Samson held Clementine close and kissed her head as Julene fiddled around in the kitchen.

"Are you heading over to the studio now?"

"Mmm, yup. As soon as I finish packing these snacks, we're walking over to the bus stop."

"You know, why don't I give you a lift across town? I've got a few appointments over there this afternoon, anyway."

"Are you sure? We don't mind the bus, we like people watching." Julene kissed the baby's head as she walked past.

Truth be told—which it would not be at that point—Sean lived on the north side of town, as well, and he would know who Linda was involved with. Hopefully he could shed some light on the origins of that baby. Samson dropped his family off and then drove slowly away, his mind on other things.

Sean was surprised to see Samson; it had been a long time. They spoke candidly while Sean locked his front door.

"Yeah, I saw her a few months ago when she was still pregnant. I thought of you, man, and that stupid party of mine. I don't know what her situation is, though, sorry. I heard you and Julene got back together. I hope everything works out for you guys."

Samson wandered aimlessly down to the shopping precinct and bought a newspaper and another coffee, catching up on the noteworthy and the mundane. He drove back to the studio because he couldn't think of what else to do.

"Don't you have an appointment this afternoon with a new client?"

Samson checked his watch. "Yes, actually I do. Thank you for reminding me. I might assume, though, that you're chasing me out."

"You need activity, you've been moping today. And besides, I didn't think my chasing you was a problem." She wrapped her arms around him and kissed him deeply. "You like being caught."

When he managed to tear himself away, Julene called out to him as he walked toward the front door.

"You might need a better phone if you're going to be forgetting your appointments, mister. I hope you won't forget the wedding."

Samson's laugh was a tad forced as he slunk out to the truck, incongruously blue in the dull rain. Or was he just on edge?

His new client lived down at the bay and with the rain and constant traffic, Samson was in danger of running up the back of the car in front of him almost the entire journey. He changed radio stations a few times in attempts to wake himself from his reverie as though he were half asleep, to little avail. Luckily the traffic was slow so it wouldn't have been a high-impact crash.

Eventually, he made it off the main road to cruise the side streets in search of the right house. It wasn't hard to find after he started looking on the right side of the road—it was the only house for a block that hadn't already received a renovation like its neighbors. Thank goodness, here was something he could sink his teeth into that wouldn't bite back.

As they walked through the house, Samson and the homeowners—a Mr. and Mrs. Dane—discussed aspects of the interior that could be repaired or upgraded during the process of renovation so they wouldn't cost a bomb on their own. The job would end up being fairly straight forward. Samson jotted notes and promised to email a full outline, including other contractors he recommended. He bid Mr. and Mrs. Dane adieu and went to a nearby café to doodle on his notepad. He ordered a strong coffee, stronger than usual. Looking down, there were pictures of sleeping babies amid drops of spilled coffee. He contemplated calling Moose but didn't want his friend to lose faith in him again.

"It was the worst kind of accident," he murmured in deep thought.

He waved to the waiter behind the café display for another strong coffee and then wondered if he would push the truck back home with caffeine power alone.

If Linda had had a baby from that awful night, what could he do? It would ruin his newly regained happiness with Julene, for one thing. It would ruin Julene's newly recovered love and trust in him, too. What a fuck up. At the absolute very least he could find out if the baby was really his. But how?

Samson didn't know any of Linda's friends, besides Sean, and he didn't want to go back to him again. He should start by finding out her last name, where she lived, worked, any family in the area. But how could he do that without going back to Sean? The obvious thing was to ask around but he didn't want to be obvious. He could get a private detective but he used to be a cop for goodness sake, he should be able to handle that shit himself. Friends still working the beat; that would be his play. And friends of friends—he might know people who knew people. His friend from university, Rick Toben, might be one of those guys, simply because he seemed to know everyone. He sent Rick a message straight away.

Samson ordered a pastry and then paid his bill at the front counter, fiddling with his phone all the while. A message came back from Rick then and there.

*Hi Dave, got your message about Linda. I don't know her much except to see her at a party or the like. She seems like a fun woman to have around. Give her my best.*

Before signing off, Rick said he couldn't remember her surname properly but gave a few names that sounded about right and then suggested the names of a few of her friends that he knew of. Samson reread the part about Linda being a fun woman to have around; sheesh, maybe Rick wasn't who he seemed.

Samson made some phone calls sitting in the truck, the lack-luster light through the clouds not helping his mindset. He tried to remember why he hadn't had Linda arrested or brought up on charges for, quote unquote, ruining his life. Something about lack of evidence or tainted evidence or witnesses not willing to co-operate or some other rubbish. It had been too late by that time, Julene already having left him. He hated rehashing all of that stuff and shook it out of his head now so he might do a better job of concentrating on driving.

It was full dark before Samson got home and Julene called out from the kitchen. She asked where he'd been all of this while as she handed Clementine to him and helped tie the wrap around his waist. He settled the baby against his chest and started his customary dance steps to soothe her.

"So they're living in this cute little house and it's one of the only ones on the street that haven't been renovated. There's not much to do structurally of course, those old places are strong as—"

"Houses, ha ha." She'd heard that joke before.

"Right, but a few things on the inside, a wall here or there, galley kitchen, update the wiring, maybe a plumbing pipe and some heated flooring in the bathroom. Standard stuff."

Julene brought the dinner plates to the table and sat down to eat; Samson took a forkful every other step or bounce and Julene watched him with a smile.

"Look, I might go out after she wakes up again, I've got a few things to take care of. If that's okay with you." He didn't meet her eyes for long.

"Oh, really? Nothing to do with an upcoming event at all, is it?"

"What? Oh, uh, no, of course not."

Now he felt worse than the heel that he was. He bided his time until he could leave, hating himself for not being able to enjoy the time with his family, *his family* for fuck's sake. But the situation was what it was, and he had to get some answers. As soon as he was able, he kissed their cheeks and grabbed his keys.

He had a crackpot idea that might just work, but he had to work himself up to going ahead with it. Samson drove around in the dark aimlessly for a quarter of an hour, stopping for a minute to remove the magnetic business decals from each door of the truck. Behind the steering wheel again, he galvanized himself into some semblance of action and drove downtown to where he knew that there was an electronics store that sold "sound amplifiers" for "bird-watching". Samson wanted answers but not confrontation and this might just work. There was so much that could go wrong, and what could he do? He could lose it all, or . . . He couldn't think of an alternative and he started sweating under his jacket.

Armed with Linda's address after searching the suggested names from Rick, he drove straight there from the city and parked fairly close to what he thought must be the house. He just sat in the truck doodling on his phone, or pretending to, while organizing his new purchase and sneaking glances out of his window.

It was dark and cold and the streetlights provided little relief. Samson walked a few blocks before crossing the street and walking back in the other direction. He moved at a normal pace and felt he took long enough that someone wouldn't necessarily see him coming back on the other side of the road and think him suspicious. He knew from experience that people didn't always want to see anything.

As he drew closer to the house, he discreetly switched on the mini dish-amplifier he'd positioned inside his jacket, and slowed his pace. There was a light on in the back of the house but no noise that he could hear. Samson kept walking until, standing near the corner, he spied the entrance to the lane behind the houses on the street. He kept to the path until he turned into the lane and then paused to pull out a cigarette and lighter—a legitimate reason for him to dawdle. At this distance he couldn't miss the conversation in the kitchen at Linda's house coming to him through the dish and the earpiece.

"Linda, can I grab a bag for later?"

"Hell no, you can pay me for what you owe me, first. Hey, can you pass me that tea towel behind you? Yeah, he's just had a little sick up. There we go, thanks."

"Um."

"Yeah, what?"

They were interrupted by the opening and closing of a door and Samson heard footsteps and then furniture scraping. A short transaction ensued and then that person left.

"So, Linda."

"What, already."

"Do you, um, is there a possibility that your kid is my kid?"

"Oh, Andy, do you want my kid to be your kid?" She laughed. "My kid has a namesake, so you're off the hook."

Samson swallowed uncomfortably, the neckline of the sweater beneath his jacket suddenly pressing against his throat. What conversation there was after that seemed trivial and after a few minutes "Andy" left. Samson left, too, walking along the back street until he came to the next corner and slowly walked back to his truck. He started it immediately and drove away.

Samson woke up to a kiss on his cheek; his eyes opened slowly when she kissed his mouth. He breathed deeply of her and dragged his arms from under the warm blankets to put around her.

"Do we need to postpone the wedding?" Julene asked between kisses.

Samson struggled to sit up, running a hand over his face and disheveled hair.

"What? No, of course not. I'm not going to miss my chance to make you mine, once and for all." He smiled and pulled her close for another kiss but she didn't stay long.

"Are you sure? You've been distracted a bit, almost withdrawn, and I wondered if it was because the wedding's so soon. And we've already jumped in with both feet. I wondered if it was all too much, right now. I mean, six weeks after having a baby? And now thinking about buying a new house? It's a lot."

Julene sat back on her calves and looked at him, giving him a chance to wake up a bit more before responding. He looked at her sitting there, her toes poking out from under her shapely ass to the long dark hair over her shoulders, tucked behind her ears.

"No chance. I'm all in. I've been thinking about a few things, but nothing I want to divulge to my bride to be, that's for sure. Now, one thing I've been wondering about is whether we'll spend the night apart before the wedding. It's tradition, you know."

"I think we've done a fine job of bucking tradition thus far, and I might want some more bucking the night before the wedding. What say you?"

"Oh, love, that might be taking things too far," he said with a smirk.

Julene headed across town with Clementine tied on tightly and Samson headed out to lose himself in work again. He took a break a few times to splash water on his face before checking out at a reasonable time to get back to what was foremost on his mind.

Samson drove past Linda's house again and pulled up a few houses away. He decided to be bold; he didn't have a lot of time. He knocked on her neighbor's door.

"Hi there. I'm sorry to bother you but I'm looking at renting a house over there," he'd spotted a few rental signs the night before, "and I can't get a straight answer from the real estate agent about the neighborhood. I wonder if you could tell me anything about any loud neighbors or noisy kids running about the place?"

His audacity was rewarded by a lonely, retired grocer who knew everyone and most of everything that went on. She invited him for a cup of tea and Samson sank into a loyal, green corduroy couch, surrounded by innumerable framed photos on end tables and side tables and coffee tables. He drank two and a half cups of tea, as penance for gossip that was solid gold, from a cup and saucer he could barely hold due to the ridiculously small handle on the side of the white china. Of course, most of the gossip was about people living in other rental properties, but he did hear that Greg next door was cheating on his wife and Susan across the road used to be Greg's girlfriend. Finally, he was told Linda next door had an adorable baby but was unmarried and seemingly unattached, and there was a continual parade of people through her doors at all hours.

"I don't speak to her much but she seems nice enough and her wee baby is a lovely little boy, hardly makes a sound. And she always has him wrapped up in one of those fabric baby wraps that everyone's using these days. I only wish I had known about those when I had my own babies."

Samson smiled at her and finished another cup of tea.

"Well now, I've given you quite an earful but I expect you'll want to be going now or you'll be stuck here with me watching *Wheel of Fortune*."

He shared a laugh with her and thanked her for enlightening him.

"Nonsense, I knew you had a crush on her when you got here."

Samson felt himself pale.

"I'm glad you were able to stay and keep me company for a little while."

She all but forced a napkin full of cookies onto him and then closed the door as he stepped back into the daylight. Samson imagined he could hear her running back to the lounge room to turn on the TV. He went slowly down the steps and walked to his truck, his footsteps heavy. He saw Linda walk up to her gatepost, her blonde hair swaying in the cool breeze. He saw her see him. He drove away and tried not to look back.

# THIRTY

The wedding was in two days and Julene decided she'd better give over her painting and concentrate, or else her inspiration would get the better of her and she'd miss the whole thing. She thought Samson might understand but her parents would never forgive her.

Today she was going to pick up the dress and take a quick look into the conservatory in the Adelaide Botanic Garden to make sure there were no last minute changes, considering that their entire wedding was last minute.

There was a rainstorm as she and Clementine arrived at the dress shop and a few drops splattered onto both of them before Julene could get inside. Clementine woke up, unhappy. Julene got her settled and then sent Samson a message for him to check in with the conservatory instead. Ursula came over to meet her after she ended the call.

"I didn't know you were going to be here." Julene gave her a side hug and Ursula peeked in at the baby.

"Oh my, she is so adorable. And you've really got this wrap thing down, don't you? She looks super comfy in there."

Julene nodded as she bounced a little bit, back and forth.

"I wanted to see your dress! I saw the sketches, of course, but I wanted to see the finished product before your big day. I couldn't help it, the drawings were gorgeous."

They both turned to speak to the seamstress who had unques-tionably woven magic with her fingers. The elves must have helped during the nights because the dress had been finished in record time, ready for the dye of the design onto the skirt.

"When my mum insisted on paying, I didn't mind! Considering how short the timing on everything was, I knew the dress would cost an absolute fortune. But Marta assured me the design was a simple one and it wasn't quite as exorbitant as I expected. Here, you hold Baby Clem while I try it on. Is that okay with you?"

Ursula could not refuse a squishy baby and said as much while Julene got herself organized behind a heavy white curtain. When she eventually came out, Ursula was delighted with the result and she could see Julene was, as well. The sheer shoulders were perfect to cover the nursing clips at the straight neckline of the dress, and the pink watercolor on the skirt had turned out stunningly.

"What are you going to do with your hair and makeup?"

Julene swept some long dark strands away from her eyes.

"I thought I'd put it up and use some of the makeup tips you showed me, but I think less is more, and I'll probably take a nap after the ceremony, anyway. I don't think I'll do much more than that."

She twirled a few times in front of the mirror and then picked up the wrap and tied it around herself, before slipping Baby Clem inside it on her back. Once again in the reflection, it was a wonder-ful picture. The watercolor skirt matched nicely to the watercolor baby wrap since there were a lot of pink tones amongst the blue, and it would keep them close and keep Clementine quiet during all of the important stuff.

Ursula offered to drive them home since the rain hadn't let up and she was pleased to hear everything was just as Julene could wish for. She wished her luck with hiding the dress until the big day and drove away.

Samson's truck wasn't in the driveway so she took her time hanging the dress somewhere he wouldn't run into it. He wasn't the type to open Christmas presents early if he found them but she didn't want to take any chances. She had a quick snack standing at the dark granite counter and then settled down for a nap.

Julene woke when there was a knock on the door; her parents had brought dinner.

"We thought that since we'll be off next week, we ought to come over and see Baby Clem while we still can. And we bought some Pad Thai as well, since you said it doesn't bother her, and we're starving."

Julene's dad organized plates and chopsticks at the table and they sat down for a bite. Clementine made her appearance mid-way through the meal and looked owlishly at her grandparents before settling into her routine position.

"So, sweetheart, is there any chance I can sneak a peak at your dress after dinner?"

"I'd rather not, in case Samson comes back when I've got it out of hiding."

"He told us he'd be home late since he had a big job down at Glenelg. That's why we went to the botanical gardens for him today."

Julene was surprised to hear that.

"I assume everything was fine, then?"

"Oh! It's going to be such a nice day for both of you over there. The lighting is amazing, of course, and there's enough space for everyone as well as atmosphere and intimacy, too."

Her husband tried not to roll his eyes.

"It is a lovely place, honey."

"Do you want to hear about the menu, Julene?"

"No thanks, Mum. I'm sure you told them about my shellfish allergy and my aversion to white chocolate, so it'll be fine. Everything else can be a surprise."

Her parents washed up the dishes while Julene settled herself and Clementine on the couch.

"Well, dear, believe it or not, we'd better go and start packing up our things. We don't need everything that we have with us, so we're sending some of it on ahead. That way, we can just take our suitcases onboard with us when we fly."

They kissed her goodnight and let themselves out.

# THIRTY-ONE

Samson had decided that he, too, needed to ease back on work in order to get ready for the wedding, but it didn't take long to collect a hired suit from the store and hang it in the truck. The rest of his day he'd use to find some information and hopefully set his mind at rest because he'd missed quite a bit of sleep last night for worrying, and rest was what he desperately needed. He glanced at his notes as he drove.

Aside from her name and address, he still didn't know much about her—where she'd worked previously or if she had or where she hung out. He would start with some of her friends. He vaguely knew one of the people Rick had suggested in his email and he knew the guy had a job, which was a relief. Samson didn't want to be calling his friend in the police department every five minutes with a different name because he couldn't remember how to locate a suspect after less than a year off the job.

"Daniel? Sure, he's over there. He doesn't have a long break so please keep it brief."

Samson walked over to a corner cubicle to speak to Daniel, one of Linda's friends. He hadn't really thought of anything to say to any of these people if and when he found them, he only knew that he was a bit desperate.

"Hi? Can I help you?"

"Hi, yes, you were recommended by an acquaintance and I'm interested in . . . " he looked around the office. He'd barely glanced around when he pulled up outside. Seeing the guy behind the desk, Samson realized he was not one of Linda's friends from Sean's infamous party. Picking up a business card from the black plastic holder, 'Insurance' leap out. "Insurance. I need some insurance and I was told you're the person to speak to."

"Oh, cool. What sort of insurance are you after? And are you shopping for quotes from different companies? Because we can do that here, too, but let me assure you rates from competitors are not as competitive as they seem, once you read the fine print."

"Oh, uh, I think I prefer your banner brand. I've heard good things."

Samson introduced himself and then settled down into one of the carpety chairs pulled up to the desk. Daniel took down his details, punched a few things into the computer, and asked about other types of insurance.

"You know what? Yes. I have a fiancé and a newborn, so I should look at a package, or something." Samson threw out some details about his work and his friends and assets, trying to draw the guy out about himself, to little avail. "Actually, I think I might have seen you around a bit, we might have gone to a few of the same parties, maybe last year. Were you with Linda Summitson at one stage? Does that sound right?"

Daniel stopped typing for a minute, looking sheepish.

"Yeah, uh, that's right, but I'd rather you didn't mention her name here in the office." Daniel lowered his voice. "She was cool to hang out with for a bit, but much more and I probably would've lost my job. She's a party girl, that's for sure."

He resumed punching away at the keyboard and asked a few

more questions then he started searching his desk and accompanying drawers for a calculator. His head popped up with the treasured machine.

"So, how do you know Linda? A family man like yourself, doesn't seem quite the ideal friendship, if you know what I mean."

"Right? Ha ha, yeah. Actually this guy I was working with a few weeks ago is a mutual friend and he recommended you. He said he'd met you both at a party last year. Sometimes he still sees her around at one of the cafes."

"Oh yeah, she always liked that one on The Parade at Norwood, not too far from the cinema. I try not to go that way anymore, just in case she tries to reel me back in."

"He said she just had a baby." Samson's eyebrows responded to Daniel's.

"Dodged a bullet on that one, then."

Samson wrapped things up pretty quickly and then scratched off Daniel's name when he got back in the truck. He'd still be interested in reading the guy's paperwork when it came through, though, because he was a family man, now. He headed off toward The Parade to reconnoiter.

Samson pulled the truck up to the curb near the cinema. He crossed at the lights and had a look around at the different cafes. There were plenty to choose from but only two could be said to be near the cinema. He went into the first one and ordered a coffee and sat down to wait, his heart waiting patiently near his throat as he tried to relax into the background of the constant foot traffic.

People-watching had always been an occupational hazard and he still utilized it when out and about if he was by himself; he watched his own people when he was with them. Now he had a newspaper and some sunglasses and a hat; and he saw plenty. He figured this was the right place to wait.

Samson had just received his second coffee when Linda walked in. He wasn't ready for a confrontation; she smiled at him when she walked past. He needed to stay cool—he wasn't sure if he should coolly walk away. Now that he'd seen her up close, his nerve was close to failing.

Linda ordered herself a drink and came and sat with him, her thin arms settling imposingly on the surface of the small table. Samson sat ramrod straight.

"Hi there, stranger."

He couldn't respond.

"I'd like to introduce you to someone. This here's little Sam."

She smiled and looked at him smugly. Sweat ran down under his shirt and he hoped the bile wouldn't rise much further. He hesitated.

"Who's his father?"

"Who do you think?"

"I'm sure I don't know. Some poor, unfortunate soul. Does he even know about this little guy?"

"He does now."

"Oh, come on. You don't expect me to believe that he's mine."

"Why not? He was born just about a month ago, which, I would say, is a perfectly-timed result of a fun time *I* remember us having." She laughed quietly at him. "Do *you* remember?"

"I remember that you ruined my life. Incidentally, I was told I didn't mention your name during the whole sorry escapade."

"Yeah, well, it was just a bit of fun."

"You're an awful bitch, you know that? Do you always ruin people's lives *for fun?*"

"Hey, it wasn't my fault if your woman overreacted."

Samson had had enough and stood up to leave.

"Oh come one, why don't you stop and stay a while, get to know your baby."

Samson didn't look back.

In the truck, he was sweating everywhere, his hands wet on the wheel. He didn't believe her for a second but he what if he was wrong? He couldn't afford to take chances. There was no telling what Linda would or wouldn't do. Did she turn up by chance or had Daniel spoken to her? It was an ugly coincidence; that was for sure. He decided to check some hospital records, to see what else he could find.

The staff in the bland, brown Registry office were dubious of his story but he still had some credentials tucked away in his wallet and that alleviated their concern enough to let him view the files. Samson didn't think he'd have long before someone changed their mind and kicked him out, though, asking him to follow standard public procedures.

Sure enough, the date was just a few days past nine months of that night and the kid's name was indeed Sam; no mention of a father.

Samson grabbed something from the vending machine on his way out of the sterile office. He felt queasy when he was behind the wheel again and pulled over to take some deep breaths. He needed to eat some proper food. He had nothing in his belly but stale coffee and now that chocolate bar, and it was going to come out the wrong way if he didn't do something about it soon. He stepped out of the truck and gulped the fresh air, trying to calm himself as he walked to another café and ordered tea.

"Peppermint, please." He received a pot and ordered toast as well. "No, just plain toast, thanks."

Samson rehashed what he now knew, which wasn't much, really, but he felt marginally better having gained some semblance of control over his situation. He sat at the small, round white table for a long time after finishing the toast, worry eating at him. A thought occurred to him, a scary one. What if the baby was his? But what if there were other babies, too? He'd been careless with women after Julene cut him loose and what if someone else had had a baby? Samson looked around, stricken, as though there might be babies everywhere, their mothers advancing on him with barely remembered faces. Surely, though, if that were true, he'd have been approached by the affected woman—women—already? For alimony or medical costs or guilt money? He tried to ignore the thought and it eventually slunk away to make room for Linda again. He had to pull himself together. He was getting married in two days, damn it. He stood up and left the café, walking a few blocks to find a barber.

"Hi. I need a haircut."

"You sure do. I can seat you in about fifteen minutes, that okay?"

He headed out for some sunshine in the meantime.

Samson felt uneasy about everything but Linda wasn't threatening. She was a bitch, sure, but that was it, really. He had to assume it was a sick joke from someone who obviously liked to tease. He was getting married the day after tomorrow. That would be his sole focus from now on. He walked resolutely back inside the barber's shop and came out feeling relaxed and looking sharp.

# THIRTY-TWO

Julene arrived home with a grumpy Clementine an hour or so after Samson; she was happy with the haircut.

"What makes you think I need your approval for my haircut?"

"Because we're getting married, remember? Happy wife, happy life and all that."

"You know, I think there is much to be said about a happy husband, as well."

He took Clementine out of her arms and rocked and rolled with her a little while Julene took a moment for herself and made up some smoothies. When Clementine was quiet, he popped her down for a nap, singing softly to her while he walked backward out of the room.

"Why don't you ever sing to me like that?"

"You rarely need any cajoling to come to bed." He kissed her and her smoothie moustache. "Mmm, strawberry wife, my favorite."

Julene laughed at him.

"You seem to have gotten over whatever was bothering you."

"I've no idea what you are talking about. Now, enough talking. I think we need to be practicing." His hands on her hips, Samson pulled her slowly closer.

"You mean bucking tradition?"

"Yes, exactly."

"Do we need to do anything else for tomorrow?" He asked sleepily as Julene nursed Clementine in bed, dreary light streaming through the parted drapes.

"You mean, for *our wedding*? No, I don't think so. I might have to buy some exotic lingerie, or some edible body paint or something, but nothing much else."

"Exotic, eh? I'd just as soon see you in nothing at all."

She laughed at him. "Yes, but you've seen that already."

"And as for body paint, you could always just get a jar of Nutella and give me a spoon."

Julene threw some pillows at him. Samson got up quickly.

"Alright, I'm out."

He dressed quickly and then grabbed his keys.

"Wait, where are you going?" She called down the hall from the bedroom.

"Well, I think I have my own exotic surprise to organize."

He closed the door behind him, hearing her laugh in delight as he did.

It was later than Samson had thought and there was plenty of traffic already. He eventually found an empty parking space near the main road shops and walked until he saw what he was looking for. He went inside the lingerie shop, feeling awkward but determined.

"Hi there."

When the sales lady turned around she was holding a pair of something Samson couldn't quite discern and he blushed.

"Oh, hi. Can I help you?" She looked him up and down.

"Um, yes. I'm getting married tomorrow and I think my wife wants to get some nice pieces, for our, um, wedding night." He tried not to look around at the posters of scantily clad women; it was sort of like a mechanic's shed he'd worked in during high school. "I thought I might come in and have a, uh, look around . . . " He couldn't finish.

"You mean, choose a few things and then let your fiancé choose from those? That's a great idea. Plenty of our clients want to choose something to impress someone special, but they often wonder about the impression they're making. You don't want to go too far, you know? Good thinking on your behalf, mister—"

"Samson."

"Mr. Samson. Come over this way and let's have a look at a few styles."

Samson laughed to himself when he left with a smart little business card, wondering how he could organize bachelor events doing something like that. He could make a fortune.

At home, he slipped the card into Julene's wallet and then polished off a smoothie he found in the fridge, leaning against the kitchen counter.

"What are you so happy about?"

"Who, me?" He grinned and came around the counter to wrap his arms around her. He pulled her close against him and she responded in kind.

"Yes, you, the cat who licked the cream. You look very smug."

"If by smug, you mean, in love, then yes. If by smug, you also mean I just went to the lingerie shop and had a sneaky peek without you, then, also yes."

"Oh, did you buy anything nice?"

"No," he said into her hair, "I left that part to you." He unbuttoned her shirt. "This is the part I like."

His hands caressed her skin under her clothes. He lifted her off her feet and took a few steps toward the bedroom before stopping and looking around. He headed back into the kitchen and set her ass on the edge of the counter and made quiet love to her in the daylight streaming through the windows. At one point he knocked some cups into the sink and they held their breaths waiting for Clementine to wake, but she was quiet until their post-coital picking up of clothes and re-dressing.

"Okay, so, we're off now." She was kitted up with the baby and required peripherals, and slipped her keys into a back pocket.

"Are you sure you want to paint today? What if you're hit with inspiration and don't come home until tomorrow afternoon?"

"I already thought of that, and the thing is, I think you'd understand, it's Mum and Dad who I'd be in trouble with."

"Yes, considering this whole, last minute, expensive wedding and all that."

"Hmm, yes, hmm, don't make me take this expense out of your hide, mister."

"I still love it when you talk about my hide. But you should go if you're going so you can get back in time for a rest before we buck tradition some more."

She smiled at him and blew kisses before walking out the door.

Samson was just about to give Moose a call when the doorbell rang. He wondered if Julene was playing a joke on him and took off his shirt before answering the door.

"Hell-lo. Oh."

He was shocked to see Linda on the doorstep. He hastily put the shirt back on before stepping out into the brisk afternoon and closing the door behind him.

"What are you doing here?"

"White pages, dude. Aren't you going to invite me in?"

Samson frowned.

"I thought we could talk about this reasonably." Her tone teased and admonished him at the same time.

"Talk about what? I think you should just go." His gaze moved to the distance and stayed there. He couldn't bear to look at her and he didn't want to look at her child, either, wrapped in a blue blanket the same as one Clementine had in yellow.

"Talk about Sammy. We had some medical bills during the pregnancy and he'll have his own bills eventually, beyond diapers and digital fucking thermometers."

"Seriously?" He spared her a disbelieving glance, crossing his arms resolutely.

"Of course. You've shown a real interest in him and that's convinced me that letting you into our lives is the right thing for all of us." She patted the baby strapped to the front of her body. "So I can send you the bills or we can just set up a monthly arrangement, if you prefer."

Samson shook his head again.

"No." He laughed at her. "No way."

"Look, you can be reasonable or I can be unreasonable. We can talk about this tomorrow, if you like."

He glanced at her and saw her beaming at him.

"I'm sure I can find something nice to wear to your wedding. And I've seen some super cute little tuxedoes for babies, too."

"How do you know about that?"

"Well, you've made it no secret. Maybe I could borrow an outfit from Julene. Then we can all get cozy together before the wedding."

"You're out of your goddamn mind, you know that?"

"No, but I am out of pocket. So, don't leave it too long to get back to me, okay? Or the honeymoon will be over for you when I come back to speak to your new wife."

Linda walked purposefully away, through the gate and then down the street. She didn't look back. Samson was glad because he probably looked like he was going to lose it and he didn't want her to see him like that. He called Moose.

"Hey man, what's up?"

Samson launched into detail, pacing the length of the hall with a death grip on his phone before pouring a stiff drink at the dining table.

"Is Julene home?"

"No, thank goodness. But Linda must've known because she said she'd come *back* to see Julene. She was probably watching the house."

"Right, okay. Well that tells me she really doesn't want Julene to know, she wants it all on the down low and it all still might be a lie. Tell you what, though, that's shitty timing."

Samson agreed, feeling miserable.

"Maybe you should go to the police? I mean, she's blackmailing you. It's not like she's approaching you with a legitimate request for child support payments, otherwise she'd have paperwork. This could be considered blackmail."

Samson hemmed and hawed and then hung up, taking his friend's suggestion. He decided to go into the station rather than phoning it in. He'd only have to go in anyway, to fill in paperwork. But doing so would make it all public, possibly. It would be awful.

"Correction: it *is* awful."

He grabbed a jacket and headed for the police station on foot.

His station had been on the outskirts of town in the other direction so he didn't know anyone at the station near his house, and he was glad no one knew him, either. He explained his complaint to an officer at the desk and was shown into a waiting area, and soon after asked to step into one of the cubicles for further discussion. Details were noted on a sheet of official notepaper and then the officer came to the point.

"But, it *could be* your baby, and *she might* present you with paperwork."

Samson nodded.

"You say you've seen the birth certificate and it lists no paternal details, so she either doesn't know who the father is or doesn't want it recorded." The two of them looked at each other across the institutional grey desk. "You need a paternity test. That's a pretty quick way to put this all to rest. And if the kid's yours, then at least you'll know."

Samson nodded slowly.

"Wait here. I'll find some companies locally who can do the test, okay?"

Samson nodded, heading toward the miserable end of the scale again. He thanked the officer for her time and read through the information on the walk home, wind berating him for his crimes the entire way.

His preoccupation showed later that afternoon; he was quiet and replied with "hmm" a lot when Julene spoke to him.

"Are you getting cold feet again?"

"Hmm."

"I bought some lingerie this afternoon."

"Hmm."

"I dropped the baby today at the studio."

"Hmm, what?"

"There'll be no dinner tonight so you can save your appetite and just eat me."

"Hmm. Actually, I did hear that one, and I demand dinner. I'll need my energy if I'm going to be taking care of you later."

But his heart was not completely in the banter.

When Clementine was down for the night, Julene brought a small glass of wine for each of them to where he sat on the brown leather couch, staring into nothing.

"Seriously, Samson, what gives? Are you anxious about tomorrow? Or something else?"

"Sure, it's a bit of anxiety about what I'm wearing or if anyone will notice my shoes." He slipped his arm around her and settled back.

"That's all very funny, but if you're keeping something from me for much longer, I'm going to get a little bit pissed off."

He silenced her with kisses.

"Maybe we shouldn't be bucking tradition tonight." Samson's heart wasn't in much of anything tonight, but Julene would have none of it.

"Uh uh, no. Opportunities for making sweet, sweet love to your wife grow fewer and further between as kids get older, or so I've heard. Clementine will take fewer naps, and our lives will become busier, so we need to take every opportunity given to us and make it count."

She undid a button on his shirt to punctuate each phrase and then tore off the last two when she wrenched the shirt open. He laughed at her and was in no position to resist, though he felt his duplicity in not telling her what was really on his mind. And she was right. Each opportunity might be his last if Linda was right and she screwed him all over again. He closed his mind to the thought as he closed his eyes to kiss Julene.

# THIRTY-THREE

Julene woke up and reached over to pinch her soon-to-be husband but his side of the bed was empty. There was a rose and a note, to the effect that he had left early so she could get ready in peace. She smiled to herself and then had a peek over at Clementine. Fast asleep, but probably not for long since her milkmaid was up and about.

Julene padded down the hall in socks against the cold floorboards and pulled her dress out of hiding. She took off the suit bag so any wrinkles might hang out between now and when she put it on.

Clementine woke up, hungry as usual and her parents knocked and let themselves in not long after. Julene happily handed off the baby as soon as she could so she could jump into the shower. She heard the doorbell while she was in the bathroom and came out in her underwear and a fabulous vintage slip to see the photographer snapping a few shots of the three of them. After that, she was quick to arrange her hair and slap on some make-up before putting on the magnificent wedding gown. Her mother just about passed out when she finally walked into the lounge room, and the photographer was ready for it all.

# THIRTY-FOUR

Samson had opted for a quiet lunch with Moose after a vigorous morning run around the oval, the city, across town to the north side, and then back to Moose's house. After a shower, he'd fallen asleep in the back room and had no dreams interrupt his sleep this time. Samson's mind was likewise thankfully still during a close shave and a lunch of steak strips with the odd piece of lettuce. A beer and a few nips afterward saw both he and Moose dressed and ready. They didn't talk about the situation with Linda, and didn't talk about much else either. They watched a few sports shows on the box and then it was time to go, and then they went.

Samson was starting to sweat in his suit under the windows in the conservatory at the gardens. He was worried Linda might have dropped round to the house again this morning to talk to Julene; maybe she wasn't coming.

But there she was, looking amazing in a dress that had a design similar to one of the paintings he'd seen hanging in her gallery. Claude's response was the most audible. And there was Clementine, peeking around from behind. What he had taken for part of her dress was actually the blue watercolor wrap they'd bought during the babymoon, wrapped around her torso. It was a beautiful picture and he teared up accordingly. More so, because he harbored feelings of guilt and deceit and blame. He tried not to let them show on his face as he looked at this trusting woman who was walking toward him.

They grasped each other's hands and said the appropriate words, waited for the appropriate responses, exchanged rings. They had both prepared vows but Clementine would have her way right then, and everyone laughed when her cries became too loud and demanding to jiggle and bounce through. Julene quickly adjusted the wrap and her neckline to accommodate Clementine and then they resumed their exchange. They enjoyed a long and joyful kiss after they were pronounced, although awkwardly, as Clementine would not be persuaded to move once she was settled. They grasped hands again and struck poses for the photographer, and then the guests were invited to meet the newlyweds on the lawns outside the glass building.

After seeing almost everyone that she could, Samson and Julene excused themselves so she and Clementine could take a rest in the manager's office next door where she'd left a blanket on the sofa before her grand entrance. Samson draped both of them and stepped quietly out of the office, peeking through the window where he could see his now-wife stare long and hard at their daughter before closing her own eyes. He tore himself away from the tableau and walked slowly back to the lawn.

Back in the swing of things, Samson was ecstatic. He felt terrible about it because it was partly due to Julene not having been approached by Linda. On the other hand, he half feared seeing the woman there at any moment. He took in the congratulations of his friends and family, felt their happiness for himself and his family wash over him, and turned from each of them as soon as politely possible to make sure no one untoward had made an entrance of their own. He led the charge for his guests with the drinks and canapés and was happy to jump into groups of photographs and sit and catch up with his guests. People asked about a honeymoon, and he explained they were deferring it until they visited Julene's parents in South America some time in the future.

Eventually Julene and Clementine reappeared to cheers and applause. At that point the photographer organized album-ready photo groups. Everyone smiled and laughed or 'ooo'ed and 'aahhh'ed when the happy couple had their family photos taken and then the full cocktail menu was served and the band struck up.

"Hey man, where's the cake? I was expecting some towering inferno of flowers and icing."

"The wife and I are, bucking tradition."

There was dancing until everyone left to find a livelier party. The happy couple said their farewells and walked through the gardens to a local hotel in which they'd booked a room. There were a few lights strung here and there along the walk and it was an enchanting way to finish the wedding.

The hotel room had been carefully made up, with a crib opposite the bed and flower petals everywhere. Samson lit some well-placed candles and they quietly organized Clementine for bed. Julene found a bottle of champagne and some flutes on the antique sideboard and they retired to the soft blankets and fluffy pillows of their own bed, the black upholstered headboard uncompromising above them.

"Well, my dearest love, my *wife*. That was a great afternoon."

"Indeed, *husband*. It was fun. We should do it again sometime." She clinked his glass and took a mouthful of the delicate bubbles, smiling at him over the rim.

"I didn't mean it like that. I had a low key morning, going for a long run and then hanging out with Moose at his place. And then in the afternoon, well, I felt like it was a warm and low key wedding, rather than a high stakes, tense wedding like you hear about sometimes."

"I'm sure that only applies to tense people. Or high maintenance people, or high stakes as you put it."

"Mmm. So tell me about your dress. You look stunning, of course, completely original, the quintessential, artistic bride." He dropped some of the flower petals in her hair as he spoke. They clinked glasses and sipped. He ran his fingers over the sheer fabric at her shoulders.

"Well, it's as you see it, and this fabric here hides the nursing clips."

"Ingenious. What about the back? Are there one thousand and one tiny buttons for me to slowly and erotically unfasten?"

She clinked his glass.

"As the parents of an infant, we don't have time for those types of indulgences. There's a zip, which I could undo myself if you were having trouble."

He clinked her glass and left them both on the bedside after they'd been drained.

"I think we deserve a bit of indulgence right about now. What do you think?" He did not receive an audible response. "And right about here."

He traced the sheer fabric with his fingers and opened the covering of the neckline, and he kissed as far as he could reach before tracing the fabric on the other shoulder. He reached around behind her and eased down the zip, tracing his fingers on the skin beneath as his hand trailed down her back. Samson kicked off his shoes and stood up; Julene contended with his belt and trousers easier that way. He moved his hands back to the fabric at her shoulders.

"No, no," Julene protested. "Leave it on."

"Are you sure? You don't want to mess it up."

"Yes we can, that's what it's for. It's not a legit wedding if you don't go all the way *in* the dress. You dig?"

He dug. He shrugged out of the grey suspenders and pulled off the tie. Julene held out her hands and wiggled her fingers for him to come back and then she started unbuttoning the shirt, slowly.

"I love it when you wear a blouse for me."

He burst out laughing and protested her choice of words. He stopped laughing when he pulled out the belt and snapped it together, cocking his eyebrow. At that, she hoisted the dress to her thighs and cocked her own eyebrow. Julene deftly put her big toe in a belt loop and dragged his pants down, and he fumbled around with his underpants. He fumbled around with her underpants, too, happy to see her choice from the previous day. He kissed his way from her knees to the tops of her thighs, and then close, closer, closest, until Julene's fingers tickled at her husband's ear and he allowed her to pull him to her by the open front of his 'blouse'. She whispered in his ear as it moved above her and he laughed at her again, almost losing his rhythm.

"Stop that. I'm the husband now, and I need, to do, my, first job, as your, husband, properly."

He kissed her mouth with gusto and wouldn't let her free to make any comments about her new husband until she was breathless and had no interest in talking. At one stage the flush of her cheeks matched the pink of her skirt and he kissed her neck and jaw and forehead until she all but ate his face right off. He buried his face in the curve between her neck and shoulder and himself in her nethers even more so until he lost *his* breath and his color was high, too. He collapsed on his elbows, his arms on either side of her, his head on her chest. He could feel her heart beating hard and fast inside her ribs, and he kissed the skin there. He eased away from her and lay beside her, his vision obscured by an overly stuffed pillow. Julene turned toward him and caressed his face.

"You can check that off your list, husband. A job well done."

She scooted off the bed and hung up her dress before turning on the shower. The bathroom quickly became steamy and it crept into the bedroom.

"Are you coming in?"

Samson lay with his eyes closed, his feet hanging off the side of the large bed, his black Misfits socks glaring dully.

"What? I thought my job was done."

"Well, as your wife, it's my job to do the washing up. So get in here."

"If you say so."

The bathroom tiles were almost as steamy as the air and he slipped a few times on the short walk to the shower. Inside the glass door was super steamy and Julene's hands slipped all over him.

They slept as long as they could, nursed and sang to Clementine, and then went back to sleep. When next they woke, they went for brunch with a view of the gardens and then returned to their room to nap yet again. Clementine woke in the afternoon and Julene nursed her in the warm bed, pillows and blankets around them all like a nest.

"I could get used to this," Samson mumbled into one of the pillows.

"Then you should have married the pillow."

"Touché."

He rolled over to hold the baby and Julene snuggled back down. Samson got out of bed to make a timely diaper change and then they hopped back into the warmth and softness until Clementine made it abundantly clear she would not settle without additional sustenance. Besides soft breathing, there was nothing else in the room and sleep claimed them all for a time.

Much as they would have liked to stay forever, or at least another night, Julene and Samson decided to go home after the nap so they could settle Clementine for the night in her own bed. It took a while to pack everything. Julene organized her dress into a bag while Samson took a taxi home to bring back the truck. He found an envelope on the doorstep that all but erased his feelings from the preceding days. Inside was a picture and a note from Linda. Samson's mouth went dry. The note read like a birth announcement or party invitation. He felt sick.

"What took you so long?" Julene was worried when he finally came back to the room.

"There was just some . . . junk mail I had to stuff into the recycling, that's all. What do you want me to take down first?"

At home they made up a plate of leftovers from the fridge and drank tea and juice. Samson brushed his fingers through his wife's hair while she lay against him on the couch.

"Is this what newlyweds do?"

Samson's mind flicked away before he could bring it to heal.

"I imagine some newlyweds would be making up for their wedding night when they were too unruly and drunk to actually consummate their marriage. Others might not be on speaking terms if one or other found out about some indiscretions at the wedding or at another time."

"Oh, that's juicy."

"Still others might be writing up annulment papers for one reason or another. Or maybe changing their legal status if they only married for convenience."

"All very legitimate activities for newlyweds, I suppose."

"Thank you."

"Now tell me, do newlywed husbands still keep things to themselves? Or do they wisely divulge concerns to their new wives, thus relieving themselves of half of the burden?"

Samson was silent for a moment.

"You know, I think newlywed wives worry too much and should think more about washing up."

Julene turned to him and laughed, kissing him with her arm around his neck.

"I don't feel like doing anymore housework tonight, husband."

# THIRTY-FIVE

Samson was gone early again on Sunday when Julene woke. She assumed he'd gone for a run since he never worked or even went to the hardware store on Sundays. She wondered if Clementine's waking schedule was changing because she had woken up, too. Julene hoped she'd settle back into the old routine soon because she was feeling the difference from lack of sleep. If not, perhaps they'd start getting up at a reasonable time and head over to the studio in the mornings and come home for afternoon naps.

Walking around the lounge room, she looked out the windows to check the weather. When she turned back to the room, she saw that Samson had left his phone on the dark wooden coffee table.

"That's unlike him."

Julene boiled some water for tea and checked the fridge. She might have to take Clementine for a grocery trip. She started a list on a scrap of an envelope from the recycling bin and hunted up a few bags to take with them. On the walk over to the main road, they saw Moose and he joined them as he was headed to the grocery store himself.

"I wondered if Samson was with you, since he left his phone at home."

"Oh, er, no, it's just me. He's probably running off the beer from the wedding. Like when he ran all the way to Glenelg. Maybe he's getting back into the swing of things."

"You're probably right."

Moose signed off and did his shopping while Julene positioned a fussy Clementine and pushed her cart around the aisles. Afterward, she walked slowly home with the few bags on her shoulders, and when Samson still wasn't there, she decided to head over to the studio; perhaps he could meet them for lunch somewhere.

# THIRTY-SIX

Samson had woken early and couldn't get back to sleep. He'd been restless during the night and felt restless after laying down again. He didn't want to wake Clementine by tossing and turning, so he'd gone out to the kitchen to pace around. The sun was just coming up—he pulled on some long pants and his sneakers, managed to find a sweater in the study, and ran out the door.

He nodded to the other crazies out for their early morning run, steam emanating from their mouths. Some of them had trendy earmuffs; some had brightly colored clothes. He preferred to keep to himself; old sweat pants and a paint-stained hoodie being fine enough for him. He'd bought himself some proper running shoes, though. At the time he'd been taken by surprise at the cost of the things but the salesperson had assured him that arch support was everything. They supported him now as he ran in circles around the oval, part of the crowd. He decided to take a step around the whole park instead. He could keep his eyes peeled to avoid any surprises pet-owners had neglected to take with them, and he would have a quieter path as well.

The eucalyptus smelt sharp in the early morning and he stopped to crush a few small leaves in his hands. He wiped the pieces under his nose and picked up the pace again. Samson checked his watch and thought he could squeeze out another hour before Julene and

Clementine would likely be awake. His brow furrowed when he thought of them because Linda automatically joined the conversation in his mind and he seemed helpless to intervene. He ran faster, crushing twigs and leaves which Julene liked to step on to hear their crunch. Clementine had been perking herself up when she heard the noise, as well, lately.

Eventually, Samson was out of breath and he slowed down to a light jog and then a walk. He didn't want to stop moving though; he wanted to run back to the house in a few minutes and knew he'd get a stitch if he stopped completely and then tried to run again.

"Hey there, wait for us."

Samson turned around and saw Linda walking with her son in the wrap, both of them bundled up against the cold, both of them wearing beanies. The baby's eyes were peeking out from the bottom of the wool while wisps of blonde hair peeked out from Linda's. The breath flew out of him.

"What are you doing, following me?"

"We don't need to follow you, Dave. We know where you live, remember? Besides, we usually walk this way a few mornings a week when it suits us, don't we, Sammy?"

Samson wanted to run away but he was also curious about the baby and couldn't hate himself for that. Besides, he still wanted information and she was probably the best way to get it, if she could be trusted for five minutes. He tried to engage her in small talk but she avoided all his attempts and merely made comment on the aspects on his own life that he was trying to get her to talk about.

"You know, you suggested the other day that you wanted me to get to know him. This might be a first step to that end."

Linda considered his comment and nodded her head, quiet for a few minutes. Sam had gone to sleep and was rugged up under a fuzzy blanket and beanie, some long elastic strings holding Linda's black coat closed around him. Samson commented on them.

"Yeah," she laughed. "You know, it's been frigging cold and I didn't want to buy a whole new coat, so I sewed a button onto the elastic and it works perfectly to hold it closed so I don't get cold, and he's already rugged up."

"If you could come up with a catchy name, you could market those everywhere."

"You know, I'm not sure that's really my style. I already have a pretty steady income."

"Well, maybe it's something to think about for young Sam here, rather than having him grow up in a house with all sorts of drop-kicks walking through the door and bringing goodness knows what types of problems into your house and your lives."

"Spoken like a true cop, always looking out for the welfare of others."

"I don't need to be a cop not to be a jerk. You should try it sometime."

Samson started running again and he made it home without further incident. He didn't feel so awful at the end of the conversation as he did at the beginning but he felt bad because he wouldn't mention it to Julene. He also couldn't expect to have any more polite conversations with Linda; he had to assume the next time she'd be demanding or threatening and he needed to be ready. He thought about talking to her about the paternity test but he thought she would definitely be hostile to the idea, and it would make it nigh on impossible to get one on the sly, if such a thing was even possible.

Julene and Clementine weren't there when he walked into the kitchen. He picked up his phone and called as he raided the fridge for a meal.

"Hey, we wondered where you'd got to."

"I was restless last night and didn't want to wake Clementine too early this morning, so I just went out for a run and I guess I stayed out longer than I meant to. Are you guys at the gallery?"

"Yeah, we've been here for a while. Do you want to meet us for lunch?"

Samson wolfed down a plate of everything then showered and changed. The walk to the bus stop was brisk but promising of spring. Walking from the bus stop in North Adelaide, he glanced around the leafy street before going inside the studio.

"There's Daddy."

He immediately came over to cuddle and bounce his child, patting his wife's ass as she walked back to the canvas. Julene pulled her hair up in a bun and wiped her hands on the apron she picked up off a stool, before picking up a brush and slashing at the canvas in front of her.

"Hey there, wife. Why so grumpy? What did that canvas ever do to you?"

"You're one to talk, husband. Besides, you're not an objective critic so pipe down over there. This style is very apt, right now. And I'm feeling inspired, so you might like to take a walk." She looked at him pointedly.

Samson unfolded the baby wrap from the table and tucked himself and Clementine into a neat package, saluting his wife before heading outside. Walking back the way he had come he saw Linda again and stopped in his tracks. She smiled when she saw him and waved. He couldn't have her walking down this way, in case she didn't know the gallery was there and that Julene was inside or especially if she did. Samson broke out in sweat all over; he started to walk slowly toward her. Thankfully, she stopped walking and waited for him at the corner.

"So, we meet again." She was annoyingly cheerful.

"I was hoping not to have a repeat performance of this morning, ever. And yet, here you are."

"I really enjoyed our conversation this morning, actually, more than I wanted to admit. And you were right, I did suggest it, so I shouldn't have been so mean."

Samson hated himself for thinking she really wasn't that bad when she wasn't being awful on purpose. But he shook his head; he had to remember what she'd done to him last year.

"Look, that's all well and good but what do you want?"

She stopped and looked at him, her body facing him with her hands resting on the front of the baby wrapped on her chest.

"I told you what I want. I want you to help me financially, *because he's your son.*"

Samson turned away from her and kept walking, Linda keeping pace. Passersby would have thought them a quaint little family, and Samson felt sick in his stomach. He needed to get her away before Julene finished painting and came out to find them.

"You know, I still don't believe he's mine. You should stop this ridiculous charade and go and have a meaningful conversation with the kid's real dad. And besides, you said you've already got a pretty steady income, so this seems like a load of bullshit to fuck me again, frankly. It might even start to sound like blackmail if you keep it up. Which would prompt me to speak to some of my friends, if you take my meaning."

"I think I do, but don't think that I've given up the idea of speaking to Julene either. That's a decision you have to make. And you can't be minding her all the time."

They'd walked along the busy main road and Samson was ready to end this now so he could head back to the studio. He wanted to have steadied his breathing by then, too.

"Okay, look, let me get back and take a look at my finances and think about things for a bit. Stay away from me and from Julene until then."

He turned and walked back the way they'd come, hastily making his way to the gallery. Julene was still inside, engrossed in a new canvas and still making dark slashes. She was using a different color but it was equally striking. Samson took a bouncy walk around the walls, glancing back occasionally toward the studio Julene was occupying and was glad this had all turned out so well for her.

Reflecting on the past, however, he couldn't help but think further back to the party with Linda. Had he encouraged her? Teased her? Embarrassed her in front of her friends? Of course, nothing he'd done could justify what she had done to him. Had he not been clear enough with her in response to what he'd taken for playful flirting? It didn't matter now, he was being as clear as he knew how without being a complete asshole. But he had to protect himself and his family, too. He made a pot of tea in the kitchen and set out some cups then peeked again to see how Julene was going.

"I see you peeking around corners, you know."

"I don't want to interrupt you."

"You'll interrupt the flow of inspiration by sticking your head in and out of the room. No prairie-dogging allowed."

He walked away, laughing.

"And be quiet out there. You'll wake the baby."

His phone beeped and he pulled it out, swiping past the home screen. It was a message from Linda. He wondered how she'd gotten his number, but of course, he had advertising in all the right places so how could she not?

*Don't forget me.*

He quickly deleted it and looked back over his shoulder. He could still hear Julene in the other room. He thought about telling her; it was a shitty thing to talk about, but it was shittier still to keep hiding it from her. It would be worse the longer he took to 'share his burden'.

"What are you contemplating over there?"

"Your navel."

"What?"

"Seriously," he laughed. "There's a drawing here similar to your piece at the hospital and the one you gave me, and I can clearly see the navel, which I'll assume is yours."

She wandered over to where he stood and inspected the picture.

"Hmm, very convenient. I'm ready to go, how about you?"

Samson helped her pack up and then they walked to the main road under the burgeoning sun to find something for lunch. They found noodles in a box and Samson could eat fairly well with the chopsticks while walking and not spill much onto Clementine as he went, so they kept walking. Julene marveled at his multitasking and he scoffed at her surprise. Clementine was still sleeping soundly when they made it into town and Julene decided she'd like to browse through the mall. "The mall with the balls," she joked. Samson trailed her at a lesser pace and eyed a few things in the window of the sports store, whereas Julene came back in half an hour with bags in each hand.

"Whatever did you find in such a short time?"

"I got a bunch of great things! I won't have time to find things for myself since you're back at work full time from tomorrow, and theoretically I am too. Plus Mum and Dad are flying out tomorrow. Anyway, I'm an independent woman, why am I explaining this to you?"

"Because I'll probably have to carry it when Clementine wakes up and realizes my deficiency. And because I have to wonder if you don't have half of that stuff at home already."

"Variety is the spice of life, my love."

He kissed her nose and she patted his ass to get him walking again.

"Are you done or shall we head home now?"

"No, we can go. Hey, wait. Is that—"

Samson had walked a few steps ahead of her and didn't stop except to speak over his shoulder. "Come on, woman, catch up."

He had actually received another message from Linda, which he quickly deleted. Julene skipped a little to meet his steps.

"I thought that was, someone."

"Who?" He did his best at nonchalance.

"Um, no one, I guess."

"Okay, good. Because those noodles barely touched the sides. What are we doing for dinner?"

# THIRTY-SEVEN

Julene thought she had seen Linda and it was an ugly feeling. But looking back again, she didn't see the same person. She just hoped it wasn't her, because that woman had been holding a little baby, much the same as Clementine. She entertained unhappy thoughts for part of the walk but dismissed them once through the door because Clementine needed to be changed and the heating needed to be turned up.

"I'll have to check a fuse or something. This keeps happening."

Julene went straight to the meat-from-the-butcher at the bottom of the fridge and cut up what vegetables there were left and threw it all in a pan.

"At this rate, we're just about shopping every single day. At least I'm seeing dividends from all of the protein." She sighed in mock exasperation.

Julene walked over to him and took his phone out of his hands, dropping it on the couch, and slowly pulling his shirt out of his waistband.

"Moose insinuated I'm wasting away the other day."

Julene put her hands on his skin and moved them around to caress the various muscle groups.

"But he hasn't seen you with your shirt off recently, has he?"

He laughed and shook his head. He leant down and cupped her face in his hands.

"Only you." He kissed her deeply, before breaking away and going to stir the smoking pan. "What are *you* eating, by the way?"

"Ha, ha. I need you to save some for me, too."

He nodded in mock resignation and then set an enormous pot of pasta on the stove.

"Husband, let me ask you something."

He walked over to her and pulled her shirt out of her waistband, nodding.

"Yes. The answer for you is always, yes." More kissing.

"Seriously. Um, do you think we should have another baby?"

Samson backed away and tried to calm himself through a coughing fit.

"What?" Samson stood up straight and ran his hands through his hair, looking at the ceiling. "Seriously? Where has this come from?"

Julene raised her eyebrows and her shoulders. Samson went back to keep an eye on the pan, stirring to buy himself some time while Julene spoke.

"Even though it was completely unplanned and happened at a rough time for us and threw a spanner into the works of our lives, it was such an amazing thing for me to experience, much less *feel*. If we were to do it again, purposefully, it would be an amazing experience for both of us, from the beginning."

Samson was stirring disjointedly.

"I love the idea, but I'm not ready for that just yet."

Julene nodded.

"Julene, this has been a wonderful thing for us. But as you said, completely unplanned, a shitty time from the beginning, in terms of other things that were going on, and it really hasn't been that long since we sorted out you and me." He came and put his arms around her. "Let's see how selling this place shakes out before we go adding even more rooms to the needs of the new house. Okay?"

"Okay. Yeah, you're right. I know you're right. I think I'm a bit hormonal and I was thinking about it all again today at the studio, that's all."

She grabbed some plates off the shelf and they ate quietly while Clementine contemplated the toys hanging above her on the blanket.

The new week was a happy return to their routine after Julene and Clementine bid her parents farewell at their hotel apartment. They'd taken a last-minute trip over the past few days, so they had a few things to catch her up on. After their emotional leave-taking, Julene walked to her studio and got straight to work.

She painted and nursed and sketched and cleaned and painted and nursed and drank tea and had snacks and went for lunches every day. It was heavenly. They went home in the afternoons, usually before the work hour rush if she remembered to finish up in time; other times they stood or sat on the bus with people heading home after a day of work, everyone's eyes glazed or out the window. Clementine loved it.

Samson ended up working on Saturday, so Julene headed back over to the gallery but gave up after an hour or so when Clementine could not settle. Julene wondered if it was from something she'd eaten at dinner last night. She walked around, buying a snack from here and a drink from there as she walked toward the city. It was an uncommonly lovely day and she was looking forward to getting home. Perhaps they would sit out in the backyard for a while. But the grassy area was small and the fence was not so pretty, which made her think of the real estate agent. She looked for the number on her fandangled phone and dialed it.

"Hi, this is Julene Somersby—er, Samson. You've been speaking to my husband, David Samson about looking for a house? Yes, that's right. I wondered if you could send the listings through to me, I have some spare time today and I'd love to see them again . . . Oh, of course. No, that's fine. I'll have another look at home for the old listing first. Thanks, good-bye."

Samson had apparently not spoken to the agent since the wedding or thereabouts. *How interesting*, she thought.

"Then what's he been doing, little love?"

Julene made it through the city after buying a smoothie from one of the street vendors, but instead of going straight home—"boring"—she dawdled along the busy main road. She browsed in a few of the shops and bought a few magazines before turning for home. She crossed the road and was about to turn the corner when she saw Samson's blue truck drive past her.

Julene raised her hand in a wave but he didn't see her; he kept driving and pulled up to where she'd been standing not a few minutes ago, at a café just down the road. She started walking, intending to meet him and then stopped. It *was* Linda with a baby, and she'd come around a corner of the café and sat at one of the black metal tables. She and the baby wore matching beanies. Samson got out of his truck and walked over to the same table. He sat down and they talked, like regular people.

Julene was shocked, robbed of her breath. Samson was a nice guy but he wasn't the nicest when someone purposely hurt him, she could attest to that. Linda had hurt him—hurt them both— badly, but here he was talking to her like he would to any one of his friends. And there was the baby, who she could see had a head of dark hair *just like Clementine* when Linda gently pulled off their respective beanies.

Julene's feet unstuck themselves but she didn't know what to do with them. Should she walk over there and casually say, "Hi, what the fuck is going on here?" Should she run over there; should she stay hidden where she was and watch; should she stay hidden but get closer; should she go home and pack her things? Had this been going on ever since? Or just since before the wedding, when Samson started acting anxious and distracted? That felt right. It felt awful. Julene backed away and turned for the house.

Clementine woke and Julene settled her to nurse in the wrap as she walked. She walked up to the gate but didn't go in. She couldn't bear to go inside the house they'd been sharing when he'd apparently been carrying on with Linda somehow. Instead, she kept walking and eventually got a bit lost in an unfamiliar neighborhood. Checking her watch, it hadn't been long but she was definitely out of her comfort zone.

Julene was in an unfamiliar street but she could hear the main road not far away, she couldn't be too far from somewhere familiar. Julene assumed Samson and Linda would still be at the café. They'd looked like regular people and regular people who don't hate each other tend to sit and visit for a while—perhaps an hour—when frequenting a café, she reckoned to herself. Julene wondered what they were talking about.

Actually, Julene wondered how Samson had left that little detail out of every single conversation they'd had for the past month or so. What in the actual fuck? *Of course,* Julene reasoned, *if he had casually mentioned he was friends with Linda from Sean's party and that she'd been pregnant with his child, I'd have run a fucking mile, so I guess I can see why he didn't bring it up.* But not bring it up at all? Julene's heart hurt.

She really needed to pee and she had a feeling Clementine was about to exceed the limitations of her undergarments so she turned back for the house, hating herself for being so stupid. She couldn't quite bring herself to think of it as 'home' in her state of mind but it was her only refuge and they both had needs to take care of. It didn't take long to find the main road again, though she was much further south than she had realized. Julene quickened her steps until she saw the beginning of the small commercial strip where the awful tete-a-tete may still have been going on a short distance further. She crossed the road, cooing to Clementine all the while, or perhaps to herself, as well, and made it back to the house in good time.

She stared idly while Clementine cooed and gurgled at some striped hanging toys. She was ready for her nap after that and Julene wasn't sure if she herself was going to cry herself to sleep or wait by the front door and punch Samson's lights out when he walked in. She decided on a drink instead. Julene poured herself a big gulp from one of Samson's bottles and threw it back quickly. She felt the burn and cringed, but she felt a little more relaxed after that and ready for a confrontation. There wasn't long to wait.

"Hey there, lover. I got some of these for you around the corner." He dropped a bag of pastries on the side table and sat on the opposite couch.

Julene felt like her head was about to explode. Should she answer him in kind or cut straight to the heart of the matter? Should she play along with this happy family routine or ask him directly what in the hell he was playing at? She was hungry, though, and picked up the bag. It smelled so good. She slowly opened the bag and looked inside, deciding on a 'less is more' scenario whereby Samson might bring things up naturally himself, and whereby she wouldn't overreact again and ruin everything. Samson reached into the bag and pulled out a croissant for himself. Julene pulled out one filled with cheese. She picked it apart and ate the pieces from her fingers as he asked about the studio session.

"We did okay."

"Yeah, it was a good day for me, too. Everyone showed up, for once, and I think the job might finish ahead of schedule. It'll be a miracle."

He laughed to himself and went to peek in at Clementine. He tiptoed back into the lounge room and sat on the other couch again, arranged his long legs abstractly over the brown leather.

"Do you want to come over here?" He wiggled his eyebrows at her, a goofy grin to match.

"You know, we must have just missed you because we were over at the shops as well, not long before you got here."

"Oh?" He put his legs down and sat up, slowly.

"We could have met for coffee."

"Oh. Well, let me make some now." He walked over and poured out some beans, got out the stovetop machine and boiled some water. "Uh, how do you want it?"

"Espresso."

Julene stood and brushed off a few crumbs before turning to look at him standing over there. Samson ground the beans, loud in the miserable silence.

"I saw the truck and I waved to you, but I guess you had other things on your mind."

"Julene—"

"Like Linda and her baby!"

"Julene, let me explain."

"I saw you get out and walk over to her table and sit down like you were old friends, like you had so much in common, like you could talk for hours."

Samson's face was red. His eyes refused to meet hers until she came to stand near him in the kitchen, nothing between them.

"I didn't know how to tell you!"

"I'm sorry I'm so hard to talk to. I'm sorry you couldn't talk to me but you could just as easily sit down and talk to her! I'm sorry you couldn't tell me that you had become besties with the woman who sort of ruined our lives and who has, apparently, had one of your babies as well. How long have you been seeing her?"

"I'm not seeing her."

"You saw her today."

"Yes, but—"

"And you must have seen her a few other times to be on such friendly terms as not to *scratch that bitch's eyes out!*"

"Julene, calm down."

"Fuck you! Don't tell me to calm down. I think I have a right to be annoyed you didn't tell me you were seeing her. Are you playing happy families with her as well?"

"How could I even do that? When do I have the time to do that? Be reasonable, would you?"

"Reasonable, you say. Fuck off. Maybe those times you said you were going to meet with the rest estate agent, you were really hanging out with your *other family*. I can think of at least two times when you said you were going to meet him. But guess what? I couldn't get a straight answer out of the guy about when he saw you last. What else have you been bullshitting me about?"

"Hey!" Samson made gestured toward the bedroom. "I'm sorry." He was all but whispering. "I said I was going to look at houses, *that's all*, and I did look at houses, just not with the agent. Admittedly, I didn't see as many as you might have thought, but that wasn't because I was running out on you."

"Are you sure? How can I believe you now? Is everything a lie?" Julene backed out of the kitchen and moved to stand in front of one of the couches where the open space could accommodate her angry arms.

"Look, will you please just let me explain!"

"You know, at this point I don't know if it would make much difference."

"Julene, come one. Look, I saw her one day when I was out—"

"Why didn't you tell me?" Her hands implored him. "Why didn't you tell me when it happened? I think that sort of thing is newsworthy, don't you?"

"I wasn't sure it was her. So I followed her to try and see."

"And it was."

Samson nodded.

"And then she saw *me* a few days later, and she tried to spin me this bullshit story."

"Why didn't you tell *me* the bullshit story? This affects me, too, doesn't it? And Clementine? Are we going to start finding out now about a bunch of other bastard children that are her siblings?"

Samson could only look at her with sad eyes, his hands hanging down by his sides.

"Is that the reason you aren't ready for another baby, because you don't know how many others of yours are out there now?"

She was yelling, and the idea of other kids was a bad one to bring up. Julene didn't want to cry; she wanted to stay angry and in control but it was too much. She sat on a couch and the tears came. She wiped them off angrily.

"It's not like that at all," he said quietly.

Julene looked up at him. She stood up. She put her hand on the back of the couch; it would not do to pass out from getting up too quickly in the middle of an argument.

"I don't believe that. You can't know that."

"I need you to believe me. I need you to try and understand."

"Understand what? That you've got another kid and you didn't tell me? That you've been having play dates behind our backs and you expect me to just *calm down* because you don't like the confrontation? What is it exactly that I'm meant to understand?"

Samson moved back to the kitchen and took the coffee off the stove. He sat down on one of the dining chairs and leaned over, his head in his hands. Julene took over the process of coffee, her movements wound up and angry. She wanted to smash it on the floor then grab her bag and walk out the door, but she had to rein in her feelings because of Clementine. She had to keep her perspective as a parent and, supposedly, as part of a family. She had to stop overreacting, try to be objective and all that, but it was hard, so hard. She stood against the wall and crossed her arms, looking at the ceiling. Samson took a deep breath and stood up, walking around slowly.

"Julene, I need you to understand how hard this is for me. I was horrified when I saw her, absolutely appalled by the idea she might've had my child. But if that's the truth, then I need to find out. And if it's not the truth, I need to find that out as well."

Julene backed away from him as he walked to the stove. He poured himself a large cup of coffee, absently stirring.

"I don't think he's mine, but I have to find out. I know a way I can and I'm working on it."

"I wish you'd told me."

"I know. I wish I had, too, but it was never the right time. There was always a breathtaking moment that would have been ruined. And then, honestly, I'd forget about it because I have an awesome wife and a new awesome life and I wouldn't remember until later."

"And when I asked you what was wrong? Multiple times, I asked. I said I wanted to help with whatever was on your mind. What then?"

Samson sighed.

"I wanted to take care of it without you even knowing about it, to avoid all of this. I didn't want you to worry. I thought I could expose her lie and be done and you'd never have to worry about this bullshit."

"Well, I appreciate you didn't want me to worry, but that *is* bullshit!"

"What?"

"You said manacle! You said you were all in. Withholding things like this is not *all in*. *That* is bullshit."

"Maybe it is, but if it comes to the worst, then at least I would know. She came to me. I didn't have to stumble across her and beg her to tell me."

Julene could say nothing to that.

"If the worst is realized, then sure, it's the worst for you, and certainly not ideal for me, having her in my life, in our life. But a child is a child and deserves what I can give him. I think you should be able to see that."

"Please don't make me the bad guy here. I'm not saying you

should turn the kid out in the cold; the point here is you didn't tell me and kept it a secret, like it was an affair. It feels that bad to me."

Samson sat slowly into one of the chairs at the dining table, wrecked.

"I don't know what to say to you, Julene. It's another shitty situation, but it is what it is."

Clementine was awake and unhappy about it. Julene wondered how long she'd been crying, they'd been arguing for a while. She went into the bedroom and closed the door.

# THIRTY-EIGHT

Samson was exhausted; the coffee hadn't helped at all and he'd drank a lot of it. Normally, he'd be spinning around right about now, if he wasn't punishing himself physically at a client's house, after drinking that much, but the argument with Julene had drained him almost completely. He grabbed his keys and closed the door behind him.

He needed to give Julene some time; he knew that. But he needed time as well. She was too quick to jump to the worst conclusion and she'd hurt him, too. She'd kept the pregnancy to herself for six or seven months. She'd purposely excluded him and when he dwelt on it, it hurt, damn it. It was all very well for her to blame him but she'd done the wrong thing, too.

Samson drove aimlessly, getting on and off the highway as his thoughts distracted him. He found himself driving out in the suburbs and the sign for a baby store caught his eye. He pulled into the carpark and sat there for a few minutes, trying to clear his head.

He didn't want to play the blame game; they would both lose. She was right to be hurt he hadn't told her, but what a shit it was that she had seen them because Samson felt he was close to exposing Linda's lie. He still thought it was a lie. Sure, little Sam looked a bit like him but only because of the dark hair; he was still too small to have his own discernible features. The timing was bad, though, no doubt about it.

Walking into the pastel-colored big box store, he was greeted by staff at every turn. He wandered aimlessly before coming to the pacifiers and bibs. Clementine was always going through burp cloths and bibs faster than they could run the laundry so he grabbed a few packs in varying patterns. Suddenly, he had a thought and took a closer look at the display of pacifiers. He picked up one after the other, turning them over and peering inside the plastic covering, looking at the shapes and angles and sizes of them all. There were age recommendations on the packaging, as well. He found a couple he thought he could use and grabbed a handful of them, bumping into a saleswoman as he turned around.

"Hi there. Do you want an extra hand?" She produced a basket and smiled up at him, her purple apron glaring under the fluorescents. "It's so nice for the fathers to take an active interest. That didn't used to happen not so long ago, you know."

"Yeah. Thanks."

Samson grabbed a few of the pacifier clips, as well, and dropped them into the basket.

"Do you need anything for your change bag?"

"My? I don't have one of those."

"Oh. Let's take a look over here. There are different styles, some dads like a backpack whereas others prefer the messenger. You look like you might be a messenger dad, if you ask me."

She displayed a few of the bags to show how they either folded open to become a change mat or had one inside to remove. Samson decided on the latter and chose a plain fabric, and was told he might pass for a smart-looking Indiana Jones. She sealed the deal with that.

Back in the truck, back in traffic, Samson's mind was as busy as ever and not in the happiest frame. He pulled over when he saw a bar. He'd been there once or twice; there was good beer, sports on

TV, attentive bar keeps. He had, actually, picked up a few times there before he started seeing Victoria, but he tried to forget about that.

Samson waved for service when he sat down and ordered a pint. After the third one he ordered a whiskey, another beer, and then some food. Bar food was fine with him; he didn't need a gourmet meal.

"No, but it helps, I think."

Moose was sitting beside him.

"When did you get here?"

Moose raised his eyebrows.

"You called me. You've drunk too much and I have to wonder if it's really that bad."

"No, yes. Everything was so good until now."

"Do you want to tell me about it or just go?"

"I think I should go. That waitress is starting to look familiar."

"Man, you're the worst."

Moose signaled for the tab and they double-checked the truck was locked before getting into Moose's tiny Mazda and driving away.

"Hey, sorry about this. And thanks."

"If and when I have massive benders, you shall be my first port of call."

"Yes, please do. Then I'll know exactly how stupid and pitiful I am when loaded and sad." He fell asleep in the car.

Samson woke up in the dishwater dawn; his neck feeling like it was made of broken glass. He turned it, expecting to hear it crack. The light was on inside the house so he gingerly stepped out of the car and went inside.

"Dude. You left me in the car?"

"You sir, would not wake up for love or money, and I all but yelled in your face after giving you a good shake a few times. I certainly wasn't going to carry you in if you were too drunk to put out."

Samson headed for the shower and found headache pills in the cabinet while the water warmed up.

"Do you want some clean clothes?" Moose asked afterward.

"No, these are okay. I'm gonna go, I'll check in with you later. Thanks again."

"Take care of yourself. Oh, and no more drinks, I've got a real date tonight, okay?"

Samson walked back to the bar. It wasn't far and the fresh air did him good. He drove into the city and checked into an inexpensive hotel.

"Why are you doing that?" Julene asked him over the phone.

"Because we both need space, right now. It's just easier for me to do this, so I can take care of some things."

It was a sober farewell on the phone. Samson had a proper shower and an early night after a day of deplorable TV. He slept amazingly well but woke up missing the fatigue he felt from hearing Clementine in the background of the night. He redressed in his clothes from the other day again, and then replied to a message Linda had sent him while he and Julene had been arguing. He would meet her for a late lunch. She suggested he come over to her house but he quickly declined. He had to remember she was a sly bitch and who knew what she'd have planned if she had him at that kind of disadvantage.

"So, how have you been?" Linda flicked her blonde hair as she spoke.

She hadn't given him a minute to sit down before she opened her mouth. Samson had only glanced around the small sitting area with its pale and plastic decor briefly when he checked in yesterday. He glanced around for witnesses now.

"Are you staying here?" She looked amused at the thought and fiddled with the tips of her wispy hair.

"No, I met a friend here for a work meeting the other day and I thought it was nice enough."

"Have you thought anymore about my deal?"

Samson's eyebrows shot up and he let out a short laugh.

"Sure, of course I have. Your deal sucks. It's blackmail. I'm still pretty sure Sam isn't mine and you're depriving the kid of the opportunity for a proper life, but that seems to be neither here nor there. I've got a meeting with my accountant tomorrow, so I'd appreciate you not sending anymore messages, okay?"

"Worried Julene might find out?"

Samson took a deep breath. "Actually, she knows."

"Well, I hate to burst your bubble but I didn't tell her, so don't let that sway your opinion on taking care of your son."

Samson rolled his eyes at her continued insistence. It was needlessly melodramatic.

"I told her myself." That wasn't exactly true but he didn't have to tell her that.

"What the fuck for?"

"Because you kept sending me messages, kept turning up everywhere. She was bound to find out at some point if I didn't tell her first. And another reason—I told her so you wouldn't be able to."

Linda feigned indifference.

"So what's in the bag?"

Samson's eyes flicked to the spotted bag next to his feet. He sighed and picked it up.

"I was buying a few things for *my* child and I thought I might as well get a few things for Sam while I was there. We go through everything about five times a day; I assumed he'd be the same."

"How thoughtful."

Samson could only scowl. There were some cloths and blankets and a beanie inside; he pulled out the pacifiers in the plastic cases to show her.

"There are so many brands with different shapes and they all say different things about the same thing. Does Sam even use these?"

"Sure, sometimes. They usually fall on the floor, so," she shrugged, "not helpful. Actually, I think I have a one like that somewhere at home, who knows."

Samson avoided looking at Linda as he rummaged amongst the little packages. Sam started making some fussy noises and Samson held up one of the pacifiers. Linda shrugged again, so Samson popped one out of the plastic and leaned closer, holding it out. The baby latched onto it straight away. Samson dropped the bag next to her chair and leaned away.

Linda pulled a container of something—puppy dog's tails?—out of her bag. She took off the lid and started to eat with a fork she pulled from the bag as well. Samson tried not to notice how she ate like everyone else, with silverware rather than with a forked tail. He got up and poured himself a glass of water from the pitcher on the white sideboard and carried it and a couple of paper napkins. He watched the baby boy when he sat down at the white plastic table. He was a cutie, but Samson was still sure he wasn't his child. What was he basing this on? Surely it was a gut feeling rather than just an aversion to being tied to this horrid woman for the rest of his life. Sam popped the pacifier out of his mouth and it predictably fell on the floor.

"See?" Linda sighed and put her fork down.

"I'll get it." Samson held up his hand to her and leaned over the arm of his chair to scoop up the lost sucker. "Let's try this one instead." Samson snagged a different version from the plastic bag he'd just abandoned, one that opened from a cover. He showed Linda how it would snap closed if dropped, and he clipped it onto the edge of Sam's blanket with a clip ribbon. "There now, that should do it."

"Are you sure you don't want to come home and take care of us a little bit more often? You know, I think he settles a bit more easily when we've been out with you."

Linda's eyebrows played with him and she smirked as she watched him squirm in the plastic chair.

"I've heard deep voices can help settle babies. But as for your question, the answer's a definite no. You screwed me up big time last year, I'm not interested in making that a permanent arrangement."

"David, I'm trying to be nice to you." She grinned at him. He couldn't help but grin back. The very idea of her being nice was laughable.

"No you're not. You're just rubbing it in."

He shook his head and finished the last of the water. He sat back in the chair and watched her push her food around before putting the container on the table beside her and smiling at him.

"Then I guess we're done here. Thanks for that stuff for Sam."

Samson sighed and looked away.

"I'll hear from you tomorrow then?"

He nodded and watched her stand up and grab her bags before sauntering outside. She paused and looked back at him once before walking away. He sat still, waiting in case she came back for whatever reason. He closed his eyes and then lifted the paper napkin from his lap and dropped it on the table. There was the pacifier Sam had spat out, back in the packaging. He picked it up carefully, carrying it upstairs to his room and hunting for a plastic bag or something to hold it in. When it was safely stowed, he let his breath out in relief.

Samson allowed himself to collapse on the rumpled bed and a few tears squeezed out of his closed eyes. This was it; this was his chance to prove Linda was lying. But what if she wasn't? What if Sam *was* his child? He felt sorry for the baby boy having such a manipulative woman as his mother. He felt sorry for himself as well, with the prospect she could be permanently in his life, if the test didn't bring the results he was desperately looking for. But he was also sure Linda would have approached him far sooner if he really was Sam's father. She only wanted the money, after all. He covered his brow with his forearm and tried to clear his mind.

Samson felt himself falling asleep and sat up with a jerk. He grabbed the bag with the pacifier inside and walked quickly out of the room, down the stairs, and out the front door. He all but ran the four blocks under a grim sky to the laboratory he'd chosen from the list the policewoman had given to him. It was on one of the side streets in a commercial pocket off the main road, subtle, hidden even. Samson opened the nondescript glass door and made himself walk calmly up the stairs rather than take them two or three at a time. He didn't want to alarm the staff by busting in, tall, dark, and angry. He silenced his phone before walking to the reception desk and then gave the guy behind it a big smile.

"You look pretty happy with yourself."

"Yeah, I'm just happy to make it here before the rain starts."

"I thought it looked pretty dark out there. What can we help you with today, sir?"

Samson leaned in slightly, discreetly.

"I'd like to initiate a paternity test."

The receptionist nodded. He pulled out some forms from a stack of trays on the desk and stood up, indicating for Samson to follow. He opened a door into a small room outfitted with a white desk and two lime-colored chairs.

"Take this paperwork and fill out as much as you can. There's a restroom just around that corner, and a water station on the opposite wall. I'll speak to one of the consultants and someone will be with you in a few minutes. My name's Laurence; let me know if you need anything else."

Samson thanked him and then sat. He took a deep breath and flipped through the pages. The questionnaire was thorough but not impossible. He grabbed a pen from the cup at the edge of the table and started writing answers as though his life depended on it. He only paused when a consultant knocked and entered the small room.

"Hi, Mr Samson, I'm Carly." Samson stood to shake her hand.

"I'm just about done with this."

"That's fine. Do you have a sample to accompany your paperwork, or are you bringing one in at a later time?"

"Oh no, I have this now. I hope it'll be adequate."

He pulled the packaged pacifier out of the bag and placed it on the table.

"Pacifiers are sometimes enough, although they aren't as good as proper cheek swabs. Do you have any questions before this is processed?"

Samson shook his head shortly.

"Okay then, that's all we need. You can pick up the results in a week, or we can mail them to you."

Samson was aghast.

"A week? That's a lot longer than I was anticipating. Are there no options for expediting the processing time?"

"Yes, there are, though the costs are quite high. Let me take this back to the lab now and you can go through the options at the front desk."

Samson was relieved and he sat down heavily after shaking hands with the consultant. He took another moment with his head in his hands, eyes closed. He ran his hands roughly through his hair and then walked back to the front desk. Laurence was talking to someone else so Samson sat and checked through messages on his phone. There was plenty of work lining up for tomorrow, which was a good thing. He could use a day of heavy labor to take his mind off all of this.

"Hi, Laurence. Carly said there are other processing options you could help me with."

"Of course. The standard processing time is one week. Then there are four-day, two-day, and one-day options and then there's also a three-hour processing option."

Samson felt his heart jump into his throat.

"Of course, they're all progressively more expensive."

Laurence handed Samson a card that listed all of the prices. His eyebrows nearly skipped off his head when he read through them and his mouth went dry. Even though the cost was prohibitive, the three-hour option was tempting. He swallowed.

"Two days. I'll take the two-day option."

Samson felt like he'd been punched in the gut as he handed his credit card across the desk, but he felt reassured when he walked down the stairs and outside. It had started raining but he almost felt like singing. He was so close to ending this ordeal and he was optimistic. But as he walked a pessimistic voice sang in his mind; it sounded suspiciously like Linda. He hung his head and headed back to the hotel, his mood fading. He thought of home.

After sitting on the end of the bed thinking through various scenarios, he decided he'd go home and talk to Julene rather than making a phone call. At least he could respond to her gestures as well as her voice, and hopefully she would respond to his. He was also aching to hold Clementine; he checked out and drove home immediately.

The house was quiet when he arrived. Perhaps they were sleeping, if they were there at all. He placed his bag in the corner by the coat closet and carefully put the keys down in the dish. Julene's keys were in the dish as well, so he straightened and walked down the hall.

They were asleep on the couch; Clementine snuggled in the crook of her mother's arm, a blanket loosely wrapped around both of them. Leaning close, he gently stroked Clementine's hair. She opened her eyes and might have smiled at him before turning her head to nurse herself to sleep again. The sensation opened Julene's eyes and she woke properly when she saw him. She held her hand out to him and he grasped it with both of his. He was standing behind the couch and he knelt down so he could rest his face on her hand, and look at them both. His knees started to ache after a while but he thought he could die a happy man in that position, now that he was home. Clementine woke up properly after a while; Samson changed her while Julene went to the bathroom then he made tea while she nursed at the table.

Neither of them knew what to say or how to say it; they said nothing as they drank the tea and ate from the cheese platter Samson put out. He held out his hands for the baby when she was done nursing and then Julene had a shower. They still hadn't properly spoken.

He stroked Clementine's dark hair and her soft cheeks. She did have that in common with baby Sam, and her blue eyes, but so did many other babies. He was eaten up with affection for this child in his arms and he was sorry Sam couldn't have that from a father, as well. If he was his child, things would undoubtedly be different, difficult. He'd feel a mixture of affection and pity for the boy, rather than sheer love and adoration from the start, as Clementine had been able to demand.

Julene leaned her arm on his shoulder as she toweled her hair with the other, looking at the both of them. She sat down cross-legged on the dining chair and ate a few more crackers, sipped the last of the tea and then washed the dishes when she was done; she obviously wanted to delay conversation as much as he did.

When Clementine was ready for a nap, Samson danced her into the bedroom and readied her for sleep, cuddling her until the last moment before laying her in her little bed. He almost couldn't make himself leave without looking back at her but he knew the consequences if he kept playing the 'are you still awake?' game. He closed the heavy white door gently behind him and came to face Julene in the kitchen.

"How are you?"

Samson answered honestly but when Julene asked if he'd been alone, he didn't. It was so close to being done, he didn't want to talk about it and then fight about it all over again.

"Why did you go?"

"I left because I wanted to give you some peace. I don't want to fight about this, even though it's completely fight-worthy. I came back because I love you and I wanted to see you and hold you both and tell you that I missed you, and then not do anymore talking."

Julene's eyes widened, in disbelief he assumed, and then she laughed and walked to him. He wrapped his arms around her and kissed the top of her head.

"What have you been doing with yourselves?"

"Watching movies and eating ice cream, and that's about it." Julene's breath was warm against his chest.

"And how's that working out for you?"

He stroked her hair away from her temple, and she sighed.

"I think Clementine was upset about the ice cream, she didn't have a great sleep last night, but maybe it was because you weren't here."

Samson nodded and then stroked the hair at the nape of her neck, slowly. He remembered what he'd said to Linda about deep voices helping to settle babies.

"I missed her."

"Are you staying?"

"I'm staying." He stepped back from her and tilted her face up to his. "I'm not leaving you again."

He moved slowly, his eyes on her eyes, until her eyes closed and their mouths met. He kissed her slowly, his hands in her thick, dark hair, long over her shoulders and still damp from the shower. Julene put her hands on his waist, her fingers holding him tightly, and then pushing him away.

"Tell me the truth." Her furrowed brows and guarded eyes were suspicious.

"I have. I love you and only you. I can show you how much if you'll let me." He chuckled into her neck. "There's no one else, and all the rest is a very unhappy coincidence and that's all."

Julene looked at him unsurely. Samson kissed her again, less patiently, while she turned her face away from him.

"I want to believe you. I want to understand, but it's hard."

Samson said something else into her neck and they both chuckled, and then they were both kissing with fervor.

Samson wanted her so badly, it was as though he'd been away for a month rather than merely two nights. But he didn't want to rush Julene into anything, in case she really did have doubts about him or really did hate him for concealing what had been going on. He could only think about how beautiful she'd looked on the couch when he had come home, sleeping with their child in her arms. He grasped her waist, working her shirt out of her waistband until his fingers found her soft skin. His hand proceeded to the small of her back and stayed there, by sheer force of will. He longed to press her to his body, to tear off her clothes with his teeth and then—

"What are you doing?" Julene was breathless, but her question was a sharp one.

"Uh, I don't know. I was lost in an extremely deep and suggestive fantasy just now. What was the question?"

"I said what are you doing? You had my bra strap in your teeth."

Samson looked at Julene properly, her hair disheveled, her shirt open and wrinkled.

"I was fantasizing about ripping off your clothes with my teeth." He kissed her throat.

"Oh, is that all. And then what happened?"

"Well, I was rudely interrupted and I don't know what was about to happen. But I can improvise."

He gently pushed off the blouse and gripped her jean-clad ass. He knelt down and kissed her stomach then her sides as he fiddled with the clips on her bra, and finally her naked breasts.

"You know, you improvise quite well."

"But only with the right props."

They laughed and the rest was less improvisation than premeditation.

# THIRTY-NINE

Julene was stiff in the morning when she woke. They were in bed now but had woken in the middle of the night, still on the floor in a heap after a thorough love fest. Her friends had been right about the make-up sex. She loved him so much but her mind was still troubled, even if her heart had quieted down. Fucking Linda, that was the problem, in both regards. Julene could hear Samson rattling around in the kitchen now and she snuck out of bed to speak to him before he set off on his run or to drive to work; she wasn't sure how early it was.

"Good morning, wife." He smiled at her as he poured his coffee and she sat down at the table, pushing her hand through her unkempt hair.

"Good morning, husband." She watched him as he threw some food into the large container he used for his lunch box.

"How did you sleep, wife?"

"Better after midnight, than before, husband. And you?"

"I slept better in my own bed than I did the two nights previous." He snapped the container closed and tightened the lid on the thermos.

"What time is it?" Julene peered at the small clock on the oven.

"Too early for you to worry about it."

He set everything down on the table and kissed her cheek as he grabbed a water bottle from the cupboard behind her. She grabbed his arm as he walked past. Their eyes met and Julene stood up to meet his gaze. Samson left the bottle on the table as well, and then his hands grasped her shoulders.

"Only you," he whispered then he was kissing her, softly, chaste but long.

She wrapped her arms around his neck. He was so tall, she was sure they were both getting calcium deposits on their spines from always bending or inclining their necks. Her foot found the chair behind her and she stood on the center spindle, giving her a full six inches of extra height. Samson peeled his shoulders back and Julene heard them crack a little. He looked at her in surprise.

"Love, this is a whole new world."

His hands could reach her bottom without him seemingly reaching for his knees, and it was funny how different it was to kiss at an even keel, rather than an angle.

"I'll have to get you a stepladder for your birthday."

"I could bring the one back from the gallery."

The phone rang and reminded them that Samson really did have to go. She went back to bed for a restless sleep when he drove away in the truck, talking on his phone.

Later in the morning, Julene decided to avoid the rush-hour bus ride and lay Clementine down for a nap in bed again, rather than wrapping and jumping on the bus. She would get to the studio in good time and hopefully in a better mood. In the meantime, she pulled out some random pieces of paper she'd found on a shelf in the study and set to work with a few lead pencils. In short order, there was a clear sketch of Clementine and it was a wonderful resemblance. She colored it with some pastels and decided it would be a perfect gift to send to her parents, who had called yesterday with all the news of their new house and village, and the details on the new job and prospects for visiting. It hadn't been too far-fetched to say Samson was at the shops when they'd called, but she'd felt bad lying by omission. She forgot about all of that when Samson walked into the house again.

"What happened? You're not usually home this early, are you?"

"There was an accident at the house. Guy got injured, taken to hospital. He should be okay but the inspector had to be called. It's routine. Aren't you usually across town by now, as well?"

"Clementine got sleepy early, and I thought we'd go over there later." She showed him the sketch.

"That's beautiful. Is she still sleeping?"

Julene nodded, throwing her thumb over her shoulder in the direction of the bedroom.

"How about we go out for lunch when she wakes up?"

Julene looked at him, wiping the crayon off her fingers. She nodded and pulled another piece of paper off the pile.

"Wait, did you get that paper from the printer?"

Julene looked at him briefly, and then returned her eyes to the paper.

"There isn't much of that stuff left, and I need it for invoicing in a day or two. Isn't there any of the heavier paper left? The stuff you're supposed to be using?"

"I couldn't find it." She was nonchalant.

Samson went into the study and came out a moment later with a thick pile of sketching paper. He dropped it on the table and took the other pieces away.

"This is why we need a new place, so you have space to do your work, even if you're not at the studio, and the rest of my stuff doesn't get thrown from hell to breakfast."

"Hell to breakfast?" Julene sat up from the drawing. "All I did was look for some paper."

"Yes. I couldn't have had a better job of turning the place over if I delivered a search warrant on the study, myself."

Julene hmphed at him and showed him her handiwork.

"Hey, that's me! I look good."

"Yeah, you do. Come here."

Samson ignored her crayon-clammy fingertips on him and concentrated on her mouth and neck, and then the front of her shirt, and then the back of her. Julene stood up on the center spindle of the chair again and Samson smiled into her ear as he settled her against himself.

"Come here, yourself. This is a whole new world of tall. I feel like I'm cheating on you with an amazon."

"I'm not sure that's the best turn of phrase to initiate sexy-talk, in your current situation, husband."

"I love it when you say sexy-talk."

"Shut up."

She momentarily silenced him with her mouth but her hands made him make noises. The height was too much, in the end, and rather than risk toppling over and hurting themselves—or worse, waking Clementine—they moved slowly to the couch. Julene marveled as she looked at him, touched him, moved with him, and then she closed her eyes and thought no more.

"God I love you, woman."

He pawed her and kissed her while she all but lay in a heap on the floor. He wiped a few strands of sweaty hair from her forehead and stared into her eyes.

"You never cease to amaze me."

Julene closed her eyes and took some deep breaths.

"Specifically?"

"Okay. For one thing, you're beautiful *all the time*. When you're sleeping, or wake up in the morning with your make-up still on and it's all smudged, or even when you're tired and upset if Clementine's been awake for eternity. You're always so beautiful."

"Now you're just sucking up."

"Obviously. I also love that you love to make love, like *all the time*."

"Please do not tell me about other women and how often they fuck." Julene threw a cushion at him.

"That's a low blow."

"You wish. Now kiss me."

Samson was tired but he wasted no time in scooting over to her and canoodling with great attention to the details. Julene felt like she was in high school again, with so much kissing and a heart about to explode from it. Samson kissed her neck and she was able to regain fresh air; Samson kissed her breasts and she was able to regain momentum until she exploded from it. He kissed her all over until she swatted him away. But he caught her hands and pulled them around his neck, smiling down at her as he came closer, as he came inside. He looked into her eyes the whole time, consuming her with his eyes, longing for her even as he engulfed her. Julene could barely stand it any longer and opened her mouth to say so but Samson ate up her whimpers with his kisses until they shuddered themselves apart. Out of breath, Samson reached for her but she rolled away from him and covered herself with the blanket.

"Don't touch me." And she was asleep.

She was awoken by their soft and cuddly baby pulling on her hair with the accompanying soft googles and gurgles.

"Hi there, baby." Julene pulled herself up to sitting, leaning against the couch and settled the babe, the blanket around them both. "You had a long sleep, didn't you?" Julene looked up at Samson in the kitchen, cleaning and clattering pots and plates. "How long was I out?"

"A while, that's for sure. I had a shower and did some paperwork and then she still didn't wake up, and now it's just about dinner time. What do you think about some Thai? I might walk up now and order some. Do you want me to wait so you can come with me when you're done, or should I just go now?"

"Go now. I'm starving, and I'm sure you're ready to eat a horse."

He kissed them both before leaving. The wind caught the door and slammed it, drawing Clementine's ire. She could not be swayed from her meal for long, though. But then the doorbell rang and Julene looked at her watch. It hadn't been long since Samson left though it wouldn't have surprised her if he had ran to the restaurant.

The doorbell rang again. Julene started to get a heavy feeling in her belly but went to the door, anyway. The blanket around her and Clementine was tucked in place well enough. She called through the closed door.

"Who is it?"

"I'm looking for David."

"Who *is* it?"

"Oh, is that you, Julene? It's Linda. We're here to see your husband."

Julene slowly opened the door. She peered around it.

"What are you doing here?"

"Well, David said he'd call me this afternoon, but I didn't hear from him. So I thought I'd better follow up. In case he forgot."

Julene started to shiver with the door open; it was really cold out there. She looked at the child wrapped to Linda's body and invited them in. She felt detached as she stepped back from the door to make way for the literal other woman, never mind that she was basically wearing only a blanket. Linda nodded to her and closed the door.

Julene had gone over in her mind so many times all the things she might say to Linda but right now, she wanted to ignore her and have Clementine nurse in peace. She went back to the couch and kept her eyes on her daughter, pretending the other woman wasn't there. She played with Clementine's fingers so she wouldn't get scratched by her deadly baby nails.

"This is cozy."

Linda sat down on the armchair and unwrapped her child. He was only beginning to wake but took to the breast immediately. Julene couldn't believe she was sitting in what might be taken for companionable silence with this woman, breastfeeding their children together. Samson walked through the door just then, the smell of noodles and rain wafting in as he waltzed down the hall.

"Phew! It's cold out there."

He went straight to the counter and heaped a pile of fragrant food onto a plate before bringing it to the side table and noticing Linda for the first time.

"Woah! What are you doing here?"

He looked uncertainly at Julene; she shook her head slightly and looked away.

"Oh, don't be like that. I said I might pop over if I didn't hear from you, and so, here I am."

Samson hung his head. "Shit, I forgot."

He glanced at Julene's profile. Her brow was unhappy; she didn't look at him. He offered Linda some noodles but she declined.

"Sam doesn't seem to like wheat products."

"These are mostly rice, I think. I can't vouch for the sauce, though."

"That's nice of you, really. But I just came to see you since I *didn't hear from you* this afternoon."

Samson looked at her pointedly.

"You need to go, now."

"When Sam is ready, I'll be happy to go since I've *made my point.*"

Samson could only frown out the window and then back at the counter where the remaining food was waiting. His stomach growled. Samson ate the noodles straight from the box, avoiding eye-contact with both women in the room but dared not turn his back on either one. When he'd finished, he stood up and said it was time for Sam to be done.

"I didn't see a car outside, did you walk here?"

She had.

"Get your stuff, I'll drive you home."

He glanced again at Julene but she refused to meet his eyes. When he grabbed the keys, she picked up the plate and started eating the noodles while Clementine throttled some of her toys. She kept her head down when Linda said good-bye and left with her husband.

Julene had just finished pushing the last of her noodles around when Samson walked back in the door. She watched him. He stood at the end of the hall, waiting for her to say something. He slowly walked to the kitchen counter and put his keys down.

"I don't suppose there are any noodles left?"

Julene couldn't tell if he was serious or trying to break the ice.

"For fuck sake, you ate three quarters of the food. Next time, you might buy a serving for me that I'm actually allowed to eat." She stood up from the couch. "I'm gonna go."

They both looked down at the blanket.

"I'm gonna get some clothes on, and *then* I'm going out for a bit."

She handed him the blanket and walked to the bathroom. His eyes followed her, his eyebrows questioning. She slammed the door. A quick shower, some clothes, whatever was lying around so she could just *get out* of there. She grabbed her bag from the front table and closed the door quietly, in case Clementine was winding down. She had said nothing to either of them before she walked past; she knew if she talked, at least to Clementine, then she'd have to stay for the bedtime routine. Then she would have to speak to Samson, and she really didn't want to do that.

There was a pub not far away and she walked there in short order, hardly seeing the dim light and swaying branches along the way. The sight of the wooden sign over the red brick was a relief and Julene pushed through the heavy door into the warmth on the other side. Having just nursed, she was confident she could put away a drink and not worry about it. She ordered two but she kept quiet and only started crying once. She ordered a soda water after a while and then made a joke in her inner monologue about nursing it. She laughed to herself, and then Moose sat down beside her.

"Tell me what's happened since you're here by yourself, knocking back drink after drink and not talking to anyone?"

"Fucking Linda."

Moose's face paled in an instant. "What? He didn't! He wouldn't!"

"No! Do you really think he's that bad?"

"No, I just, your explanation didn't help."

"Right. Well, I mean, she is the problem. She came over tonight."

Moose looked sympathetic and pissed off at the same time. Julene gave him a few more details and then hung her head on his shoulder.

"How did this happen to us, Moose?"

He had no explanation, other than perhaps they had tempted fate for so long with their perfect happiness, that someone up there had smited them.

"Being smote sucks."

Just then, Samson plonked down at the small table.

"What are you doing here? Who's with Clementine?"

"I called one of your friends, the one who lives around the corner. She brought a bunch of textbooks with her so I've got some time up my sleeve, I think." He covered her hand with his. "I'm sorry."

"Dude, what the fuck was Linda doing at your house?"

Samson looked at his friend and then at Julene and ordered a beer.

"She wants money."

He drank half of the beer in a draught and burped for good measure.

"I love it when you talk sexy." Julene picked up her water.

"And I love bringing the sexy talk." His eyes were more Doberman than puppy dog.

Julene finished her soda water and looked away, but she was still listening.

"I went to the cops, like you suggested, and there wasn't much they could do. But the cop I talked to suggested a paternity test."

Julene turned to him.

"You didn't tell me that."

"Like I said, I wanted to take care of it without you having to worry about it."

Moose interjected. "Well that approach hasn't worked out so well, has it?"

Samson heaved a sigh and finished his drink. "Yeah, well. I'm picking the results up tomorrow."

"How did you get Linda to consent to the test?" Moose sucked on a rind of lime and waited.

"I didn't. I gave the little guy a pacifier and when he spat it out, I snagged it. She didn't object to me keeping it, or rather, not throwing it away. If the issue comes out about consent, my position would be that since she insists I'm the biological father, my consent should be enough."

"Right on, man."

They clinked their glasses and drank. Samson waved to the waiter and ordered some snacks, "For my lovely wife."

"It's a shame about the baby, though." Moose glanced at both of them and then around the room. Perhaps he was waiting for someone.

"Yeah, it's a shame." Samson snuck a glance at Julene, too.

Moose ordered another round and then the food came. They ate and drank in silence for a while before Moose wandered over to the jukebox and keyed up a few songs. He came back to the table looking pretty pleased with himself.

"Tell me you did not request 'Wuthering Heights' by Kate Bush, again."

Moose ignored Samson's withering gaze and beamed at them both.

"Dude, I love that song!"

Julene high-fived Moose and then launched into the chorus; Moose making it a duet. They were both shushed by Samson and then by Kate Bush herself. After it was over, Samson insisted on dragging Julene onto the dance floor and slow dancing her as though they were in high school to another awful song from Moose's playlist; Julene's hands were around Samson's neck, their hips moving but not their feet. She tried to stay mad at him but he was so damned good looking. She thought she could quite easily go to hell with him, hand in hand, on his path paved with good intentions.

The song ended but Samson didn't let her go. He stepped one of his large feet closer to her and held tight around her waist. She turned her face to his.

"How are you going to talk your way out of this one, husband?"

He was maybe an inch from her mouth; he could only smile and laugh at himself.

"You're a troublesome husband, indeed. I didn't think we'd have these kinds of problems quite so soon."

Another song had come on; Samson started moving with her again.

"What do you mean, *these kinds of problems*? We have an extraordinary life, we can't expect to have ordinary problems."

"I'd settle for no problems, frankly."

"Well, I'd settle for some kissing in the meantime."

She acquiesced. Moose joined them to dance with a lady friend of his own and they waved to him when they headed back to the table.

"We'd better go." Julene signaled for the bill.

When they were outside, jackets pulled against the cool night air, Samson clasped Julene's hand. He kissed it.

"We should do this again, sometime."

"What, fight over another woman and then go dancing?"

Samson stopped walking. He stepped off the side of the path as a few people walked past them and then stepped in front of her so she'd have to look at him.

"No. I mean, get a babysitter and go out once in a while. Clementine is sleeping pretty well at night and I know you have your routine at the gallery, but I think it'd be nice for us to go out once a month or something. Go somewhere, eat something, have an adventure."

Julene nodded and shrugged. "An adventure?"

"Well, for a few hours, at least."

Julene started walking again. "What kind of adventure? I don't want to try a new place in town and end up chewing disco biscuits with my goat cheese by mistake and wake up to someone harvesting my organs in the desert or anything."

Samson laughed at her.

"Julene! Ha, how we would even get to the desert?"

She laughed and shoved him.

"Well, what then, smart ass?"

"I mean like, an entrée here and dessert there, a whiskey somewhere else, maybe a paintball gun in someone's back yard or something afterward."

"You know, I think we'd do well to avoid people's backyards."

"Point taken." He was silent for a few minutes as they walked. "Wait! I've got it!"

"Do tell."

"Let me think this through."

They'd arrived back at the house but were waiting outside for Samson's inspiration to work itself out. He sat beside her on the brick fence, folding her fingers back and forth through his own. Then he stood and pulled her to her feet, kissing her hands before putting them around his neck.

"What about your inspiration?"

"Mmm, you know I think better on my feet." He kissed her slowly, caressing her shoulder with one hand, down her side to her ass.

"Are you . . . sure you don't . . . want to go inside?"

"I told you . . ."

"Is there an end to that sentence?" Julene wondered.

Samson's breath came out in a rush. "I'm thinking on my feet."

"Yeah well, mine are about to come out from under me."

"I'd like to come from under you. Maybe we should go inside."
But he stayed there, kissing her, holding her almost off the ground.

"I think you're about to lose your, uh, inspiration."

He laughed and picked her up and walked up the steps, just
about kicking the door in before she could unlock the damn thing.

"Hello?" A head peeked out from the end of the hall.

"Hi, Justine, it's just us. Hey, thanks for coming over."

"It was no problem. She hardly made a sound. I had a few peeks,
just in case. So adorable."

"Do you want to stay and have a drink?"

"Thanks but no. I've got heaps of work to do over the next few
days. And, um, you guys don't look like you need company right
now." Justine smiled and hefted her book bag.

Julene nudged Samson and he went out after her, offering to
help. Julene could hear the exchange.

"Are you kidding? I don't think the firepower is in your biceps
right now. I'll see you guys later."

"Did you hear that?" Samson closed the door gently behind
him, leaning against it. "I'm not sure what she was insinuating but,
it was . . ."

Julene stepped out into the hall, her clothes clearly in a pile
behind her. Samson took two long steps and scooped her up.

# FORTY

Samson was awake early. He was wide awake. He slipped out of the room and got dressed in the laundry from the clean clothes in the basket. He tip-toed down the hall and eased the front door closed behind him. He walked up and down the main road, hands in his pockets, and then into town. He walked past a handful of people here and there, readying their stores to open for the day ahead. He walked through town, past the garbage collectors, past the early-morning commuters. He walked across town to Julene's gallery. The cafés were starting to open for breakfast and he grabbed a muffin and coffee to go. He hopped a bus back to town and then kept wandering, this time through the commercial district. He found himself at the testing lab and supposed this had always been his destination, regardless of the hour. He sat on the steps and contemplated the traffic.

Eventually, he stood up and double-checked the hours of the lab and then worked himself up to a run on the way home. It was still early and his job wasn't set to start for a while; he headed to the oval for a few laps, falling into stride among the runners and walkers already there. He was approaching double digits when he spied Linda and Sam entering the park so he peeled off toward home. He wasn't quite ready to go home yet, though, so he kept to the side streets and then ran up to the intersection of the noisy main road into the hills. He remembered their drive up that road two months ago and wished for that untroubled feeling again, when his biggest concern had been the other woman he'd been sleeping with.

Traffic on the road was mostly trucks and they were loud. He turned the corner and ran down the hill, zigzagging into a few more side streets. There were one or two nice-looking houses for sale as he ran toward town, and Samson realized he couldn't hear the main road anymore. He searched around for the house numbers and a street sign and repeated them to himself as he ran, adding extra names as he went when he saw another house or two that looked nice. By the time he got home, he was later than he wanted to be because he'd stopped to grab a few sale flyers at some of the houses. He dumped a handful and then scrambled around in the loose notes and paperclips for a pen to write down the street names he had been chanting on the way back. There were quite a few to look up later, but he was hopeful something nice would turn up among them that had everything they wanted or could be easily converted.

"That's an oxymoron," he said to himself in the shower.

Julene was in the kitchen with Clementine when he got out and he smiled at one and kissed the other. He asked Julene what she was having for breakfast and got out the big pot for oatmeal.

"You can have some of this if you want."

She wrinkled her nose.

"No thanks, oatmeal isn't my favorite."

She pulled a tray of vegetables out of the oven and mixed it with some rice and soup.

"I don't have much time this morning but do you two want a ride across town?"

Julene did and Samson dropped them off outside the studio as soon as they were organized. He blew kisses to his wife and child and watched them go inside. The wind blew a hearty gust and some camellia petals showered past the front door after it closed. Samson could only see that as a positive omen and he drove away, hopeful.

It was an eternity between each time Samson looked at his watch, though it was only every twenty minutes or so. He was pretty busy and the house had four or five other contractors working at the same time so it was also loud. It should have been distraction enough. He managed for a while but eventually the tension built up in his shoulders and neck and he needed to get out. He managed to stick around for some paperwork but not for the conversation afterward. He drove single-mindedly to the city, and then irritably, as he looked for a spot to park the truck.

Sitting in one of the lime chairs in one of the small rooms again, an envelope was passed to him across the white table.

"Do you want to discuss the results?" Samson shook his head. "Do you have any questions about the process?"

"No. I'm just, I think I need time to gather my thoughts before I open them. I appreciate your time with this, Carly." Samson excused himself and left the office. He sat in the truck without moving for a long time. Thoughts were racing through his brain and he could feel a headache coming on. He wondered if he should go and buy a drink somewhere before opening the envelope, but then he tore the end to shreds without further thought.

Negative. The DNA comparison was negative. Samson leaned over the steering wheel and relaxed his shoulders until they moved up and down from the force of his feelings. He wiped his eyes and then called his accountant, for a referral. He was lucky enough to get an appointment to have his Will drawn up that day and drove downtown for the interim. The salesperson at the jewelry store remembered him.

"You haven't been back so I can only assume things went well with your perfect ring?"

"Yes, very much. There's something else I've been thinking about, though, and I wondered if you could help."

The salesman was all ears. He picked up the drawing Samson pushed across the glass and smiled.

"Actually, we have something very similar to this in stock. Let me bring it out for you."

It was late when Samson made it home. Julene and Clementine were sitting at the table, playing and laughing.

"Oh, Daddy, you're home late."

Samson picked up his daughter and held her up to his joyful face. He kissed her cheeks and then snuggled her into the crook of his arm. He danced her to and fro while Julene massaged the side of her neck. Samson looked questioningly at her.

"Adoring neck. It gets me every time."

"I get that, too, but it's just as much from looking at you as it is from looking at Clementine."

Julene swatted him.

"Ha ha. There are benefits to being short, you know."

"Yes, small packages and all that. Speaking of which, I have a small package for you."

"That's not exactly how I would describe it."

Samson grinned as he sat beside her and watched her face as he held out a small box on the palm of his hand. Clementine reached it first. She chewed it a little but quickly lost interest when it didn't reflect the light or make crunchy sounds. She dropped it onto her mother's lap, her sleepy baby eyes blinking at both of them. Julene looked into Samson's eyes questioningly as her fingers closed around the box.

"Small package," he said, and kissed her neck. "Come here, baby, let Daddy wrap you up."

He whisked the sleepy baby away to the bedroom, returning when Clementine was quiet. Julene had the box open and was looking at what could only be described as a golden manacle.

"This is seriously beautiful."

She looked up at him before taking it out of the box. Samson took it gently from her and then pushed it onto her finger. It was too big for the ring finger on her left hand so it went onto Julene's right hand and fit snugly under the knuckle.

"I did say manacle, and today I found one. Consider it an eternity ring, because that's how long you've got me."

"Aren't they for ten years?"

"Yes, or after the first child. We can catch up on the rest later." He smoothed her hair away from her neck and kissed her again. "I've got something else. Something for both of us."

"What's the occasion? I'm feeling pretty spoiled, right now."

Her eyes were glued to the shining, miniature handcuff while Samson walked over to the front door where he had dropped his bag and keys. He rummaged around a little.

"The results came today, and they're negative."

He brought the large envelope to the table for Julene to read and sat down beside her. Julene looked at him and sighed.

"So that's it then."

"Yes. It is, actually. I took a copy of it to the police and they drafted an official letter to Linda which is probably getting hand delivered," he checked his watch, "right about now, if it hasn't been already. And I also managed to get in to see a lawyer and write up my will. They said we can update it at any time but in its current format, everything is legally squared away for you and Clementine, and no one can fuck with that."

Julene put her arms around him, resting her head on his shoulder. He pulled her into his lap. She whispered her thanks to him as he held her tightly.

"And therein, hopefully, ends our *extraordinary* problems."

He nodded, stroking her hair.

"But not our extraordinary life."

"No," Julene said, "but I'll settle for some kissing in the meantime."

# Acknowledgments

My husband always encouraged me, and my boys took it as a given. For that I am grateful. To the team at She Writes Press, thank you for helping me on my journey.

# About the Author

Micayla lives in Oregon with her husband and 3 adventurous boys. Prior to full-time parenting, she worked in Sydney, Australia. More recently, she's let the boys fend for themselves while furiously writing a handful of novels, and enjoys sewing clothes and hats, and reading until the wee hours.

## SELECTED TITLES FROM SHE WRITES PRESS

She Writes Press is an independent publishing company
founded to serve women writers everywhere.
Visit us at **www.shewritespress.com**.

*A Drop In The Ocean: A Novel* by Jenni Ogden. $16.95, 978-1-63152-026-6. When middle-aged Anna Fergusson's research lab is abruptly closed, she flees Boston to an island on Australia's Great Barrier Reef—where, amongst the seabirds, nesting turtles, and eccentric islanders, she finds a family and learns some bittersweet lessons about love.

*Appetite* by Sheila Grinell. $16.95, 978-1-63152-022-8. When twenty-five-year-old Jenn Adler brings home a guru fiancé from Bangalore, her parents must come to grips with the impending marriage—and its effect on their own relationship.

*Conjuring Casanova* by Melissa Rea. $16.95, 978-1-63152-056-3. Headstrong ER physician Elizabeth Hillman is a career woman who has sworn off men and believes the idea of love in the twenty-first century is a fairy-tale—but when Giacomo Casanova steps into her life on a rooftop in Italy, her reality and concept of love are forever changed.

*Play for Me* by Céline Keating. $16.95, 978-1-63152-972-6. Middle-aged Lily impulsively joins a touring folk-rock band, leaving her job and marriage behind in an attempt to find a second chance at life, passion, and art.

*Shelter Us* by Laura Diamond. $16.95, 978-1-63152-970-2. Lawyer-turned-stay-at-home-mom Sarah Shaw is still struggling to find a steady happiness after the death of her infant daughter when she meets a young homeless mother and toddler she can't get out of her mind—and becomes determined to rescue them.

*Keep Her* by Leora Krygier. $16.95, 978-1-63152-143-0. When a water main bursts in rain-starved Los Angeles, seventeen-year-old artist Maddie and filmmaker Aiden's worlds collide in a whirlpool of love and loss. Is it meant to be?